I0593185

STRANDED
FOR THE
Night

NEW YORK NIGHTS
BOOK THREE

KIA CARRINGTON-RUSSELL

Dedicated to all the women who want to be treated sweetly in their relationship but rough in the sheets. I hope you find your happy ending. But until then have some fun.

CRYSTAL
✦ PUBLISHING ✦

Chapter 1

Cassidy

Miserable, dehydrated and hungover. I stirred my turmeric and ginger juice with the straw, idly in a daze as I sat across from my two best friends in one of our favourite Manhattan cafés for breakfast. I was painfully hungover and the sunglasses I still wore even inside did nothing to prevent the light from penetrating my pounding headache.

I'd naturally gone to a friend's New Year's Eve countdown party and under usual circumstances, I would've flirted the night away and probably taken someone home. But instead, because of my sworn celibacy from my serial-dating life over the last three months, I didn't even have a New Year's Eve count-down kiss.

And although that should've been the least of my worries, all the tequila I drank felt like it'd been for nothing. It would also be the last night I'd be partying in Manhattan anytime soon. The moment my parents sent through the text message a month ago saying they'd be meeting me in New York in the New Year, I quit my job, packed my apartment, and hired the first rental car I could find to escape. I'd intended to spend the next few months with a friend in her ski lodge in Canada until my parents gave up and went back home. Because I knew exactly why they were coming to town and I wouldn't have any place in their scheme.

Clover and Issobelle were both eating their meals; both of them seemed in far better condition than me. Especially Issobelle, who could drink her weight in booze and still walk in a straight line. She looked polished as ever. And Clover apparently had a quiet one with her boyfriend, Damon. A heavy silence fell over us. I hated the silence.

"It's not like I'll be gone forever," I reiterated. "I'll be back before you know it."

Issobelle chewed around her meal, speaking unapologetically with her mouth full. "If I didn't have so many damn projects coming up, I'd join you." Being one of the most famous photographers in New York, she was running a tight schedule. One that even she didn't appreciate nowadays that she was exclusively contracted to *Candice Magazine* for twelve months. The only form of change she could make recently was coloring her lopsided sharp bob from blue to pink and even that didn't seem to satisfy her.

"No, I wouldn't want you to come anyway. It'll probably be super boring at my friends." Because the mini vacay I told everyone I was leaving on didn't actually have an expiry date. Not until I knew it was safe to come back to Manhattan.

"Sounds like you don't want me there," Issobelle mumbled skeptically. I scoffed, giving her a deranged expression. Well yes and no. My other friend circles outside of Manhattan were very different to the friendships I'd formed here and I never wanted those two worlds touching.

Clover politely dabbed a napkin at her lips as she spoke. "I doubt anywhere you go would be boring." She pushed back the sleeve of her blouse and looked at the watch on her wrist. It was right before the hustle of everyone's day starting. And now that she was working at *Be True* magazine as their travel columnist, she had a flight to catch shortly. "But it still seems kind of risky to me, Cassidy. You just up and quit your job at *Candice Magazine* and are now randomly going to Canada for... how long did you say? Are you sure everything's okay?"

No. "Yea of course it is. I just need a change of scenery." I giggled throwing back my blonde curls with a bright smile. A motion that gave me a head spin—I was officially swearing off tequila. "I'm so sick of the New York men, and work's drab, and yea you know, I just feel like I need a fresh start."

"But you are coming back, aren't you? Because you're making it sound like you're never returning," Issobelle said with a skeptical stare.

"Of course. You know what I mean, just a little vacation," I said, tapping her lightly on the hand.

"Without an end date?" Clover clarified.

"Mhmm," I nodded with a beaming smile.

Sitting on the same side in the booth, the two looked at one another with a worrisome glance. Why was this starting to feel like some sort of intervention? It's not like I could tell them that I came from a completely different world and was running away from my parents as my past catches up to me. And I wanted anything else but to live that life again or even talk about it—as if the mere whispers of it would manifest it into being right in front of me.

"Do you have enough money saved?" Issobelle queried. We'd gone over this so many times already. And yet I found it endearing that they cared so much. Genuinely. It wasn't superficial like all the other friendships I'd had before and even then, we didn't speak about money, we just showed it off with flashy materialistic items.

"I'll be fine." I rolled my eyes. Did I save money? No. Was I dependant on the credit card I'd received since I was ten? Yes. Was it hypocritical of me to use it since I was running away from the very same parents that didn't look at those expenses twice? Probably. But my infatuation with beautiful clothes and accessories was never going to change. Even if I did change my life and identity.

Clover and Issobelle didn't seem convinced.

"Promise us if anything happens and you need help with anything, you'll call us," Clover pressed.

"And the moment you arrive in Canada send us a text," Issobelle insisted.

"Yes, guys, okay." I laughed, taking a second sip of the juice.

"I still find it weird you're driving up to Canada. I didn't even know you could drive," Issobelle teased.

I rolled my eyes. "I told you, change of scenery." The truth being I didn't want to purchase a flight ticket with the credit card in case my parents tracked where I landed. I also couldn't afford it on my own because I was still waiting on my final pay check for another month. Was I a confident driver? No. Had I considered taking public transport on a bus? Absolutely not.

"Alright, well, I have to go so I don't miss my flight," Clover chimed as she stood up to give me a hug. Clover, although only a few years older, always felt like a mentor of sorts. Saying goodbye to her was the complete opposite of comfort. I didn't want to leave them or my fun life in New York. But I didn't want to confront my parents either. I held back a tear.

"Make sure you tell us if you need *anything*," Clover insisted.

Issobelle, not much of a hugger, stood up as well with hands in pockets. "And remember no fuckboys. You swore to celibacy from them. But make sure to have a hella time."

I laughed. Yea, I was over all the flings and boys in New York anyway. They were all the same and it took me a while to realize maybe I deserved better. That's why I came to New York in the first place.

Hoping to find my Prince Charming but it turned out most of them were either toads or secretly married.

But, gratefully, I'd discovered incredible friends along the way.

Chapter 2

Eric

The crunch of snow under my boots was loud. I'd arrived just before nightfall and the mountain back roads in the winter had taken a beating. I'd had to manoeuvre around multiple fallen trees, arriving just barely at a reasonable hour. Only those who had a truck would be able to manage it, anything small would get bogged. And that was probably part of the reason why I liked the secluded location. I readjusted my backpack over my shoulder, admiring the wooden cabin and fiddling with the key. How bad could its maintenance be this year?

When I opened the door and switched on the light, the cabin echoed with a low whistle of wind pushing past me. I let out a chilled puff of breath. It was just as beat up as the roads. It'd be a full day's clean, especially the dust and spiderwebs. But it was home. Despite its pristine making and design, I imagined my twin brothers were to blame for having left it in this mess when they visited midyear uninvited.

I looked down at Shadow, my dog, scratching him behind his ear. The great big, brown German shepherd was sitting by my side loyally. He inspected the cabin with the same resolve that I did, slowly stepping in and sniffing about. This year, in the small town of Rosefield, the air felt more frigid than usual. I hoped the locals received enough wood for their fireplaces until I was able to make it back for the New Year.

"Looks like we've got our work cut out for us this year, boy." Before I could properly inspect the frigid cabin, a set of lights danced through the trees. Damn. I thought I'd at least get a few days in without any visitors.

A beat-up, gray truck parked behind my red one. "Well, well, well, if it isn't Eric Dawson himself." Coots charmed a grin. The old man had half his teeth and a few gray scraps of hair on his head and chin left. "I had a feeling you'd be pulling in today." He must've seen me drive through town first.

Shadow sat obediently at my feet, coming

between me and anyone I conversed with. And I loved how it intimidated the shit out of everyone in the process.

"It's been a while," I said extending my hand to shake his.

"I'm assuming you missed your pa and uncle before they left town for hunting?" he asked. The same time every year the two left for a month. And that's why I came back, to help out my mother. Unfortunately, the locals had also gotten used to the tradition.

"It would appear so," I grumbled.

Coots stared down at Shadow, licking his lips as he looked between us. I had nothing personally against Coots or any of the locals. I just wasn't much of a people person—and that was putting it politely.

"Ye cabin's looking pretty beat up, had a few storms run through these past few months if ye need a hand."

"Nothing I can't manage on my own."

He shook his head, agreeing as if we'd had a full conversation.

"Always a man of few words," he joked. When I didn't entertain it, he went sombre. "Anyway, ye pa wanted me to give ye a new axe for the new year."

"What happened to my old one?" I growled.

Shadow shifted his front paws impatiently. *I know, boy*, I thought. Coot's attention dipped back down to him, probably assuring the dog wasn't doing anything scary. "Ye brother broke it apparently."

I huffed. "The twins?" I asked.

"Nah, Thomas," he said. That little shit. I didn't give a flying damn if he was the youngest and my mother's favourite, he was in so much shit when I saw him next.

"Ye pa left it with me to bring it up when ye got into town. So, it's in the trunk, I'll grab it," he cheerily said. He eyed Shadow as he warily stepped away. The moment his gaze shifted elsewhere, I smirked, rubbing my hand through the fur on Shadow's head and scratching the black patch at the back of his ear.

Shadow would never hurt anyone unless commanded. But like owner, he had a certain "charm" about him that let others know he was grouchy and best left alone. It filled me with male pride. Man and his best friend, that kind of shit.

"Here she is." Coots hauled the new axe out. "Me and Ann were hoping we might be first to receive some of ye wood."

Ah. That's why he'd driven all the way out of town to greet me. The axe was just an added excuse.

But I didn't mind chopping wood for the locals. It took my mind away from other things while I was here in town. "Sure. I'll drop some off over the next few days."

Coots seemed pleased with that, patting a hand on his stomach "Also, be careful around these parts, some locals have been reporting wolves howling lately."

And by "reporting" he meant "gossiping." "Around these parts? There hasn't been a sighting for years," I scoffed. I'd grown up here most my life and not once had there been a sighting. I doubted it was going to happen now.

"I know, that's what I said," he agreed breathlessly as if we'd finally found communal ground.

He was discontent when I said nothing again.

"Ye going to see ye mother while ye in town?"

I eyed him. With a population this small, I was certain there was no way to avoid her, even if I wanted to. Not to forget to mention I'd be managing our family café, like always, so the question was rhetorical. As if sensing my displeasure in the conversation, his throat bobbled.

"Well, I best be heading, it's been a long day and what not. Good to see ye, Eric. Ye looking..." He seemed to try and find the words and flexed his muscles instead. "Ye know, as giant as ever."

At that, I did offer a smirk, one that seemed to intimidate him even further. He waved as he all but ran toward his truck. As soon as he threw it out of park, he reversed halfway down the mountain at a speed he hadn't come in on.

I let out a whistle, scratching Shadow on the head, who hadn't left my side. "Let's get to work."

Chapter 3

Cassidy

S even hours into my drive, with plenty of scenic stops and photos taken on the way, I stopped into a small lake town called Rosefield about an hour before reaching the Canadian border. In another two days, breaking up the trip with long enough stops, I should be happily lodging at my friend's ski resort, sipping on Mimosas. As great as that sounded, I still had a ways to go, and I'd been on edge driving the entire way so far. The snow hadn't stopped since the moment I'd left Manhattan.

I appeared to be driving down what looked to be Rosefield's quaint main street and, with closer inspection, their only street that had any shops or services. I pulled over in front of what looked like their local café, noticing the little sign that read "open." I stepped out of the car, immediately frost-bitten by the cold. The depth of the snow worsened the further out of Manhattan I drove, and this small town was certainly no exception. Looking down the main street there wasn't much in this town and I wondered if they got a few tourists in the summer because of the lake and mountains I'd been driving alongside for the better half of an hour now.

I held myself tightly as I walked into the small café, immediately relieved by the fire crackling and warmth that hit me. The café had a couple of retro red booths and singular barstools along the counter. A woman with beautiful red curly hair greeted me with a smile as she looked me up and down. I definitely did not look like a local. I self-consciously adjusted my designer jacket.

I froze the moment I saw the huge looking wolf that barked and ran for me. I squealed closing my eyes and throwing my hands up. My heart pounded. But nothing happened. Slowly, I peeled one eye open and then the next. A cold chill ran down my spine. Oh God. It was sniffing my shoes. Oh God, was it going to pee on them? *Please don't pee on them.*

The redhead now seemed a lot more interested

as she leaned over the counter. "You friendly with dogs?" she asked with a slight Californian accent.

I tried to smile through it. "Ummm, friendly isn't a term I would use. But perhaps unfamiliar with them."

She chuckled and called out to someone in the back. "Hey, boss man, your dog's harassing a customer."

Two older ladies sitting in one of the booths stared in bewilderment, their jaws dropped in shock.

"Is it legal to keep wolves as pets in this town?" I squeaked.

"He's a German shepherd," a robust voice growled. An even colder shiver washed over me. My eyes almost bulged at the sight of the ginormous man that stepped out from the kitchen. How the actual fuck did anyone grow to six foot six and the width of a doorframe. I was guessing he was in his late thirties. His green eyes narrowed on me, a thick black beard and eyebrows covering what might've been an attractive face. Not to say he wasn't with the beard… but it covered a lot. And I wasn't so used to seeing men with full-grown beards in Manhattan. He whistled, the dog immediately returning to his owner's side.

"And he doesn't go to anyone but Eric," the redheaded woman beamed with a smile. "My, my, my, ego must be rather bruised right now, huh?" She pressed the tongue inside her cheek as he gave her an effective look. I gulped, terrified. The woman only found it more amusing.

"What are you in for, hun?" she called out. "A cup of joe for the road? Flat tire? Wood?"

Disheveled from the confrontation with the dog and the modern-day version of the Hulk walking through the door, I tried to muster my thoughts and pulled down on my pink marshmallow-looking jacket. I tucked back some of my hair, feeling significantly out of place. "Umm do you do any types of juices here?"

She politely mulled over a smile, although I could tell she was trying not to laugh.

"We've got orange juice. A whole big bottle for the trip if you're willing to pay the right price for it." She winked.

I smiled politely. "Um just a glass will do, and can I use your bathroom?"

"Straight through that way," she said, pointing. I noticed the smirk she offered the tower of a man. He stood with his hands strapped across his chest, staring at me walking away and brooding the entire time.

The bathroom was, well, as expected at a place

like this. And I'd been in far worse predicaments on a night out in Manhattan, especially after someone had vomited. I pulled my phone out to text my friend Alice in Canada, checking in that I was safe and going to find a hotel to stay in for the night. I wasn't a confident enough driver, especially on these snowy and wet roads. And now that it was turning dark, I wasn't going to risk gray hairs over it. I'd been driving like a grandma the entire time, my knuckles turning white over the steering wheel as I considered my demise every time I hit a corner in the mountain range. I cursed under my breath when my cell appeared to have no reception.

I finished up applying lip gloss and then ducked my head out the door. When I peered down, the great big hulk's beast of a dog was standing outside the door, tail wagging.

I grimaced. Shit. I was cornered. "Umm, hi." I curtly nodded and tried to swoosh it away. My experience with animals was near to zilch. Anything with fangs was in the "not to be trusted basket."

"Yo, Eric, your dog has the poor girl cornered in the bathroom," the redhead called out. I tsked, embarrassed that I'd been spotted but also grateful that someone would save me. I heard the grumpy man grumble and a whistle drew away the dog's attention again.

A sigh escaped me. "Thank you." I curtly nodded as I readjusted my handbag.

"We don't get a lot of your type out here," the older lady in the booth said to me as I walked past them with a smile.

"Type?" I asked, furrowing my eyebrows. I'd received various names in the past, known for my party-girl habits, but these women didn't even know me.

"The pretty kind," her friend crooned.

I felt red spread across my cheeks, embarrassed I'd thought the worst. "Oh, thank you, that's so sweet to say." Although flattering, I wasn't entirely sure if it was a compliment.

When I turned and sat on a stool at the bar, a glass of juice was already waiting for me. I looked at it, intrigued, and then to the redheaded woman. The hulk and his dog had vanished into the back. The woman was wiping down the counter. "Juice straight from the carton." She winked.

I looked down at it ominously. I was certain this wasn't made on sight. "Thank you," I said sweetly. I got out my cell, disappointed to find the lack in reception again. How was I going to find the closest town to find a hotel? "Um, excuse me. Where is the next big town from here? I'm wanting to stop over somewhere for the night?"

She whistled thoughtfully, throwing the tea towel over her shoulder casually. "It's going to be about an hour drive and heading over the border. We're central in the mountains here, you're not going to find any major town for a while yet. Sorry, hun."

I gulped. I wasn't entirely comfortable with driving another hour in the dark, but I supposed I could manage it. I took a sip of the juice, almost keeling over from immediate sugar overload. "Oh wow." I gasped, covering my mouth, deplored that I'd said it out loud.

She openly laughed at my misery. "Not what you're used to huh?"

"It's different," I charmed. And definitely not freshly squeezed. "Can I have this in a to-go cup?" I had no intention of drinking it but didn't want to seem rude. I pulled out my credit card, idly trying to find reception on my cell again as I handed it over to her.

I started swiveling on the chair, hoping the angle I positioned the cell would make a difference as I tried to hit send on my text message.

"Sorry, hun, your card's declined."

I looked up at her slowly, dragging myself away from trying to manifest cell reception. "What has? My credit card?"

She swiped it through again in front of me, a big red message appearing. My eyebrows knitted together. "That can't be right," I laughed. I flicked through my purse. "Here try this one."

Again, the same message appeared. "Is this because there's no reception here?" I asked.

"Sorry, hun, but this worked for Ann and Patrice, just fine."

Confusion and dread coiled in the pit of my stomach. My parents wouldn't have... Did my parents cut off my credit cards? "Oh, umm. That's fine sorry." I flicked through my purse finding my personal card that I'd almost entirely maxed out until my next pay and handed it to her.

What is happening to me right now? Dread filled me, and I wasn't sure if I was nervously laughing on the inside or openly, probably looking like a psycho. Oh my gosh. I only had a quarter tank of gas left for the rental car. It couldn't possibly get me to my friend's ski resort, I'd have to fuel up somewhere. But if they've cut my funds off as consequence for running away... I was completely screwed.

Fuck, suddenly this juice needed vodka or prosecco in it ASAP.

"Yep, that one went all through fine, hun," the redhead said cheerily. "And here's your juice to go."

Go? Go where? How was I going to get anywhere with a quarter tank of fuel. Were my parents purposefully doing this, so I'd have no choice but to call on them? My back straightened. There was no way I was calling them. If I did, I'd only be admitting I depended on their money and would have to fall back into their agreement. A cold sweat ran over me. But hadn't I been, since I'd been using the credit card all this time?

The doorbell chimed again and an old man missing half his teeth and only a few strands of hair waltzed in with a limp. He stopped dead in his tracks and looked at me, his hands wringing nervously. "Woah, we don't get girls like you here in Rosefield."

"Your wife is sitting here," one of the ladies harrumphed from the booth.

He gave her a smile and walked over, pressing a kiss to her cheek. "You're still my everything, my beautiful Ann." There was something oddly sweet in his endearment. "It's looking bad out there."

The could-be-secretly-Hercules man walked back out, his width filling the doorframe. He watched me from the corner of his eye and then spoke to the older man. "What is?" The dog sat at his feet, an intimidating glare aimed at the older man. I felt almost bad for him. Together, the duo was terrifying. And yet somehow, this man seemed misplaced in this town. He looked like he should be a part of some mafia or motorcycle club. Oh gosh. What if I was stranded in some dangerous town?

While I spiraled into way too many thoughts, movies, and subplots about how I'd ended up stranded in the deadliest town possible, the man continued talking. "The winds pushed an old tree over the main road heading into the town over, I'm going around and letting the locals know now in case anyone needs to get out any time soon."

"Wait, in the direction I need to go?" I clarified with the redheaded woman.

She grimaced and nodded. I stared at her. This could not be happening. "Well like there's back roads and stuff, right?"

The attractive brute, Eric, kicked up a sneering smirk. "In that little car of yours out there, it's a surprise you made it even this far. You won't get out on any back road without a truck."

Despite his reasonable response, I certainly didn't appreciate his tone or attitude. A tight smile crossed my face and the redhead seemed almost apologetic. What was I going to do? I took a breath and stared at the juice. Great. I had no money. No reception and my only way out had been blocked. How could my luck be that bad?

I held everything in, making sure not to laugh at my circumstances because I was certain I was about to cry. I couldn't go back to my parents or *him*. It wasn't an option. *Come on, Cassidy, you're creative, think of something.*

"Are you going to have somewhere to stay?" The redheaded woman worriedly asked. I looked up at her, surprised since I'd been in my own thoughts. *A place to stay?* I couldn't even afford a place to stay. I had my car, but what would that do in this snowy cold weather? I'd freeze.

At my lack of response, the locals glanced around at one another. Oh shit, now they were taking pity on me. "Oh yea, I'll be fine. It's no problem whatsoever. I'll just..." I fell short. I'd just what? Chop down the tree in front of my path? Magically make money? Shit, I didn't get my last pay check for another month.

Amongst the awkward silence, I chewed my bottom lip. I could work something out. I wasn't anyone's responsibility here. Absentmindedly, I noticed the dog's ears prick up and he walked over to me, my shaky breath coming out in short bursts. He began to nudge my leg.

The old man gasped. "Well, I'll be damned," he said to his wife, Ann. "Ye seeing, this?"

"You should've seen him when she walked in. He walked straight up to her," Ann crooned with the same bewilderment.

Immediately, my gaze snapped to his owner, who was once again unimpressed with arms crossed over his chest.

"Why don't you stay with one of us for the night until the fallen tree's sorted," the redhead suggested. "And by one of us, I mean my brother Eric here."

"What?" Eric and I snapped in unison.

His gaze sharply landed back on me. "I can't take her in."

"You know we already have a full house back at Mom's and what are you going to do, let a poor woman freeze to death?" Now she crossed her arms, a scary, intimidating demeanor kicking in. Now that she'd mentioned "brother" I kind of noticed the resemblance. Not in the hair color but in their nose and eye shape.

"Lori," he gritted out in warning.

"It's fine honestly, I'll figure something out," I said quickly.

"The snow's been picking up again too, it isn't safe driving at night. Not in a car like that," the old man said and whistled, obviously making Eric feel bad.

The dog nudged against my leg again. Slowly and cautiously, I reached down. He sniffed, then rubbed his head against my open palm, its soft silky fur threading through my fingers. A tension rippled through me. This wasn't so scary. Despite the circumstances, it was somewhat soothing even.

"And what would Mom say?"

"Fine," Eric threw his hands in the air. "You can stay with me," he gritted out.

I quickly found myself saying, "It's fine, really." Because who knew where this man was actually taking me. For all I knew he was taking me out into the woods to chop me into tiny pieces. Again, the scenes from movies and plays ensued.

As if reading my mind, his expression softened— if that was even possible—and he uncrossed his arms. "You'll be warm with me tonight." His eyebrows knitted together. "Well not with me but in my home."

Lori threw back her head and laughed.

"Shut up," Eric gritted out.

I noticed then the slight blush on his cheeks. Was he embarrassed?

"That's very gentlemanly of you, Eric," Ann crooned and offered me a wink. I had no idea what was happening, but I suddenly felt like I was the one being used for a personal prank. But what choice did I have? If I at least had a place to stay for the night, I could gather my thoughts and plan of action. I suddenly questioned why I'd been so reckless with my money and every impulsive purchase I'd ever made. Why didn't I have savings like normal people?

"I'm just closing up the shop," he grumbled and then called his dog back. "So, get your stuff out of your car."

"Please," Lori added, looking at her brother with disbelief. "Do they really not have women where you come from?"

His gaze snagged hers again and he looked at me, then back to her again. He simply grunted and said, "You'll need to leave your car out front because it won't make the drive up the mountains. So grab your bags, please."

"Mountains?" I squeaked. But he was already gone.

Chapter 4

Eric

Meddlesome. That's all they were back at the café. Especially Lori. She'd purposefully set me up, enjoying every part of it. I had no doubt she'd be giving me crap for this in years to come. It'd be even worse when she got my brothers in on it as well. I internally grumbled.

I peered through the rearview mirror at Shadow, who was sitting on the back seat with his tongue hanging out of his mouth. He looked dubiously happy and that only irritated me more. Replacing his usual spot was a pretty blonde that was the furthest thing from local.

Her overpowering sweet perfume filled the car, flaring my nostrils. My knuckles were turning white over the steering wheel. It suited her to a dime. Anyone with eyes could categorize her as beautiful— in a high-maintenance way. Her light-blue eyes danced with life, with a complexion so smooth it was hard to believe she was even real. And that hair... How did anyone manage perfect curls in weather like this? It was unimaginable. *She* was unimaginable. Like some Hollywood actress that stepped straight off her private jet. One now stranded in Rosefield with a vehicle that would get her nowhere.

I grumbled internally again. How did this little star end up under my care? I used this month to get away from people, not take them in as charity cases.

"So, like, how far up the mountain are we going?" she said nervously. I fixed my gaze on the bumpy road. My silence clearly didn't unnerve her which I found even more irritating.

"I'm Cassidy by the way." Silence. "I usually at least know the guy's name who's taking me to his home," she said lightheartedly.

"I'm not taking you to my home," I gritted out, not liking her sexual innuendo- which seemed to ooze so naturally from her.

"Right," she said nervously, peering out the window. "Well at least you finally spoke."

My knuckles whitened over the steering wheel

again as I peered through the rearview mirror at Shadow, still happily panting.

"So, were you born in this town?"

"You like to talk, don't you?" I replied. We hit a pothole in the snowy dirt path. She clutched to the side of the door as she bounced in her seat. Shadow and I might've been used to these roads but she certainly wasn't conditioned for them. Slightly remorseful, I slowed down slightly.

"Well, I figured I'd try to make you like me at least a little before you chop my body into tiny pieces and scatter me in the woods," she said, nervously laughing.

My eyebrows knitted together. Had she been thinking that the entire time we'd been driving up the mountain? I didn't even consider how uncomfortable and bizarre the situation might've been for her. I was only foreboding how bad it was for me. Man, I really am an asshole.

"I don't plan on chopping you up," I said in a no-nonsense tone, attempting to soothe her nerves.

"Oh, that's nice to know. I'll be one of the spontaneous victims." She nervously chuckled again.

This time, I did look at her. She was still staring out the side window intently. Although she held a brave smile, I felt guilty for forcing any woman to be scared around me.

Another jolt in the road. Her eyes snapped shut as she took in a sharp breath. "We're almost there," I said trying to shift into a friendlier demeanor. I tried to ease my own tension. I shouldn't be taking out my irritation on her. But, man, it was hard; she was so unnaturally beautiful. Lori was out of her mind sending a woman like this to the cabin with me. Did she really think I was that noble? I pushed away any tempting thoughts. I really needed to get a grip. She looked way too young for me. "Where are you from?"

She peeled her eyes open slightly, surprised that I'd finally taken interest in any form of conversation. "Manhattan."

"I would've picked you for a LA girl."

She seemed taken aback by that. "What is that supposed to mean?"

"Just regarding your three oversized suitcases. We don't get a lot of girls like you out here. So, I just assumed LA." I wasn't going to openly say because I thought she reminded me of some superstar that either just strutted off a studio set or runway.

"Oh, well I'm leaving Manhattan for a vacation, so the three suitcases were necessary."

"With that much I thought you were moving."

Silence. I peered over in her direction again. I had the sense that when this woman went silent it wasn't a good thing. *Secret.* Instinct told me she was tight-lipped about something.

But the silence suited me just fine.

"So, are you like, the mayor of this town or some-thing?" she quietly said, changing the subject.

A cold dread passed through me. And as if know-ing, Shadow's tail momentarily stiffened before wagging again and his tongue continued panting.

"No," I gritted out. "That would be my uncle. Although my father and siblings help out from time to time."

"Okay cool. And do you have many siblings?"

I was already exhausted. This had been the most conversation I'd had to maintain all week. And I couldn't tell if it was nervous chatter or if she just didn't enjoy silence.

"There's five of us."

A breath of air rushed from her. "Oh my gosh! That's huge!"

Silence. Her small, delicate finger stroked the inside of the door handle, fiddling as she became uncomfortable by the silence. My shoulders sagged in defeat, sensing she was about to speak again.

"And are you like the oldest. What are you, like

fifty?" My gaze snapped to hers as we hit another pothole and this time, she hit her head. "Ow."

Okay maybe I'd accidently hit accelerate on that one.

She rubbed her head, wincing but laughing. "I was joking. I was just trying to grab your attention. What are you really, like mid-thirties?"

That eased my heart slightly and I was embarrassed by my fragile ego.

"Forty-two," I found myself gritting out. Why did my age and appearance even matter? "What are you like sixteen?"

Her laugh filled the truck, twisting a confused knot in my stomach. It was light and carefree and perfectly suited to this woman I barely knew anything about. And yet I felt like this was her most natural state.

"You're funny," she teased. "I'm twenty-six."

Twenty-Six. Shit, she was young. Sixteen years younger. Wait—*funny*. I don't think anyone had once described me as funny.

"You know where I come from everyone gets lots of stuff done to their face so everyone's practically ageless. You never see wrinkles or crow's feet or any of that stuff. Just everyone looking half their age." She seemed to find that amusing.

I found myself self-consciously looking into the rearview mirror again, assessing the few wrinkles Lori had kindly pointed out on my face last year. I also had a consistent scowl that was stapled to my expression. I had the urge to touch my wrinkles. I'd had supple skin like hers at her age, hadn't I? And then I quickly grew grumpy again. Why was I even worried about this?

We slowly crawled to a stop the moment the headlights hit the cabin. Two deer peered up, quickly dashing off into the woodland.

"Wow!" Cassidy grabbed my arm and pointed. I stared down at her small hand now wrapped around mine, feeling too warm. "Did you see that? Those are like real deers!"

Shadow barked as if in agreeance. I stared over my shoulder at him. Traitor. Her smile was bright and genuine until she realized she was clinging on to me. She pulled away as if I burnt her. And the feeling had been mutual. Yet I felt almost disappointed the moment she pulled away. My mood couldn't have been any fowler.

"Oh sorry, I get excited quickly," she nervously laughed.

One night, I thought to myself. That's all it would be. Surely, I had enough patience and restraint for one night. And how presumptuous of me to even think this little bombshell would be attracted to me? Not that I'd ever had any woman complain and I'd never struggled to take women to my bed. I internally cursed myself. Why was I thinking with my dick in this situation?

I suddenly realized the dread on Cassidy's expression. A little muscle in her neck was strained as she kept a tight appreciative smile staring at the cabin. I'd never met anyone with such transparent and honest expressions. The cabin certainly wasn't the five-star hotels she was surely used to but it wasn't a beat-up shack either.

"I just want you to know I've sworn to celibacy," she blurted out, quickly facing me, expression dead serious.

I was so taken aback by the ferocity and sheer determination that I couldn't help the slight tick of my mouth, a smile daring to break free. Well at least I hadn't been the only one thinking about it. She also seemed serious. Was she so used to men only expecting one thing from her? With a body and face like hers though, I imagined she could have any man she wanted.

"Cassidy, I'm not using your body as currency," I said cautiously, unsure as to what past this little transparent snowflake was running from. "I'm offering you one night to stay until the road is cleared up and you can continue passing through town. I'm not going to touch you. And besides, you're not my type."

Her eyebrows knitted together. Either in confusion that I'd admitted she wasn't my type or because I wasn't after her body. She slowly nodded and threw her long blonde curls over her shoulder before weakly opening the door and jumping out.

When I opened the back door, Shadow lunged out and began his usual inspection of sniffing the trees. Shadow must've found a trail because he meant serious business. Maybe the deer. I watched him, making sure he didn't stray too far as I emptied Cassidy's suitcase she'd pointed out onto the snow. She'd limited herself to only one out of the three.

"How did you put these bags in here yourself?" I asked Cassidy. There was a ridiculous weight to them, and I highly doubted she'd be able to lift them past her shins let alone into the car. She had no chance of dragging them out of my truck considering her height only came up to my chest.

She tucked back part of her hair. "Well, I didn't, I had help."

Ah. I imagined a woman like her always had

help. She wrapped her hands around herself self-consciously, that pink marshmallow-looking jacket clearly doing nothing to keep the chill away. "C'mon," I instructed with every intention of setting up the fireplace so she wouldn't freeze to death. Then I really wouldn't hear the end of it form Lori and my brothers.

It felt strange inviting someone into my space. This little retreat I'd created for myself for over a decade now. No one else had been welcome. And welcome was a stretch even now. It was just one night. I could babysit this little snowflake for one night.

Chapter 5

Cassidy

There were so many rolling hills, cliff edges, and woodland. Completely in the dark and stranded with the biggest male I'd ever seen in my life. The tension on the way up here was palpable. I was an inconvenience to him and although this wasn't my ideal situation to be in, I certainly didn't have the sense he'd hurt me. It was simply how much he unnerved me that put me on edge.

And despite that, I only had one night to figure everything out. What would I do tomorrow when the tree was lifted? I was completely broke—worse then broke. I was jobless. Homeless. And stranded in a town that didn't even have a dot on the map. Issobelle and Clover would've been better suited in this situation. They were more versatile than me. I, however, was certainly not cut out for nature and wildlife.

And what would I do, call them after only one night away to express the dilemma I was in? There was no way I could do that because then I'd have to come clean about everything and that was something I refused to share. I was too scared, as if the very mention of my parents and *him* would manifest the situation. I'd just lay low for a few months and they'd give up—surely. But then again, they'd never cut off my credit cards before.

No, I could manage one night with this real-life-looking barbarian.

With little effort, he carried my suitcase and he'd been right. I would've struggled dragging that through the snow, but he made it look like it weighed nothing. When he opened the door, it exposed the edges of a living room in the darkness. I couldn't see a damn thing beyond. It was eerily quiet in there.

I was just so used to the constant chatter and life of Manhattan and this was the furthest thing from my comfort zone. And it made the situation with this stranger somehow feel intimate. I wanted to slap my cheeks. Was my mind really only trained on one thing? I was literally in the shittiest predicament I'd been in... ever, and all I could think about was how ridiculously handsome this older man was. I needed to go to therapy ASAP.

I tried to peer over Eric's shoulder as he opened the door further and flicked on the light. The cabin sparked to life and when he stepped in and placed the suitcase beside the door, my jaw unhinged as I swept my gaze over the entire room. "Wow." I whistled, genuinely surprised.

The outside of the cabin was deceivingly small compared to the ample space inside. On the left was a brick fireplace. In front of it was a cozy leather sofa. The colors of deep gray and brown decorated the space, matching the man standing beside me. Across the room and up two steps on a raised level was the main bedroom with a king-sized bed. My mouth widened at the view behind it. The large floor-to-ceiling windows showed off the dark outlines of what might've been rolling hills and mountains. I could've only imagined what that view might've looked like during the day.

Eric walked to the fireplace, his expert hands tending to it quickly. On the right was a long kitchen and island bench, the grays of the bench somehow deepening the space. Beside it was a closed room, in what I imagined to be the bathroom, and another door which might've stepped out to a balcony in the back.

Shadow nudged me in, reminding me I was still standing at the door with my mouth gaping at the sheer and unexpected beauty of the cabin. I chastised myself for being judgmental, having thought that it was a run-down little shack. And instead... it was this glorious hidden oasis.

"This is your home?" I asked, stepping over the wooden threshold.

"Did you expect me to live in a cave or something?" he asked, blowing on the fire.

"Would you be annoyed if I said yes?"

He peered over his shoulder, somewhat unimpressed. I laughed, thinking myself hilarious. So, charm and jokes did not work on this brute. Unfortunately, they were the two things I fell back on when nervous in any situation.

"All of this looks really new," I said, still appreciating the space. I felt like I'd just walked into some luxurious cabin resort.

"Well, I only built it about ten years ago."

My jaw dropped. "You built this?"

"Do you not have men who can build things where you come from?" He grunted. He had his back to me, hands on hips as he surveyed the fire as it grew in size.

"Well sure, I guess. So remind me what it is you do again? Café owner?" I asked, admiring the wooden chandelier above. The furnishings were simple but beautiful. And although I didn't know Eric at all, it very much felt like him. It even smelt like him. That bold, woodsy earth cologne perfuming the air. And I wasn't certain if he used cologne or that was his sheer sweat. The man was built like a god. *Celibacy*, I reminded myself. I'd sworn off men until I found the right one.

He walked over to his kitchen, opening the fridge and scooping what looked like a home-prepared meal for Shadow, who obediently waited for his dish to be filled.

"Something like that."

"So, you're a café-owning, dog-training fifty-year-old?"

His sense of humor was practically non-existent which made me even more nervous. He grunted, not necessarily in approval but as if that was all the effort he could muster in the conversation thus far. "Eat or drink whatever you like. The bed's all yours. I'll sleep on the sofa."

My gaze drifted from him to the bed. "I can't," I

gushed. There was no way in hell I was sleeping in that bed. Gentleman or not, that bed oozed testosterone.

And then my gaze dropped and narrowed on the giant axe beside the front door. A thick lump bobbled in my throat. I began to nervously laugh, catching his attention again. He looked at the axe and offered an exasperated sigh in realization.

"Cassidy, I don't think I've ever had to tell someone so many times that I'm not intending to chop them into little pieces and scatter them into the woodland. And trust me, there's a lot already on that list."

I wasn't sure if he was joking or not. I suddenly found something fascinating on my jacket and nodded. "Well of course. I know that." I didn't fear this beast of a man but nor did I know this world either. "I feel as if every teenage horror movie I watched always started in either a cabin or a tent," I rambled. "So why do you own an axe?"

"I cut wood for the locals daily."

My eyebrows knitted together. "Wait so you're a café-owning, dog-training lumberjack?"

He downed a glass full of water. "You forgot the people chopping part," he growled with a straight face. I stared at him stunned. Another joke? So, this oaf of a man could actually manage them?

He waltzed over to a cupboard, pulling out a thick woolly towel and handed it to me. So close, he loomed over me, and I'd never felt so comparatively small to someone else. And I hovered at five ten myself.

He cleared his throat when I said and did nothing, nudging the towel into my hands. "Take your shoes off and have a shower so you don't get sick."

Shadow came to my side, licking his lips, evidently well fed. His head nuzzled against my fingertips and I found myself curling them through his fur, kind of enjoying the experience Despite how bizarre it was.

"Thank you," I stuttered out. Eric nodded and walked back into the kitchen. "Are you hungry? I can cook something." He opened a freezer full of meats and I paled.

He seemed confused and then realization dawned on him. "You're a vegetarian, aren't you?"

I offered him a tight smile. "I'm not very hungry anyway. And it's not that I can't stand the sight of meat or anything but that's a lot, do you eat all of this?" I did a double take of him and then rolled my eyes. Of course he did. Look at the size of him? "Or is this just a week's worth of food for you?"

"Should last me the month. I have fresh—"

"Thank you but there's no need," I quickly spluttered. I couldn't be any more of an inconvenience and besides, there was no way I'd be able to eat right now anyway. My stomach was in knots the moment the cold dread washed over me at the reminder there was still so much to be dealt with tomorrow.

He didn't seem to like my answer but slowly closed his overflowing fridge of fresh supplies. "Well, if you want anything it's there."

"Thank you." I peered down at my cell again, that knot in my stomach wrangling tighter. Something just felt off. "Also do you have Wi-Fi or something up here? My cell doesn't have any reception and I'd like to message my friend my whereabouts."

His eyebrows knitted in confusion. "I have reception up here, show me your cell?"

Reluctance traveled through me. Was this where he stole my phone and—

As if reading my thoughts, he rolled his eyes. *Actually* rolled his eyes. "I'm not throwing you to the wolves, Cassidy."

"There's wolves?" I squeaked.

His penetrating stare assessed me dryly. "Not

sighted since the late nineteen hundreds." His hand was still outstretched. Slowly, I pulled out my cell realizing the ridiculousness of it, with its pink cover and fluffy keychain that hung over those thick calloused hands. He could certainly crush it with one squeeze.

He assessed it for a moment, flicking through a few settings. I peered over his shoulder curiously, making sure he wasn't going through any of my private pictures. Not that he seemed like the type. But he was a guy after all.

"You're not out of reception, snowflake." Snowflake? "Your service has been suspended."

"Suspended?" That dragged my attention away from the "snowflake" comment.

"Yea did you forget to pay a few bills or something?"

I laughed. Oh, he was serious. "No, I've paid everything."

"Hmm that's usually the main reason why they'll suspend it. Unless someone else has access to your account and suspended it," he said as he handed me back the cell.

A cold sweat rolled over me again. No. Surely, they wouldn't. My parents and I might've had our differences right now, but surely, they wouldn't cut off my cell as well?

With my credit card and cell, were they basically holding my necessities for ransom, so I came scurrying back?

"Does someone else have access to your cell?" he asked.

I perked up, plastering on a fake smile. "Not that I know of. It's too late, I'll deal with this tomorrow," I beamed. His gaze narrowed on me as I fluttered to my suitcase. "That shower sounds pretty good now."

I didn't even know where to begin processing this new information. What if they'd cut off everything? I was literally stranded. I flicked open the suitcase, my face paling. Shit I'd grabbed the wrong suitcase. I was in such a fluster that I'd grabbed the one with all my makeup, hair accessories, panties, and bras. I wanted to burst out into tears. How had I managed to screw up so badly? And this suitcase now seemed to be the final catastrophic catalyst to send me over.

"What's wrong?" Eric's voice boomed over my shoulder. I snapped the suitcase shut before he could peer in, embarrassed. I also wasn't going to strut out in only a thong and bra to sleep in.

I cleared my throat. Why was I being so embarrassed around this man? Did I feel judged? Self-conscious? I didn't care any other time, and besides, most people *liked* me. I was determined that this big brute would be no different. "I grabbed the wrong suitcase and don't have my pj's." There I said it.

"What else could be in that suitcase?" he asked suspiciously as he backed away and began to sift through his own wardrobe.

"Do you really want the answer?" I asked skeptically, considering he came across as a man of few words, he seemed awfully chatty since we'd walked in. Or was he maybe nervous as well?

"Here," he instructed. Just in time, I'd caught the long, oversized flannel shirt he'd tossed. "You can wear this."

Red heated my cheeks, and I couldn't look directly at him. Wasn't this just getting weirder? I didn't even know this man. But I couldn't sleep in skintight jeans either. "Thank you."

Without delay, I scurried into the bathroom, again surprised by its sophisticated arrangement. How on earth did he build something so beautiful here in the middle of the mountains?

I stared at myself in the mirror as I stripped, the gravity of my dire situation weighing on me. Tomorrow I'd be able to leave. And then what? I had a quarter tank of gas which would barely get me over the Canadian border. I had no cash. And no cell apparently. I took a shaky breath, doing everything I could manage to supress the tears that wanted to overflow.

I stepped into the hot shower, grateful for its heat as it thawed out my bones. Slowly, I found myself sinking to the bottom of the shower, curling my arms around my legs and dipping my head, allowing the hot water to wash over my back as I quietly sobbed.

I couldn't go back to my parents because it meant I'd have to deal with everything I'd worked so hard to run away from at this point. Having my credit cards and cell suspended only reminded me of how truly owned I was by them. But I never thought it would come to this. I cried, angry at myself for not creating a safety net for myself. Why had I been so naive as to think I could play out this new life I'd created in Manhattan without consequence?

And now what was I going to do? As of tomorrow, I'd have to leave and go where?

Maybe it was all the driving that had me beat down. Usually, I would've thought of an alternative exit strategy by now, and yet nothing came to mind. Only what appeared to be rock bottom as I sat on the tiles of some stranger's shower.

Thoughtfully, I squirted some of the shower gel into my palms not surprised by the intense masculine smell of it. I massaged my body with it, much preferring the smell of this than feeling cold and gross after the full day's drive.

But I couldn't hide in here forever. As much as I wanted to. I stood up, a slight head spin from the steam and crying as I stepped out, turning the shower off.

I curled the fluffy gray towel around me, patting my face before my entire body locked up. On the middle of the bathroom floor was a spider. I screamed, almost ripping the door off its hinges and bolting out of the room.

Eric jerked up, and in two strides he was tucking me behind his back, confused. Shadow growled at the ominous presence coming from the bathroom.

"What is it?" Eric asked, looking back and forth.

I pointed, hot water still beading down my back and legs. "There's a spider," I gushed, my voice shaking.

I saw the noticeable tension ripple away from him until it was replaced by something else. A booming laugh.

Disheveled, I tightened the towel around my chest, now suddenly self-conscious that I was standing so closely to this man naked. And yet it did nothing to deter his thunderous laughter that created ample butterflies in my stomach.

"It's big!" I said, popping out my hip with my hand on it.

"Of course it is, snowflake."

I peered over his shoulder as he so effortlessly scooped it up in his hand and walked toward the door. Okay maybe in his hands it didn't look so big. Shadow was by his side the entire time, curious by what Eric was handling.

Heat flushed my cheeks as the crackling fireplace grabbed my attention. Wow it was so warm in here now.

Eric dusted his hands and closed the door. When he turned, his gaze quickly drifted down to my toes. His gaze diverted as he quickly looked away from my almost-naked state.

A new kind of heat rose to my cheeks. I'd never been embarrassed to show my body before. So why now? Was it because of the celibacy I'd vowed when leaving Manhattan? It had been three months since I'd been intimate with any man, and considering my track record, that was a while. *And why was I even thinking about this?*

"I'll go change," I quickly gushed, dashing back

into the bathroom. My heart pounded. This was way too close to be spending time with a gorgeous lumberjack. Not only had I hit rock bottom but the fates were playing a cruel joke to boot. I took a shaky breath, trying to relax. Stop being so conceited. He's probably not into you. There. As easy as that, I was able to clear away the immediate thoughts that came to mind as to what I would do to him... climb him like a tree for example. This time I did slap my cheeks. Enough.

It felt strange not having my usual night routine with my creams and lotions, and my hair was going to be a giant mess tomorrow morning without my sprays. I sighed. Wow I really had hit rock bottom.

I put on a thong and threw on the oversized flannel. Wow did this really fit him? It came to my knees. I looked back and forth in the mirror kind of surprised that I liked the style. It didn't flatter in the way that I'd usually wear tight dresses but it was, well kind of cute. A pinup of "boyfriend/girlfriend goals." Not that a stranger for one night held that kind of magnitude but I wasn't as uncomfortable by wearing it.

When I walked out, the lights had been switched off, all but two lamps. One beside the sofa I'd be staying on that already had a multitude of pillows and blankets thrown over it. And the other light was on Eric's bed side table. He was already rolled over to the side in his bed, with Shadow on a pillow by the floor. His larger figure was noticeable under the blankets and the dark outline of mountains through the ceiling-high windows stretched behind him.

I went to say goodnight but tightened my lips. He was probably already sleeping anyway. I tucked myself under the blankets, surprised by the sofas comfort. I hadn't slept on many sofas, but there was something strange and beautiful about staring into the fireplace. The crackling seemed to break through my worrisome thoughts. Tomorrow, with a fresh mind, I'd figure out what I'd do.

I couldn't help but notice the eerie howling wind, a twist in my stomach unable to unfurl even as I focused on the calmness of the crackling fire. An uncomfortable tension rippled through me, the sense that something bad was yet to come.

Chapter 6

Cassidy

I quietly hummed as I cooked the only thing I knew how to. An omelette. I swayed in the kitchen, surprised that Eric was a heavy sleeper. I imagined he might've been the type to wake up at the pinprick of any noise.

I'd been awake since the fireplace ceased crackling and the charcoal barely remained to glow. I'd at least managed a few hours' sleep and had been trying to form some kind of game plan ever since. When I'd only come up with a few painful ideas, I decided to make myself useful by way of a kind of gesture for Eric's hospitality. He had said I could use or eat anything, after all.

I studied the omelette as I hoped said game plan miraculously came to mind. I had to figure out my next move after leaving this town. If a larger town up ahead wasn't too far away, maybe I could sell a ring or two? The thought mortified me. I loved all my accessories but if it gave me enough cash for gas to make it over the border and to my friend's, then it'd be worth it. But then what? I'd be stranded there with no money and Alice wasn't the type of friend I could express my worries to. She was nice and all but she loved to gossip more than the next person. Hearing that I had nothing in my bank account would spread like wildfire. I'm sure my parents thought the same thing, that I'd contact them or reach home just as quickly, begging. And I refused to do that. *I couldn't do that.*

Shadow had been by my side the moment I woke, and he silently watched me with his tail wagging. He looked up at me as if begging, probably for the food I assumed. That's what dogs did, wasn't it? But he'd only want meat, right? The way he looked at me spoke volumes, that he'd eat anything I'd throw his way. But weren't dogs allergic to certain foods? "Sorry," I mouthed to him. That was a risk I wasn't taking.

The sun had slowly begun rising in the distance and I found myself peeking over in Eric's direction often, my attention immediately drawing to the magnificent window and view behind him. Rolling snowy mountains rippled off into the distance, slithers of sunlight peeking through while the cabin was still shrouded in darkness. It truly was a breathtaking view and something I hadn't been able to appreciate last night in the dark.

I poured the whisked ingredients into the fry pan, admiring my handiwork as I hummed to the beat playing in my head with hips swaying as if I were at the club. When I peeked over my shoulder a fourth time at the mountain view, I took a sharp startled breath as my heart rapidly pounded.

Eric was awake; his gaze narrowed on me as he lazily ran a hand over his face and blinked numerous times. Interesting, a not-so-morning-person lumberjack it appeared. My gaze absentmindedly dragged over his naked but hairy chest. A heat flushed my cheeks as I looked away, surprised by my immediate attraction to the older man.

"Good morning," I chirped, focusing on the omelette at hand as he groggily made his way over.

"What's this?" He yawned, slipping past me in the kitchen and setting up the coffee pot still half asleep. He yawned again, stretching with the motion. I peeked over my shoulder, embarrassed by my shameful wandering gaze that glided over his back and shoulder muscles. Was that much muscle even possible on a man? On a real one anywayand not someone on social media through an edited lens. He had muscles bulging against muscles. I looked away, internally slapping myself for my gawking.

"I'm making you an omelette, it's my way of saying thank you."

He leaned over my shoulder, peering into the pan. His warmth and very naked upper body seemed to ignite a heat that scorched my back. I pretended to be unfazed by his proximity but it suddenly became hard for me to breathe.

"Mmm," he hummed. What did that even mean? Slowly yawning and dragging his feet back around the island bench now with coffee in hand, he lazily opened the door for Shadow to go out and do his business. He combed through his hair and twisted back and forth. His abs were ridiculously chiseled, the skin pulling tightly over every muscle. Eight defined clumps of pure masculine muscle, dipping into a V at his loose gray sweats.

He took a mouthful of his coffee and his lazy gaze snapped to mine. Suddenly, I realized I'd been staring at him the whole time. Bashful, I looked away, focusing on flipping the omelette.

"How much snow are you used to in Manhattan?" he casually asked through another yawn. Wow he was the furthest thing from a morning person.

With spatula in the air, I considered it. "A normal amount?"

He pointed outside. "This much?" he asked through another yawn.

Intrigued by the most initiative he'd taken in any of our conversations, I rounded the island bench and squeezed between him and the doorframe. *Wow.* There was so much snow.

"I haven't seen snow like this for a long time," I beamed excitedly. "Not since I was a kid creating snowmen when we'd ski in Europe and Canada. And certainly not in Manhattan." He was watching me quietly as I squealed with excitement by the sight of snow. I supposed to him, I was probably just a cliché city girl. And I didn't care—I wasn't going to let it take away the magic and bewilderment of what I saw right now.

It was still mostly dark outside the cabin, the glimmer of sun only just peeking around the house. The cold frost-bitten air swept past my exposed legs. Idly, Shadow pushed back past my knees, preferring the warmth of inside once he'd finished. And I couldn't entirely blame him.

"Is the omelette burning?" Eric asked.

"What? Oh shit." I ran around the kitchen bench, cursing as I removed the fry pan off the stove top. "Damn."

Eric closed the door and peered over my shoulder as I panicked. He took another mouthful of coffee from his now near empty mug in his giant hand as he assessed the damage.

"It's not so bad but I'll make you another one."

His hand paused on my wrist. I could hear my heartbeat in my ears. Maybe it had something to do with the roughness of his calloused hands compared to mine, but he was a *man,* and my loins were screaming to jump his bones. I was certain it came down to some weird primal urge. Gently he said, "I'll eat it. Just make yourself something as well."

I nodded curtly, startled by my hot fiery reaction to him. My ovaries were basically jumping out at him. I mean he was obviously hot, but we couldn't be any more different and then there was the age difference. I internally grimaced, why was I even thinking about this when I had much more pressing matters to consider? And I'd sworn celibacy! I was completely off men. *But maybe because all the guys you dated were boys in Manhattan,* a little voice antagonized me.

I made the omelette as directed, but I couldn't

remember the last time I'd actually eaten breakfast, well unless it was a juice of some sort.

A heavy silence filled the cabin. I glanced over my shoulder at Eric. He was shoveling the food into his mouth. Perhaps a guy his size needed more than one omelette.

As if feeling my gaze, he said without looking up, "It tastes good. Thank you."

A satisfied warmth filled me. "One of my college friends always told me the best way to show your gratitude was cooking for someone heartfelt. And I kind of liked that sentiment," I hummed in my singsong way. I enjoyed cooking, although I barely made time for it.

"Out of gratitude, huh? Is that why mine's burnt?"

I swept around, abhorred, only to find a small smile curved at his lips. Was he, toying with me?

"I mean that was an accident."

A low chuckle rumbled from the depths of his stomach. And I found it... mesmerizing. Why did I have the impression that this man couldn't laugh at all? Probably because of the constant scowl on his expression, or his obvious dislike of me crashing at his place.

"And besides," I continued, flipping the second

omelette, not entirely comfortable with how unnerved he made me feel. "That's all you're going to ask? Not about what I studied in college or what my friend's name was or anything like that?"

"Are you trying to teach me social etiquette?" he mocked.

I harrumphed, suddenly preferring the grizzly version I'd met yesterday. And I wasn't entirely sure if his sexy change of tone was because he was still half asleep or he was purposefully messing with me.

"I mean you do quite literally live in the mountains. Maybe you need the lesson." I pointed the spatula at him. His mouth twitched again, and I couldn't help but smile at him, satisfied to at least get this much out of him. I'd dealt with some of *Candice Magazine's* toughest clients at reception and it was my philosophy that I could make anyone my friend. And this man beast would be no different.

I flipped the omelette, satisfied. I didn't have the chance to make many people omelettes back in Manhattan. Everyone was always busy and only able to schedule time for parties or café catch-ups. And the few dates who actually stayed through the night, always left before there could be any discussion about breakfast. A sullen dread sunk in. At first, Isso-belle and I'd joked about my terrible luck with men and serial-dating lifestyle. But the longer I clung to my celibacy, the more I realized I really was shit with men.

"So just to confirm, we'll be going back down town this morning, right?" I asked quietly. I didn't want to be a burden on his schedule since I'd already inconvenienced him. But the sooner I could make it to the next town to pawn something—anything—and contact my friend, Alice, that I was on my way, the better. It was a stepping stone, and at least I'd be able to afford gas. A heavy weight sunk into my stomach. But then what would I do?

The cold air had settled in the room, circulating a chill and forming goose bumps on my bare legs. Quietly, Eric went to start up the fireplace again.

"Yes, and we'll check in to see whether the tree's been removed and if you can drive though," Eric replied matter-of-factly. I played around with the omelette distractedly, scraping at the edges. Shadow demanded my attention, nudging me, and obliging, I began scratching the top of his head, which I'd recently learnt he enjoyed.

Minutes later, once Eric was done with the fire-place, he asked, "Didn't you look at the forecast before driving through the border and to your friends?"

No. I hadn't thought of that, because I didn't drive all that often. "Well yes and no," I lied with a small laugh, agreeable because I didn't want to sound like a complete ditz. I scraped the second omelette out and back onto his plate.

His eyebrows furrowed in confusion at his second dealing.

"I'm not a breakfast kind of person," I confessed. "So, here's another plateful of gratitude," I brightly beamed. My mind ran away with me again as I absentmindedly began cleaning the fry pan. What happened if I couldn't get to Alice's lodge? But returning to Manhattan wasn't an option either because I had no doubt my parents were still there and waiting. I was not going to fall into their hands, exactly how they wanted me to. But damn this was hard to figure out on my own.

Chapter 7

Eric

The way she'd looked wearing my shirt was near criminal. I couldn't take my eyes off her as she casually strolled out of the bathroom and into the lounge room, the hem reaching her knees. Behind the perfected makeup was a naturally beautiful young woman, those big blue eyes captivating. I'd ground my teeth in irritation. It had taken me hours to get to sleep as I considered why she might've been passing through town. Not that I cared but some of her answers didn't sit right with me. I had the niggling sense that she was in trouble, but I didn't know what kind and what she might've brought upon our town. And yet I also considered what those blonde curls might feel like wrapped around my fist, or how soft her skin would be, or what those lips would taste like.

After hours of wrestling with the discomfort of someone else in my space, sleep finally took hold. And then when I'd woken up, she was making me an omelette? I wasn't sure what to think about this little snowflake that had waltzed into our town. But the sooner she left, and I could fall back into my routine, the better. Her staying her for only one night had already distracted me beyond measure.

Driving down the mountain she said very little, unlike the nervous chatter she'd filled space and time with on the way up. When I dared a brief glance her way, she was looking outside the window, deep in thought. I noticed her fingers wringing each other. Was she still nervous around me or was something else upsetting her?

My thoughts drifted to her cell being suspended. Was she in some financial strife? She didn't look like the penniless type, but I'd learnt over the years appearances weren't always what they seemed.

Lori had already opened shop and as I'd promised Cassidy, her car had remained on the street untouched.

"We'll check on the update about the tree and

see if you can get through yet," I said, turning the engine off. Her head whipped up, shaken from her deep thought and she gave me a beaming smile.

"That sounds great, thank you," she said, unbuckling her seat belt.

She jumped out of the truck, opening the back door for Shadow.

When we walked in, my face slackened at the sight of my youngest brother, Thomas, swiveling on the barstool. A mischievous smile stretched his goofy handsome face and I knew the shit I was already in.

"So it's true that you took in a young lady for the night? What a gentleman," he charmed, standing to attention. I threw Lori a threatening gaze. She just laughed, shrugging her shoulder casually as if she were none the wiser. And certainly not the instigator.

"I'm Thomas, Ricky boy here's youngest brother." He offered his hand out to Cassidy. Shadow growled at him in warning—and I wanted to join him. I hated that name he called me. What annoyed me even more was the way Cassidy seemed charmed by his introduction.

"Ricky?" she queried. I ignored her, walking past my younger brother and rounding the counter, the chance of me being in a good mood today, gone.

"You want a juice, hun?" Lori asked Cassidy.

Cassidy's smile faltered. Yea she certainly wasn't a fan of the one poured straight out of the carton yesterday. She thought I wasn't looking when she'd poured her to-go cup down the sink in the cabin. "No but I'll have a green tea, if you have it?"

"Coming right up," Lori charmed. It was abnormally quiet at this time, usually by now a couple of locals would've stopped by for their coffee and breakfast rolls.

"I apologize sincerely that you got stuck with my brother for an entire night, he isn't exactly friendly-making material," Thomas jibed.

"Oh no he was very hospitable," Cassidy quickly countered.

Thomas raised an eyebrow and looked in my direction. "You're probably the first that's ever used that definition to describe him."

Cassidy seemed unsure what to say.

"Any update on the log blocking the road?" I asked Lori, purposefully ignoring him, although I kept an uneasy eye on Thomas and Cassidy. It irked me how well they already seemed to get along. Thomas always had been charismatic in that way, probably the type she was used to fawning over.

"Yea about that," Lori said as she poured hot

water over a tea bag into a mug. "They're not going to be able to get rid of it for another day or so. Apparently, we've got some heavy snowfall on its way. Most of the locals are preparing for it."

I frowned; most mornings I'd usually check the reports to see what the weather was doing but this morning I'd been distracted. I eyed the reason for that. Cassidy was absentmindedly brushing through Shadow's fur as she laughed at a joke Thomas had made at my expense.

I wasn't at all comfortable with the way Shadow sat at her feet, in that protective way he had always and only ever done with me. Why had Shadow chosen this woman? He didn't get along with anyone other than me. *Traitor,* I glumly thought.

"Did you hear that, hun?" Lori asked as she handed Cassidy the mug of green tea. "You're not going to be able to head out today either. We have a bit of a nasty snowstorm on its way so no one can drive from the neighboring town to chop it down.

"Oh." Cassidy frowned. She stared at her tea.

"Don't worry you don't have to stay with this grump," Thomas jokingly said. "If you want you can crash with me?"

"Absolutely not," I growled. They all looked at

me, surprised. A playful smile jerked at Thomas's expression which pissed me off even more.

"Why not? Don't think I'm dependable enough?" he asked, leaning back in his chair. He and Lori were enjoying this way too much, and it was grating on me.

"She'll be staying with me," I growled out. Taking in her startled reaction, I felt the need to add, "I don't think she wants to stay with you and the twins keeping her up all night."

Thomas offered a sly knowing smile.

"The twins?" Cassidy asked.

"Our other brothers. Worse than this one, those two are." Lori pointed a finger at Thomas, who seemed affronted by her accusing finger. "And maybe she doesn't want to stay at all. She could still go back."

"Not if the snow will be picking up shortly," I piped up. All eyes were on me again.

"Sounding a bit bossy and possessive there, Ricky boy," Thomas teased.

My jaw tightened. "I'm not. It's just in Cassidy's best interests. That car isn't the safest on these roads and we all know it."

A silence fell over the room. Especially on the

back roads; lives had been lost with even the most experienced drivers losing grip and crashing.

"Um, if it's okay and safer, I'd rather stay the night," Cassidy said quietly. "I'm not the most confident driver." A protective tug in my stomach. Maybe it was because of all those we'd lost previously, and I didn't want the same thing for her. "But would it be possible if I could call my friend off someone's cell to let her know I might be a few days late?"

Before Thomas could scoop his cell out of his pocket, I offered her mine. "You can call off this."

I could feel Lori's and Thomas's gazes burning into me. Why wasn't I letting Thomas help her? Wouldn't that make it easier for me to go back to my daily routine and be free of her? But I wasn't giving him the satisfaction of trying to hook up with her either. His arrogance in that way annoyed me.

"Thank you," Cassidy said carefully as she plucked it out of my hand and glanced around at the interested onlookers. They were making it damn uncomfortable, but that was to piss me off and had nothing to do with her. Comparatively her hand was half the size of mine. *Delicate,* was the best description. I mean she was easily half my size, after all. She'd be like throwing around the weight of a shoulder bag. I cleared my throat, pushing away the thought of throwing her around in anyway.

"Why don't you show her around the town today before we get snowed in?" Lori suggested as she put a few utensils away. "Thomas and I have got it covered here. I don't think it'll be much of a busy day anyway."

"If we're going to be snowed in, I should cut some more wood for the locals."

Lori rolled her eyes. "Please I think everyone has enough wood to last them the month."

"Or if you're busy, I can take her?" Thomas suggested with a nonchalant shrug. I could feel the muscle at my temple pick up in tempo. He was purposefully pushing me today.

"I think they have enough wood," I gritted out, agreeing with Lori.

I could sense Lori's smirk as she turned around and through to the kitchen. I didn't much like what these two were up to.

Not that there was a lot in Rosefield to show her, but I certainly wasn't going to let Thomas sweet talk her for his own amusement. But didn't that make more sense? They were around the same age. A hot irritation ran through me. This wasn't like me. This was meant to be my escapism from everything, so why was I creating a busier schedule to accommodate this strange woman who'd randomly found herself stranded in our town? And yet I wanted to wipe that smug expression off my younger brother's face immediately. Man, my family knew how to get under my skin.

Chapter 8

Cassidy

Thomas looked like a younger version of Eric, except where he might've once been a redhead, he'd bleached his hair blonde. And where Eric had a persistent frown marring his face, Thomas had a goofy demeanor about him and was probably around my age. I wondered if the twins they'd mentioned had red hair like Lori or black like Eric.

I'd left them taunting Eric in the café; he looked like he was about to explode. I now stood outside, holding myself tightly in the frigid air. It hadn't stopped sprinkling with snow since I'd arrived in town but it had definitely picked up. I'd entered Alice's number in Eric's cell hoping she'd answer.

Surprisingly, she did. "Hello?" She yawned audibly. "Who is this?"

"Oh, thank goodness. Alice it's me Cassidy!"

There was a shuffle, as if she was doing a double take on her cell.

"Something weird happened with my cell," I assured her. "But I'm still on my way. I've just been delayed by a few days."

"Oh, was that this month?" she chimed on the other end. "I thought that was next month?" A jab spiked my stomach. I'd been texting her and we'd spoke about it twice already. Granted both times she was at a party and perhaps she couldn't hear me properly when I'd called. "Okay cool. Whatever, I'm having some awesome parties lately and there's some smoking backpackers here. While my parents are away, I've been having a delicious time. You know the whole boy from the wrong side of the tracks thing, it's got me hot and heavy," she laughed.

"Oh, that's cool," I said, not entirely finding the appeal. Usually, that would've had me excited but now I felt... indifferent? "Well, you'll never guess it but I've sworn to celibacy so that won't be a thing for me but I can't wait to party," I laughed.

"What? Ew gross? Who are you? Don't give me

that celibacy bullshit too. Monica tried to pull the same stunt last year and she lasted four months until everyone stopped inviting her to parties and stuff because she went all weird about guys trying on her. It was a total bore."

My heart sank. Shit, would they kick me out too? I hadn't spoken to any of my friends in Canada for a while, but had we always been this guy centric?

"Oh by the way," she continued. "Fredrick was calling around for you this past month too." A cold sweat poured over me and I felt the lump in my throat thicken. "But no one knew where you were besides Manhattan. Should I call him and let him know you'll be here?"

"No," I blurted out. At her silence, I continued. "No, not yet. I just want it to be us girls for a while, you know?"

She seemed to mull over that. "Okay well sounds kind of boring, I mean you have to give him some kind of attention now and then, Cassidy. I don't know much about lasting relationships and what not, but that sounds like a good start."

"We're not in a relationship," I quickly blurted. Why was Fredrick asking for my whereabouts? Shit, was he in on this with my parents?

"Whatever you say," she said through a yawn, disinterested. "By the way, where are you calling from? The reception sounds really bad, like some-things blowing in the cell?"

I looked around at the small-town square and the main street blanketed in snow. Someone casually walked their dog on a lead, waving at me when I looked up. Awkwardly, I reciprocated the action. Did strangers always greet one another like this outside of Manhattan? Was this that small town feel I'd heard people describe?

"Just a small stop in," I gushed. "Okay I'll see you later. Big kisses!" And I hung up.

My heart churned and a heavy dread washed over me. *Frederick.* Fuck. Why was he trying to find me? Hadn't I made it blatantly clear I wasn't inter-ested those many years ago? Wasn't me running away enough of an answer for him?

"Hey," Eric growled from behind. I jumped, almost dropping the cell. In the movement, my leg gave way and I slipped on the icy surface. I screamed and closed my eyes, clutching at my chest and waiting for the fall. He caught me, peeling one eye at a time open. His eyebrows were knitted together as he held me up, suspended in the air like I weighed nothing.

"You shouldn't sneak up on people," I breathed, a cool air escaping me. The legs he propped me back on were shaky and that jumbled feeling of emotion left me vulnerable, tears threatening to escape. Or maybe that had been the result of my call with Alice. I couldn't cry in front of this brute of a man. He'd just think I was some city girl that couldn't fend for herself. But wasn't I? I had no cash. No cell. And was running away from a past I was suddenly realizing I had no control over. Because my parents and Frederick still felt like they owned me.

And with a difficult swallow, I realized after my brief call with Alice that I really had outgrown that world I'd left behind. I might've still gone to parties and been a wild child in Manhattan but at least I'd made genuine friends like Clover and Issobelle. Hadn't I? They didn't care about boys and parties like I did. And they reprimanded me when I was in the wrong. I clutched at the thought of what they might say to me now.

"Cassidy, is everything alright?" Eric asked. My name on his lips was like a calming balm. Because wasn't it? Right now, I was okay. I was safe. And every self-help and new age book I'd read over the past two years as I tried to reinvent myself taught me to focus on the now and remind myself that right now, I was okay.

I clutched at my crystal necklace with a little feather attached to it, absorbing the strengths the market lady claimed it harbored. Self-love and protection. Well at least that's what I vaguely remember she said it possessed. Or maybe that's what I'd decided it to be.

"Mhmm," I said, realizing I hadn't spoken for a while and if this man had his way, we'd freeze out in the cold in absolute silence. I handed him his cell. "Thank you. All sorted."

He didn't seem very convinced going by his expression and with a brief glance through the window he grunted in irritation. I followed his gaze where his brother now gave a thumbs-up and then as if busted waved my way cheekily.

"Did you still want to look around town?" Eric asked, ignoring Thomas. I tried to hide the sly smile. His brother seemed to keep him youthful at least. And as an only child, I had to confess I kind of enjoyed watching the dynamics between the three siblings. And to think that there were another two, I wondered what that might've been like.

"I'd really like that," I said, despite the growing need to go back into the warmth.

"You might want these. They're Lori's," he said, offering me a beanie and mittens. "It's colder today than usual. And we won't stay out for long. I don't want you getting sick."

I peered at him from the corner of my eye. For someone who pretended to be impersonal and indifferent, he certainly seemed easy with caring for others. I shuffled them on, grateful for the extra layer of warmth.

"You look like your brother you know," I said to start conversation, hoping that he might not find it such an inconvenience this time.

He tsked as if the thought was more a nuisance. "He's a runt."

I laughed and he seemed stunned. Shadow barked, bouncing beside us on the snow as we walked. With a flush over his cheeks, Eric stared ahead.

"Compared to you, I think anyone would look like a runt. But it's kind of nice seeing you all get along. I don't have any siblings so it's nice to watch," I admitted with hands in my puffy pink jumper.

He seemed to consider this for a while as we rounded the corner of the main street and toward a lake. It was so serene and quiet here. The lake had frozen over, the sun glistening over it effortlessly.

Snowflakes created small droplets all over my jacket, and yet somehow it made it feel more magical.

"Come under here," Eric instructed, directing me toward a wooden rotunda. It did the best it could to block out the snow, revealing the vastness of the lake and the mountains beyond.

"During the summer you'll often see the locals fishing here. They don't catch much but I think that's more about their skill than what's available in here. And sometimes tourists will back up their boats and just party on the lake for a day or so. Most of them coming from the bigger town over." He pointed at certain spots, creating a life outside the desolate view now. I couldn't imagine any of those things.

"And do you fish?" I asked.

"No. It's never been my sport and I'm not here during the summer. My uncle and father love it though."

"Where do you go during the summer?" I asked curiously. Did he hibernate when it picked up in population?

He seemed to consider me for a moment, as if revealing any more information might give away his deepest and darkest secrets. Or perhaps it was more information than he'd been willing to give a stranger, who as far as I was aware was stranded with him for another night.

"I only ever come here for the winter season for the whole month of January to relieve my father and uncle of their duties around the town."

"So where do you come from?" I inquired also curious about his parents. I'd just assumed he was local. For some reason, I was taken back by that. So, this wasn't his home? And yet I couldn't imagine him anywhere else.

Again, he seemed to consider my question as he guided me outside of the rotunda and back toward the main street. "I live in Chicago."

My jaw dropped. "Wait you live in a city? With actual buildings and suburbia?"

He seemed just as mock-shocked by my admission. "Is it so hard to believe?"

"Yea, well you know for the most part you don't seem like the city man type?"

"The city man type?"

I shrugged nonchalant. "You know there's heaps of them, the artist, the business man, the husband with a wife and kids but says he's single, the crypto guy, the entrepreneur, the—"

"You seem to know a lot about these types?" he queried, caution in his tone.

Eric pointed out the local grocery store. I'd driven past it on the way in but had thought it was an abandoned building. The town needed a makeover, but it held a certain charm. I sighed, defeated in the admission I was about to make. Would he think less of me for it? Everyone dated in Manhattan like it was a professional sport. Didn't they? "Well, you could consider me a serial dater or a socialite depending on what way you look at it."

His eyebrows knitted together ever so slightly, his expression unreadable like usual. "You don't have a 'type' then?"

I shrugged. "I don't know, I just think you know when you know, you know?"

Again, he held that scornful expression as he pushed his shoulders back. I hadn't realized how much he'd been trying to cater to my size by dipping his gaze to my eye level as we walked. "No. I don't," he said bitterly.

Okay that definitely sounded like someone had been burnt. I couldn't see any wedding ring so I'd assumed he was single, but it wouldn't be uncommon for someone his age to be married and divorced by now, another sport in Manhattan.

Pretending like I didn't notice the change in his tone, I bounced along as he pointed out a fabric store.

It looked like a shop front but was also obviously someone's home as well. Inside the first room was Ann rocking back and forth on a wooden chair and knitting. "Well, what about you, what's your type?"

Immediately he growled. "I don't have a type. I don't do women."

"Oh." I was taken aback. He seemed confused. "Sorry I had no idea that you preferred men."

"I'm not into men," he quickly blurted out, red crossing his cheeks once again.

I furrowed my eyebrows in confusion, finding myself laughing at his outright reaction.

"As in dating or women, I don't do it," he clarified. "It's too complicated and distracting."

"Uh-huh," I said in a singsong way, satisfied by the way it flustered him. It was rather entertaining being able to get under this hulk of man's skin. I understood why his siblings picked on him. But also, if that was the truth, then I found it sad that he found women "complicated and distracting." Then again, how could I comment, I was a serial dater. Well ex-serial dater. And dating had only become complicated because it never lead to anything more.

"You should give it a go, who knows maybe you'll even like it."

He grunted by way of response.

"I've dated heaps of guys," I casually said, continuing the conversation. "And obviously none stuck around but I still met some amazing people and learnt new things. Maybe you shouldn't put so much pressure on it and just see where it gets you. Maybe you'll find an uncomplicated woman."

He was quiet for a while. When I looked at him from the corner of my eye, it was obvious he was confused about something. "When you say you've dated a lot of men, you do it to have fun?"

This was traction. He was asking questions. And that was what I told everyone, it had covered time and been fun in the past. But it had also been a roller coaster when I liked someone who didn't reciprocate the feelings—or attracting the same type of men who only wanted flings. I had told everyone it was just for fun and to pass time, and yet something compelled me to tell Eric otherwise, part of the truth perhaps. Probably because he didn't know me and also because in the coming days we'd never see one another again. I wondered what this "non-dater's" take might be on my truth.

"I tell everyone it's for fun," I admitted. "But the truth is, I've been looking for the love of my life the day I flew into Manhattan. Kind of corny right?"

He listened intently instead of laughing like I thought he might've.

"And I'm not even a hopeless romantic or anything, but there was a lot of pressure from my parents to go down a particular path. And I assumed if I were to create a life of my own and start my own family, I wouldn't have to do that." I contained my nerves, the mere thought of my parents and their "conditions" bubbling over.

"Why do I have a feeling you're only telling me half the truth?" he queried as we stepped back toward the store.

"Because maybe I'm one of the complicated women you avoid," I laughed lightly as I absentmindedly reached out to catch a snowflake. The snow had continued to pick up since we'd left the café. I wondered how foolish I sounded to him, but he said nothing.

"Do you really think you need a husband to prove yourself to your parents?" he asked and watched me intently.

I shrugged. "I'm not overly ambitious like my friends back in Manhattan. If you met Clover and Issobelle you'd be shocked as to how they could even be friends with me, we're completely different. I don't have goals and my parents never really expected anything of me because they'd already decided what was best for me. I just want to live a content life with people I love. Not be forced into a box that my parents decided for me. Sounds weird coming from a twenty-six-year-old, right?"

"I think everyone has their own pressures and there's nothing wrong if you don't have a career ambition. But don't you think you do in a way, since you're trying to pave your own path from your parents' trajectory?"

I considered him, a smile spreading across my face. His words made me feel good in my decision. Almost brave. I'd felt like a spoilt brat for years. I didn't have the same drive as my new friends in Manhattan, and all my old friends only cared about wealth and a good time. I sat somewhere in between, not entirely sure as to where I belonged anymore.

He opened the café door for me; no doubt we'd ended the town tour early because the snowfall had picked up too much. I was scattered and soaked, even more grateful for the added mittens and beanie Lori had let me borrow.

"Wise words," I charmed. "And thank you for listening. I don't know how we ended up talking about me, when we were talking about your love life?"

Thomas gasped, still swinging back and forth on the barstool. "My brother actually has a love life?"

"Shut it," Eric growled.

Lori was reading a book and never looked up, but a smile toyed at her lips.

Thomas laughed, reaching out a hand to Shadow, who purposefully stepped wide so he couldn't touch him. I realized then the truth the others had insinuated. Shadow was rather... was snobby the right word to use for him? He pranced behind his owner, the dog fully aware of his luscious coat. Perhaps picky was more accurate. An amused but heartfelt relief flooded me, liking the idea that I was one of few he'd taken a liking to.

"I think we should close up, boss," Thomas said. "No one's going to come in today. Not with this weather."

"Remind me what work you were doing again?" Lori accused with a squinted gaze in his direction. "I'll tell Mom you've been slacking off."

"Not that she expects him to do anything," Eric grumbled under his breath.

"Hey, I can't help it if I'm the favorite," Thomas defended.

"You're the youngest," Lori corrected.

"Therefore the favorite," Thomas said teasingly

as he patted the chair beside him, inviting me to sit next to him again. "But you two are his perfect little soldiers. Did you know these two come back this time every year to look over the shop and Mom while Dad and our uncle go south for hunting?"

I looked between Lori and Eric. "Really?" I said, intrigued. Although Eric had briefly mentioned it.

"The moment one of you magically obtain a partner you might have to skip a year, could you imagine that?" He gasped, still childishly swinging on his chair.

Lori harrumphed, snapping her book shut. "And shouldn't you be studying and doing something with your preadolescent life?"

He kicked up a cocky boyish grin. "I can do both. Shouldn't you both be running your oh so very important businesses and lives back home? But no, they always find this as a little escape and sanctuary."

"You both own your own business?" I asked curiously.

Lori sighed, defeated by her little brother. "We do, I run a catering company in LA and Eric runs an IT company in Chicago."

Eric seemed uninterested in the discussion. IT,

huh? I would've never picked him as an IT kind of guy.

"After the Christmas and New Year's period I give my team a break. My second-in-charge organises all the small events and venues while I'm recouping for a few weeks when I come back home. It works for both of us," she said, shrugging her shoulder.

Thomas snorted. "Her 'second-in-charge,'" he quoted. "More like her very handsome assistant who she hasn't been able to make a move on yet."

"Watch it." She pointed a finger at him. "Or I will come around there and pull your hair out."

"I'll tell Mom." He poked out his tongue.

Part of me was sad that he didn't mention anything further about Eric's' business, but I could tell by his brooding demeanor it wasn't something he wanted to talk about much during his visit away.

"But I think he's right, Eric, we should close up and go home before the snow gets worse," Lori said, looking over her shoulder at Eric casually scratching under Shadow's chin.

He sighed, agreeing. "Then let's close up."

Thomas clapped his hands together, celebrating being let off shift early. I liked him; he was goofy and childlike but had a certain inviting charm about him which I imagined made it very easy for him to make friends.

Lori shook her head as she stood up and began closing the café. Admittedly, it looked like she'd already done most of it before we returned. "What are you making for dinner tonight?" Lori asked Eric.

He shrugged. She sized him up and he gritted out, "What?"

"You have a guest, cook something."

Both of their gazes landed on me. "Oh no, don't worry about me. By all means, in fact I should be cooking for you, since you're letting me stay."

"You can cook?" Thomas asked sounding impressed.

"Well, I could only cook him an omelette this morning, and that's as far as the skillset goes." I felt rather deflated by the admission.

"She made you an omelette this morning?" Thomas perked up in his chair, raising an eyebrow between us.

Eric slipped a disapproving glare at Thomas before walking into the hidden kitchen.

"I can give you a recipe and a few ingredients for a casserole if you'd like?" Lori suggested.

"She doesn't eat meat," Eric's voice echoed through the door.

"That's no problem," Lori sung back. "I can make it a vegetarian one. If you're up for the task?"

Excitement and nerves began to flutter in my stomach. What if I was really bad at it? But if I could be useful and show my appreciation, then I was more than happy to experiment. "I'd love to. Thank you."

Chapter 9

Cassidy

Silence yet again filled the truck. He didn't seem grumpy and so I tried to embrace the silence as much as possible. I was so used to people who were always talking, trying to grab the spotlight with their bigger, more extravagant story, and I found myself oddly enjoying the quiet and companionship.

I sat with the small hamper on my lap that Lori had given me, particularly eyeing the two bottles of red wine. I peered out from the corner of my eye at Eric, curious as to how he handled his alcohol. Or was he an "only beer" type of guy. Studying his profile, I noticed the few specks of gray through his black beard. I'd been around older men before, but I never felt this unusual sensation around them like I did Eric. It wasn't intimidation but something close to. It unnerved me. My head still whirled by the bizarre encounter and how I'd ended up halfway up a mountain in a small town, stranded for a second night.

I considered the siblings conversation earlier about the predicted snowfall tonight. It'd picked up throughout the day. And if what they said was true, then it was possible I'd be stranded for another day and night if we were snowed in. Maybe even more. I clutched onto the hamper as if it was my only means to make it up to Eric. He didn't know me, and yet he took me in. A small swirl began in my stomach at his kindness. He might've come across as a grizzly bear but maybe deep down he had the temperament of a teddy bear instead.

"You seem quiet," he commented.

I pulled my gaze away from the mountainside and stared up at him, surprised he'd initiated conversation.

"I've just been enjoying the scenery. It's pretty out here." In the afternoon, I could see it clearer unlike the night before in the scary dark. The mountain range and drive were beautiful, in its stark wintery way. And I understood now why he said only trucks would manage to get up it.

He settled into silence again, with an almost approving and understanding gleam to his expression. I'd learnt with Eric it wasn't so much as to what he said, because he tried to say as little as possible, but it was the subtle changes in his body language and the simple air about him. I'd never had to study someone in such a way before.

By the time we'd arrived at his cabin, I was excited to stretch my legs. It was only a twenty-minute drive out of the town but there was something freeing about standing out in the open and stretching my limbs. I opened the back door for Shadow. He leapt out, immediately following a scent trail and walking off into the distance.

"Does he do that every time?" I asked curiously as Eric pulled out another one of my suitcases. This time with my pj's in them.

"Sometimes, only if there's been other animals close to the cabin," he said, yanking the suitcase out with little effort. The most I could do was drag it on its wheels. Eric's gaze narrowed as we walked toward the door. I peered around the bulk of him and down at a set of paw prints.

"Are there other dogs around here?" I asked.

"Not usually" was all he said before he whistled to Shadow, who came pounding back obediently.

Shadow stopped at my side, his tongue out and panting as he nuzzled himself against my leg. I laughed. I'd always been scared of dogs, especially ones his size. And yet I found it rather endearing and a newfound comfort.

Eric unlocked the door and waited for Shadow and me to step in first, an odd expression filtering through his features for only a moment before it was gone. I wondered if it was strange for him as well to have his dog like me so much.

He dropped my suitcase to the side and went straight to the fireplace. I was starting to consider it was more for me and my comfort than anything else, since I felt the cold easily. I placed the hamper down on the kitchen island and tucked my hands on my hips. I read over the instructions Lori had given me to make the casserole. This shouldn't be so hard, right?

Eric slipped off his jacket and placed it on the hook once the fire was roaring. He suggested I do the same, and when I did, he took it and placed it beside his. "I'm going to chop wood while there's still sunlight. Are you sure you're okay in here?"

I nodded, optimistic I could do this much. "Question, does that plasma work for music?"

His eyebrows knitted together. Yep... I considered him as someone who never listened to music, if the silence on the drive up in his truck was any indication.

"It does."

"Cool, then you can leave now." I gave him a bright smile. "Don't worry, Shadow and I'll hold the fort."

He looked between Shadow and me expressionless before nodding curtly and slipping through the back door. His boots had left a trail of snow through the cabin as he left. I flicked through the channels on the plasma, still surprised that he had internet connection up here. And yet my cell was as useless as a paperweight. It felt strange and almost liberating not checking it every few minutes. I was addicted to my cell, always checking in to see who liked my posts and how many followers I had. And now that it was all gone, by way of no reception, I found it liberating... after my freak out of course.

I put a remix on, one without lyrics but had a beat that I could sway my hips to as I cooked. I'd purposefully decided to go for something different rather than my usual festival music I'd listen to. It didn't feel like it'd fit in here. And I imagined the music I was playing currently also seemed mismatched to the brute of a man outside, not that he could hear it.

I opened the red wine and poured myself a glass, smelling and taking a sip. Its deep robust flavors had me excited to start cook this dish. I got to work, reading over the instructions again carefully before I stared peeling the vegetables and measuring everything. I was going to deliver the best casserole anyone had tasted, and if there were leftovers, I was determined to take some to Lori as well. Well assuming we would make it down the mountain tomorrow.

I danced and swirled to the beat, sometimes clapping at Shadow as he wagged his tail at me.

"Want to be my dancing partner?" I asked him, tapping against my stomach. Without delay he jumped up and we awkwardly swayed from one side to the other. I threw back my head and laughed. "Such a good dancing partner," I encouraged, rubbing his head. I'd grown fond of the furball. I'd finally understood what it was the Lori and Thomas had explained about Shadow, that he didn't go to anyone and always sat at Eric's feet when someone spoke to him. I also noticed how he began doing the same for me, and I'd be lying if I said I didn't feel rather special because of it.

Finally, I placed the vegetable casserole in the

oven. Then I grimaced at the thought of frying up some meat. But Eric liked meat. By the size of him, he looked like he'd take down a whole animal and eat it in one sitting. I considered it for the moment. I hadn't always been a vegetarian, but it'd been ten years since and I'd never cooked it myself. I'd seen people cook it, it didn't look so hard.

Looking at the time, I wondered if Eric would really be okay with a vegetarian casserole. Or was he just settling because of me? I grabbed a piece of steak from the fridge staring at it. I'm sure I could manage to cook one piece of steak—it'd be fine. I just threw it into the fry pan, right? I placed it on the bench. Should I wait a little before I cooked it or would it take just as long as the casserole to cook? I looked up at the time again. Lori's instructions stated the casserole would take forty-five minutes. I took a gulp of my red wine.

How long had Eric already been chopping wood for? Almost an hour? I looked out the window behind his bed, noticing how significantly the snow was falling. I grimaced, wouldn't it be too cold out there for him?

I grabbed a glass of water and went out through the back door and onto the veranda.

"Wow," I found myself saying out loud. The

view was stunning. Past the veranda and the small bit of land surrounding the house were rolling hills and mountains blanketed in snow. His bedroom window had only been a snippet of the endless view outside. The sun was dimming and when my gaze landed on Eric, a hot heat fluttered into my core.

His dark-gray shirt clung to every hardened muscle, leaving nothing to the imagination, including his impressive eight-pack abs, as he slammed the axe down on a piece of wood, splitting it in two. He added them to the pile, grabbing the next chunk of wood. His arms were the size of... well... I don't know, two minivans? I shamelessly ogled him; even his thighs were as thick as tree trunks. There was something primitive about watching him come down heavy again, swinging his axe. Every time the axe hit with a definitive smack, a little jolt ran through me and heated the pit of my stomach.

Eric cleared his throat, grabbing my attention. My gaze snapped to his. I'd just been caught red-handed, basically frothing out the mouth over him.

"I brought you some water," I quickly flustered, taking two steps before my footing gave way and slipped. I bounced down the next two. I landed on my ass in the snow, a big rush of air escaping me.

"Cassidy!" Eric was by my side in a few strides, his eyes scanning over me to make sure I was okay.

The glass of water had spilt all over my hand, and my ass was sore but other than that, nothing but embarrassment. I nervously laughed before quickly finding it pretty hilarious. Quite literally, the universe had knocked me on my ass for being such a pervert.

I wiped away the tears from my eyes, noticing the slight twitch at the edge of Eric's mouth. Was he smiling?

"I was meant to bring you water but..." We both peered at the mouthful that was left.

Gratefully, he took it out of my hand and drank the remains. Up close, I was even more aware of how tightly his shirt clung to him. Small beads of sweat in his hair and on his face. It was disgusting how much he sweated, and yet oddly... arousing.

A panic ran over me. No, no, no. I was celibate. And I should not be ogling the man who was showing me kindness and offering me a place to stay while I was stranded in some small random town.

I tried to find conversation, my mouth opening and closing, and then I froze. We both watched Shadow strut past with a thick piece of bleeding steak in his mouth. Our heads inched closer together as he moved closer to the trees and started gnawing on it.

"Was that a piece of steak?" Eric asked casually.

I gulped, conscious of his arm that was still resting on my elbow. Was he even aware that he was stroking his thumb back and forth over it? And that created far too many butterflies.

"Um... well I was going to attempt to cook it for you and I left it on the bench to bring you some water... sorry."

Again, Eric's mouth twitched. "He'd never be so daring as to steal that with me."

Sheepishly I said, "But you look more scarier than me."

"True," he said as he helped me to my feet. We stared at one another, a tension twisting between us. His gaze dipped to my lips and I wondered if he was going to kiss me. He cleared his throat, pulling away. It felt as if a cool air swept between us and that warm fluttering energy between us was severed. I dusted myself off, focusing on the pounding ache on my ass. That was definitely going to bruise tomorrow.

"No point in taking it off him now," Eric mused. Shadow had already demolished half the steak. "And you don't have to cook me meat, Cassidy, I look forward to whatever it is you're making."

A heat rose to my cheeks. "You say that before trying it."

"Call it intuition," he mused, grabbing my hand and gently putting the empty glass into it. "And thank you for this. I'll be done in about twenty minutes."

I nodded, trying to push away the heat that flooded me. Maybe it was from the red wine making me slightly tipsy, or was it the realization that Eric was a nice guy? And I tried to recall how long it'd been since I'd met one of those. I mean, hadn't I been questioning why I'd only been attracting time wasters and unfaithful fiends? Was that because they all lived in Manhattan or because they'd all been around my age?

But I'd had friends who'd found love with incredible men. And what I'd concluded was there must've been something wrong with me. Those few insecurities bubbled to the surface again and I tried to push them down. I almost felt guilty for ogling Eric; he was a nice guy. And I... I didn't attract the nice ones... ever. I had no right to look at him that way and it was inappropriate. Wasn't it?

Chapter 10

Eric

The moment Cassidy had slipped down those stairs, my heart dropped and my body acted of its own accord. I'd thrown the axe into the snow and was on my knees beside her in seconds. When she began laughing, a wave of relief—and humor—swept through me. Alongside slight confusion. I didn't warm to many people, and yet I found myself worried for her safety. Maybe it's because she looked so misplaced and vulnerable here, like some bizarre natural instinct.

Then when Shadow had strutted past with that piece of steak hanging out of his mouth, I'd realized how much my world had turned upside down housing this strange bubbly brat.

A brat, that's what I'd saw her as. But when she

looked at me with those big blue sparkling eyes, something primal yanked at me. Probably seeking a woman's touch. And I had to remind myself she was completely off-limits even after I had multiple filthy thoughts of her. She was way too young for me and I was hindered by the thoughts of getting close to any other woman again. Especially since the last one cost me everything. I'd promised I'd never allow myself into a woman's web again. Sexual partners, no problem. There were clear rules and expectations. But with Cassidy... it was different. There was something homely about her, and the way Shadow took to her irked me because it was something I couldn't entirely understand myself.

But the moment she began laughing again, that flutter of heartfelt joy and amusement eliminated all the tension and worries I'd been carrying throughout the day. I wondered how many people she touched in this way and if she was even aware she had such a charm about her.

I piled away the wood, grateful for the depletion of my energy. I'd felt on edge around Cassidy and needed something to exhaust the jittery nerves. And I wasn't sure if it was because of Lori and Thomas's meddling ways or if having Cassidy in my personal space was effecting me unreasonably. But after the physical exertion of chopping wood, I found myself steady and in control once again.

Stepping into the cabin, it felt like a sauna thanks to the fireplace. I'd noticed Cassidy felt the cold easily, probably because she wasn't used to the temperature dropping this low, so I'd made a point to set up the fireplace whenever we returned.

An outlandish form of music filtered through the cabin as I walked into the kitchen. Cassidy was swaying from side to side with Shadow standing against her, like some fill-in dancing partner. I leaned against the doorframe to the bathroom, watching them thoughtfully. Part of me didn't want Shadow learning bad habits, and yet another side of me... found it peculiar to watch.

With one hand, she reached back for her glass of red wine and took a sip, still swaying flawlessly to the beat with Shadow, tongue hanging out of his mouth, quite literally looking like a lovestruck puppy.

I cleared my throat. "Oh shit," she cursed, startled and gently pushed Shadow off as if she'd been caught in the act. My smile twitched. "Dinner won't be too long." She avoided my gaze, either from embarrassment from earlier on or something else entirely. She didn't seem injured by the fall but that could've been the liquid courage filling her.

She'd already set up the small wooden coffee table beside the fireplace with plates, a second wine glass and a bottle of red in between. "You have time for a shower," she added, still avoiding looking in my direction. Granted, my shirt clung to me and a curious interest peaked. Was she finding it difficult to look at me, because of that?

"Okay," I agreed, kicking off my boots and walking into the bathroom. As I peeled off my long shirt, I deliberated over the second toothbrush and hairbrush that sat on the opposite side to mine on the basin. I stared at her toothbrush as if it were some ill omen. How strange it was to have someone else here. It felt like it changed everything in the cabin. When I'd reached the shower, the pink loofah hanging off the shower rack grabbed my attention, along with a shower gel and various facial cleansers stacked.

My eyebrows furrowed. How many products did she need? I picked up the shower gel, curious. I opened it and took a whiff. A light florally and sweet tone flared my nostrils. It was very much Cassidy. Against my usual dark and wooden cologne, she was all spring, sunshine, lollipops, and unicorns.

That thought again, startled me. Why was I even comparing how opposite we were? I placed the bottle down as if it scorched me. The last time I had a woman's belongings in my home, she'd taken me for everything I was worth and I couldn't help but have the sensation I was being honey trapped again.

I scrubbed my body, trying to shake the thought. Cassidy was a random woman who needed somewhere to lodge until she could pass through town. She wouldn't be my problem within the next few days. A blip in my usual quiet getaway. So why did I have the strong urge to stroke my cock with filthy thoughts about her. I internally debated with myself, furious over the temptation.

I towel dried my hair and wrapped the towel around my hips, cursing under my breath. I was so in the habit of living by myself that I hadn't considered modesty on her behalf. Wouldn't she be uncomfortable when I waltzed out in a towel? I grunted to myself. Now who was being conceited?

Steam followed me out the door as I walked out, patting Shadow's head as he greeted me. Cassidy sat at the end of the coffee table, her drink suspended with mouth agape as she watched me walk to my chest drawers to grab a change of clothes. When my gaze met hers, she quickly diverted, staring at the fireplace instead.

The woman had no poker face. Sure, I knew I had a body most women were interested in, but I certainly didn't act on it all the time and nor was I stranded in a cabin with them. My jaw ticked. This was probably why Lori forced her to stay with me in the first place.

"I won't be too long," I grumbled to Cassidy as I made my way back into the bathroom, curious about the casserole that sat in the center of the coffee table. Surely, with instructions, it couldn't be that bad.

I sat down, pouring a glass of red, and that charged sensation came back to a jittering buzz. For the first time in a long time, I was starting to not feel so in control. And I didn't like it.

Chapter 11

Cassidy

Silence. The moment he sat down, cross-legged at the coffee table, Eric poured himself a big glass of red wine and downed a quarter of it before lifting his gaze to meet mine. I'd since turned off the music and now the crackle of the fireplace was almost deafening.

My first glass of red wine had already gone to my head and effectively bruised my ass when I'd lost my footing outside. I was still trying to navigate around Eric's intensity so countering it with my best charm, I gave him a bright smile and offered him the giant spoon first.

The vegetable casserole sat between us. "I hope you like it. I haven't made it before, but Lori's instructions helped."

"Thank you for making this," he said politely as he scooped a heap onto his plate. By the time he was done with it, half the casserole dish sat on his plate. Well, for a man of his size, I supposed he would eat a lot. Especially after all the exercise he'd just done. My mind drifted to the image of him chopping the wood and how tightly the shirt clung to his perfectly molded body—which was incidentally confirmed moments ago when he walked out of the bathroom in only a towel. I gulped and felt heat rise to my cheeks.

I was no innocent but the way Eric looked was sinful. I'm sure women fawned over him all the time. I imagined he had ample of options back in Chicago. It was surprising he didn't have a wife or a girlfriend, but he'd made it very clear he wasn't interested. I wondered if he'd recently had a bad breakup. Maybe that's why he looked sour most of the time.

"What's it like living in Chicago?" I asked, trying to create polite conversation as I served myself. He was already shoveling down his meal. Quietly, I added, "Is it good?" Maybe he was eating it out of obligation.

He waited until he'd finished with his mouthful, then said. "Good and good."

Right. He studied me as I picked at a small piece and ate it slowly. I turned it over in my mouth, surprised by how good it tasted. I raised my hand in front of my mouth. "Oh wow."

A warmth spread through his features as I laughed. "Wow it actually tastes good," I said surprised. Was I turning into the new hot chef on the block?

"Why don't you cook much, you seem to enjoy it?" Eric asked.

I shrugged, running a hand through Shadow's fur as he lay between me and the fireplace. It created a certain ambiance in the air—nice and comfortable— and charged with an energy I tried not to acknowledge.

I picked at my next bite. "It's kind of busy in Manhattan. I always have events and parties on. Everything just seems on the go, you know? It's much easier to grab a juice that has everything I need than to cook anything. I just don't have time, I suppose."

"You know juices aren't actual food, right?" he said matter-of-factly.

I raised an eyebrow. "That could be a very controversial opinion, Eric," I teased him.

"Maybe. Well, it remains the same, you should cook more often for yourself. You seem to enjoy it."

I smiled shyly into my food. What was happening? I was never coy or shy. But I didn't get to show this side of myself to anyone either. Around Eric, I had no inhibitions and that was worrisome. In Manhattan I was expected to be and act a certain way and unapologetically. And that was me—authentically. But I hadn't been able to explore this side of myself either. I'd been too focused on finding Mr. Right the entire time as I ran away from Mr. Wrong that I kind of lost myself in the process. The realization left a sour taste in my mouth, and I pushed the meal away.

"What's wrong?" Eric grimaced and frowned at my plate.

"Nothing, I'm full."

"You've hardly touched your food."

I cocked my head to the side, studying him, a teasing smile playing at my lips. He seemed to watch me warily. "Eric, despite you're big broodish size, you're more like a mother hen."

Red streaked his cheeks, and I found it adorable. "No," he quickly snapped. "I just don't like wasted food."

"Then you can have my plate too," I challenged, noticing he was already done with his. I handed it over to him, and with no complaints, he ate it. I found myself rather smug as I watched him eat.

There was something rewarding about watching him enjoy the meal I'd made. It was so out of my comfort zone, and yet I felt content.

I stood up, grabbing the bottle of red and topping both of our glasses. I grabbed his empty plate and the casserole dish. "Do you feel like playing a game?" I asked, looking over my shoulder as I stacked the dish in the fridge, then washed the plate. The moment I mentioned "game," his expression changed, and I felt a heat flood through my core. *Oh fuck.*

"What kind of game?" His gravelly voice broke through the cracking wood and straight to my pulsing heat. Wow that red wine really had gone straight to my head and three months of celibacy was really starting to bite me in the ass.

"Lori added a pack of cards to the hamper. I thought maybe we could play a few rounds?" I said holding up the deck of cards.

He cleared his throat, as if relieving himself from whatever thoughts he'd been having. Despite the age difference, we were still a man and woman, stuck in a stunning cabin with a crackling fireplace, the mood couldn't be any more inviting to be tangled in his bed. Another wave of heat. Okay, I really needed to slow down on the red wine.

"Okay, what game?" he asked, bringing my now

empty plate to the counter. His large frame spread a heat across my back like an inferno pinpricking goose bumps. My breath hitched. Damn it, why'd I have to see him chopping that wood. Everything in my body sparked at the thought ever since.

I let him gently push me out of the way as he washed his own dish. There was something comical and endearing watching this brute of a man hunched over and doing the dishes, a most domesticated display.

"Poker?"

He looked up at me, a twinkle in his eyes. "You play poker?"

"Well no, but I'm sure I can learn. Why, is it a bad idea? We can play something else."

He shook his head, that twitch playing at his mouth again. I wanted to make him laugh. Almost yearned for it, like another reward.

He leant across from me, his arms folded over his chest. "Don't take this the wrong way, sweetheart, I just didn't think you'd have the best poker face."

Sweetheart. There was something about that endearment that put my heart into overdrive. Damn, the way I was going I'd have to pull out my friendly intimate toy ASAP just to relieve myself.

"I have a poker face," I blurted out, not even convincing myself. "In fact, let's make it interesting."

"Oh?" He arched an eyebrow, a smug expression slipping through his neutral and controlled mask.

Like a teenage girl, the only thing cheering in my mind was *strip poker, strip poker, strip poker*. I swatted away the images that came alongside that devilish dance.

We'd unconsciously leaned into one another. He smelt of fire and wood, everything earthy and grounded. "Whoever wins each hand gets to ask the other a question. And the loser has to answer honestly."

He considered it, rubbing at his beard thoughtfully. "Okay," he agreed. "Poker it is."

I gulped as he inched closer. "Yes," I breathed, my heart hammering. Only then did he realize he'd pushed off the bench and was looming over me. And it might've been because he enjoyed the prospect of the challenge but there was something else in his gaze that in my experience always only led to one thing.

He grunted and pulled away, that cold breeze sweeping through us once again. I almost fell back into the bench not realizing how much I'd also leant forward, my traitorous body acting of its own accord. I was sexually hungry and deprived. After going cold turkey for three months, I realized now how badly I wanted to be touched again.

I followed Eric to the coffee table, sitting across from him cross-legged again as he shuffled the cards. The bottle of red wine was mostly gone already. I decided to stay on this glass for the rest of the night. If I got carried away, I was certain my carefree self would try to seduce to him, thinking with my pounding pussy instead of logic. And wouldn't that just make things awkward. He wasn't like a fling in Manhattan. I'd be taking advantage of the man who offered me a place to stay.

Celibacy. Celibacy. Celibacy, I reminded myself. Wasn't that the promise I'd made to myself? No sex until I met the right guy? And how quickly my body was to forget that.

Eric explained the rules to me, and we trialed a few rounds. By then, Shadow had laid his head in my lap and I absently patted him as I looked at my hand of cards. Okay, so turned out poker had a lot of rules. And I'd only ever played it in the past when it involved strip poker and most of the time I didn't mind losing.

But this time I wanted to win. Firstly, to prove I did have a poker face. But mostly, to learn more about this big brute. It was so hard to get any personal information from him and the more time I spent with him, the more curious I became.

We revealed our hands. Nonchalant, Eric said, with a smile. An actual smile. "You lose, sweetheart."

I harrumphed in irritation; I'd actually thought I'd had a good hand on that one.

Eric swirled his red wine around in the glass thoughtfully. "What's your most embarrassing moment?"

My jaw unhinged. Wow he was actually going to have fun with this. And I was definitely going to need another sip and scan through the large file of embarrassing moments. "Crap," I grumbled as one particular memory sprang to mind. I needed another sip of wine for this one. He crossed his arms over his chest expectantly.

"Okay so one time, in my early twenties I was at a party in Paris and was wearing a skimpy little top that tied up at the back. We were dancing and partying and maybe I had way too many cosmos. Me and two of my girlfriends thought it would be a great idea to jump up on the booth near the DJ and dance.

So we were dancing and having fun and then when we decided to finally leave, I took a step down behind them, except the ties on the back of my shirt hooked on the edge of the DJ booth and took my entire top with it. So I was left there standing in front of an entire nightclub my boobs on for show. I was so humiliated. And then what made it worse was I struggled to get the top back and so security had to come and help me unhook it because I was so fucking drunk. I drank so much after that I can't even remember what happened. I threw out that shirt the next day."

There was silence and then a monstrous laugh shook the room. As embarrassed as I was reliving the moment, Eric's laugh was contagious, and I began to laugh with him despite it being at my expense. I mean the whole thing had been pretty ridiculous. But there was something magical and endearing about his laugh. And I wondered if people often got to hear it, because selfishly, it felt rather rewarding to hear. Like I was slowly starting to chip away at his tough demeanor.

"Okay, that was a good one. Next round."

Second hand. Eric won. What's your favourite color? Lavender.

Third hand. Eric won. Do you know any other

languages? I rattled off Spanish, Japanese and French. At that he seemed surprised. My parents had given me an extensive education; one that I now rarely had a need to use but being taught at such a young age they were engrained into my mind.

Fourth hand. I squealed, actually squealed as I bested him with a two-pair hand. Shadow perked up, startled, and I rubbed his head apologetically.

Eric's eyebrows knitted together, surprised he'd lost. I poked out my tongue. "No poker face my ass!" I teased with delight. That twitch of a smile edged at the corner of his mouth again.

"Hmmm, what should I ask?" I pondered out loud, tapping my chin.

"We don't have all night, snowflake," he goaded

"For all you know, we might be snowed in together for another day and in that case we do." I poked my tongue before whiplashing at how boldly I'd said that. Would he think I'd want us to be snowed in together?

"What's your question," he said, taking a sip of his red.

Relief swept through me. Hmm, what did I want to ask this man? So many things, and yet all of a sudden nothing at all. So many personal questions that I was certain the moment I asked, he'd lock up again. So, I needed something easy, right?

"What's your favorite childhood memory?"

He seemed surprised by this and thought about it for a while. "You know, it might sound strange but probably when all of my siblings were born."

My heart fluttered. I wasn't expecting such an... innocent answer. Without my need to prompt him to continue, he did.

"I remember how happy it made my parents and when they introduced me to each of them. My memory's a little hazy around the twins' birth because I was only four, but I remember my parents promising me they'd be my new best friends. And in a town like this, there wasn't many at my age. And then when Lori came along I felt almost protective of her in a way, probably because she was my little sister. But it was a little different when Thomas came along. And by then I wasn't a child anymore either."

He abruptly stopped, and so I cautiously asked, "Why was it different? The age gap?"

He seemed to regard me, uncomfortable in the direction the question had turned. And I was certain he'd lock up on me, but carefully he said, "Yes and no." And then he looked into the weakening fire.

"There were more complications with Thomas. My parents, although they haven't always had much, gave us everything. They'd always been loving and somewhat stern, but they still let us be kids. But as I became a teenager I realized that the world wasn't so easy. That there could be complications and mixed opinions involved.

Five years after Lori, my mother wanted one more baby, she just felt like our family wasn't yet complete. She had a heap of miscarriages and it began to take a toll on the family for those four years. She was just so desperate to have another child and every miscarriage chipped away at her mentally and physically. It also began arguments amongst our family at the risks it was involving. I'd even called her selfish once." He winced at the memory.

"But she was right. Eventually she did have Thomas, completing our family. I felt guilty for not believing in her and the grudge I held towards a baby that wasn't even born yet. I just thought it'd be a disappointment like all the rest. It was hard watching my parents go through that and try to answer the twins and Lori's questions."

"You were worried about her health," I quickly reminded him, a tight knot forming in my stomach at watching him paint himself as the "bad guy."

He raised an eyebrow. "Perhaps. Or maybe I wanted to move out of a small town and didn't want the responsibility of the family business and their expectation of me. And maybe I begrudged my mother's ill health and depression at the time from all the miscarriages." He shrugged, an awkward grimace twisting his expression. My shoulders had sunken in. He still tried to paint himself as the "bad guy" here, and yet I couldn't even comprehend going through something like that for years. How else was a teenager supposed to interpret that? "Wow, that was meant to be happiest memory, huh?"

"Thank you for sharing it with me," I gently said, placing my hand on the table. I had the impression Eric didn't often open up to others and I felt grateful he'd shared a little hidden piece of himself with me.

"I think I've had enough for one night," he said, politely excusing himself as he grabbed our two empty glasses and walked over to the sink. I sighed, disappointed that he'd slipped through my grasp again. Just when I felt like I was getting something substantial from him—a glimmer into how he functioned—he slipped out of my grip.

I patted Shadow, considering how he might've been the only friend Eric opened up to. Or perhaps I was being presumptuous. He did, after all, live in

Chicago, a life beyond this small town. Surely, he had friends. Surely, there was a different side to Eric there, just as there was for me in Manhattan. And I wondered if I'd ever discover what that Eric was like before I left this cabin.

Chapter 12

Eric

I watched Cassidy as she twisted and contorted on the wooden floor, nothing but a towel coming between her and the hard floorboards.

I sat there eating my second serving of omelette that she'd insisted on making. I was beginning to wonder if the cooking had become a novelty for her, but I wasn't going to complain.

"It's called yoga, Eric," she said simply. My head leant to the side as I tried to follow her movement, her arm wrapping under her stomach as she twisted. Fuck me, wasn't she going to put her back out doing that? "And it's very soothing for the soul."

Shadow barked in agreeance; he'd tried a few times to replicate her *downward dog*, trying to mirror her as if it was a game. The most distracting part, besides the contorted flexibility, was the tight leggings that clung to Cassidy's figure and the small crop top she wore, barely enough to cover her bralette underneath every time her arms reached for the roof.

"And you should join me, it'll be good for you." She leaned back into what she claimed to be *child's pose*. My gaze dropped to the outline of her violet leggings and the way she pushed back, everything spreading and on display. I closed my eyes, partly convinced she knew exactly what she was doing. No, I wasn't into the singsong types like Cassidy. But I was still a man and fuck did she look good in that getup.

"Sweetheart, if I get down onto my hands and knees on that hard floor, I can assure you I'm not getting back up," I said, taking a mouthful of coffee.

She tsked, a smile spreading. "I'll convince you otherwise. If you can split wood with your bare hands you can benefit from a few stretches."

"I don't split wood with my bare hands," I said matter-of-factly. "I cut it with an axe."

"And cut it well you do..." she quietly drawled out.

An arrogant male pride filled me. "What was that?"

"Nothing!" she stammered as she quickly stood bolt upright, realizing she'd said it out loud. She put her hands on her hips. "Well come on, we have a whole day together. Let's try something new!"

I raised an eyebrow. "Cassidy, you realize the point of being snowed in is that you can't go out and do anything, right?"

She rolled her eyes, sauntering over. She walked over to the fridge and pulled out the oranges and apples I'd bought for her the day before. Comfortable in my kitchen, she pulled out the juicer and began to squeeze.

When I'd woken up this morning, I didn't need Lori's message to confirm we'd been snowed in. The moment I opened the door and snow flooded the doormat, I realized we were stuck together for another day at least. The snow was so thick I wouldn't even be able to chop wood for the day, forsaking me to deal with this edgy tension around the little snowflake.

I was tempted to pull out my laptop and utilize the day to work and check up on any issues the company was dealing with while I was gone. I had an efficient team, but it had become habit to fall back on being productive. And yet somehow, I was curious as to what great ideas Cassidy had.

"Just because we're locked inside, it doesn't mean we can't have fun." She raised an eyebrow as she continued twisting the orange over the juicer. It might've not been the type of fresh juice she was used to but at least I knew she was taking in some kind of nutrients. Her small appetite unnerved me.

"What did you have in mind, snowflake?" I said, placing my plate in the sink. There was something comical about her twisting around the juicer with maximum effort. "Here," I offered. "You look like you're struggling."

She harrumphed but moved out of my way. "I'm not struggling, we just can't all squish an orange with one hand until it turns into putty."

I chuckled, and she stared at me as if I'd grown another head. "I'm not the Hulk."

"Depends who you ask." She smiled slyly.

The air electrified again; it was starting to grind on me how effective her words and attention were. This cabin was too fucking small and how had I ended up juicing this woman's breakfast?

"Ideas for today?" I growled out.

"Right." She clapped her hands together, all energized again. "We could play cards again, or watch movies, or bake..."

"Bake?" I asked.

She squealed, actually squealed as she jumped up and down excitedly. "Yea like I don't know cookies or something. The only time I ever made cookies was with a friend and they were 'special' cookies. And in reality, I didn't actually help with the cooking, but I was there for it."

"So, you just got high?" I confirmed.

She shrugged. "Well yea of course but it looked like a lot of fun. *And* I might even have a bottle of champagne in my suitcase." She raised a provocative eyebrow.

"You made me carry that second suitcase because it had a bottle of champagne in it? I'd hate to know what your essentials are in the third case we'd left behind."

"Actually... there's two bottles of champagne in there." She beamed a playful smile and grabbed onto my arm enthusiastically. "But think about it. I know it's like 10am or whatever."

"It's 8am," I corrected.

She swatted me with her other hand, the manicured nails on her other one still digging into me excitedly.

"But if we put the juice *in* the champagne then it kind of like makes it a liquid breakfast, just with a little bit of fun sprinkle in it. You know, a mimosa."

I pulled a long face at her, and she tugged at my arm again like a child.

"Come on," she whined. "It could make for a fun day." She shimmied her shoulders. "And what else are you going to do all day? Journalize and mediate?"

I grabbed another orange squeezing it over the juicer. "So, your idea of fun is day drinking?"

"No. *Our* idea of fun is day drinking." She winked. "Don't make me do it on my own, I'll be climbing up the walls going crazy."

You could be climbing up something else. Just as my cock registered the thought, I swatted it away. No. "Do you ever spend much time with yourself?"

She seemed taken aback by the question and considered it thoughtfully. "Not as much as I probably should," she admitted.

I felt uneasy with her response, almost guilty for asking such a direct question. And besides, I could always work in the afternoon; I supposed it wouldn't kill me to have one drink with her. "So day drinking it is, sweetheart. I'll message Lori for some cookie recipes. We should have most of the ingredients here."

She squealed again, jumping up and down. "Thank you, thank you!" She laughed and gave me a hug. Her little arms squeezed tight, barely able to reach around my chest. "You won't regret this!" She pointed a finger at me as she sauntered over to her bag. As soon as she left me, I fought the urge to pull her back. To properly embrace her. Instinctively, it felt like she needed a hug much more than I did. Behind her smiles and charm, I was certain she was escaping something. But maybe this was the most I could do for her—oblige in her day-drinking, cookie-baking fun. For now.

Chapter 13

Cassidy

Two hours later and one champagne bottle down, I'd discovered the upmost betrayal. "You didn't tell me you had vodka in the cupboard," I challenged, mimicking that I was offended. I'd just finished my solo performance to the Spice Girls, ensuring that Eric was thoroughly entertained. I realized with satisfaction, that my over-the-top self actually tempted him to break out into a half grin—sometimes. Other times, he'd rolled his eyes at me, but I knew deep down, he was having fun too.

He went to take a mouthful of the liquid breakfast. "Ah!" I pointed at him. "The way we practiced."

Eric grumbled his complaint but with a comical glare, he raised his pinkie ever so slightly showing his sophistication. I was certain the only reason he did it was because of how much it elicited fits of laughter from me. A guy his size posing like a lady with pinkie poised was everything I'd missed in life. I needed it printed somewhere on a shirt or it needed to be created into a meme.

"Having fun?" he challenged, pouring almost the last of the ingredients into the bowl. "Or would you like to come and join in on baking these cookies?"

I swatted him away with a smile. This had now been the third time I'd fluttered off, distracted by something else in the kitchen. "Right, sorry." I grabbed for the sugar in the cupboard, like he'd instructed me to find a moment ago. Another wave of Spice Girls hit, the urge to use the whisk as a microphone coming in strong.

"Okay so we put all the ingredients together and scramble it right?"

He cocked an eyebrow at me. "Scramble it?"

I bit my bottom lip, containing the laugh. That gentle smirk toyed with his lips. It was distracting and delicious all rolled in one the fact that Eric still hadn't pulled on a shirt since waking up. And who was I to stop a good thing? He'd caught me a few times eyeing him, reminding myself of the celibacy I'd sworn.

"Read the next instruction," he commanded. He'd given me the lead role on reading out the ingredients from his cell. Under careful instruction, by way of the step by step points Lori had sent through, we threw ingredients in and when it came to the mixing part, he handed over the reins. With absolute glee, I took another mouthful of mimosa as we scuffled around each other, cautious not to touch. On my way past, I grabbed Shadow's face, smooshing it in my hands and rubbing furiously as I baby talked to him, and he absolutely loved it. Eric, not as much.

As I began to whisk, Eric chopped the block of dark chocolate into small pieces. We didn't have choc chips, so we'd improvised.

I stared at the chocolatey goodness. For the most part, I had a restrictive diet and watched everything I ate. But we were making cookies after all, shouldn't I enjoy the process and the ingredients, just to sample the product? Eric was looking at me and then the chocolate. "Would you like a piece, snowflake?"

I smirked. "Eric, you might just be a mind reader."

"I doubt it's mind reading when I can see you salivating for a piece."

I grabbed a piece and plonked it in my mouth. The smooth, velvety swirl danced along my tastebuds, an odd mixture with the orange juice and champagne.

I grabbed another piece under his watchful glare. "Catch." I said without warning, throwing the piece into the air. He caught it with his hand. I pouted and snatched the piece back. "Not like that. With your mouth."

His eyebrows furrowed. "But why would I..."

I arched an eyebrow and crossed my hands over my chest.

"Fine," he gritted out and looked as if he was attempting to brace himself, with knees lowered. I laughed as I threw it up. Both him and Shadow looked hopeful as they both watched it fly through the air. The chocolate piece landed on Eric's tongue.

"Victory!" I shouted. "You're so good at it." I nudged him with my elbow.

"Well, I am used to putting other things in my mouth," he growled. My lower abdominal flooded with heat, and I looked up at him, almost startled that he'd said that out loud.

He arched an eyebrow, a suave kind of smile crossing his features. "When I said I'm not into women, Cassidy, it didn't mean that I didn't fuck."

I choked. "Did you just say, fucked?"

His features twisted. "Please, I'm not the innocent one here claiming celibacy."

With mouth open, I popped my hip out. "I'll
have you know that I *chose* celibacy."

"And how's that working for you?"

"Three months strong," I said, although my
knees pinched together as I grazed another glance up
and down him.

Amused he dipped his giant finger in the bowl of
mixture and ever so slowly sucked, scraping with his
teeth. I found it fascinating that he didn't get any
food stuck in that glorious beard. Wait, was I into full
grown beards now? "That's a shame," he purred.

I melted, a fire blistering over my skin. The
leggings and bralette were too suffocating, I needed
them off.

He chuckled under my stunned expression,
collecting a small amount of the batter again and
plopping it on the end of my nose. "Don't worry,
snowflake, I'm not going to eat you up. It was a joke."

I pretended to fall backwards. "And now he
jokes?" All in attempt to slow my pattering heart and
the roiling tension in the pit of my stomach. "Give
him half a bottle of champagne and he turns into a
dirty slut."

"Did you just call me a slut?" Eric asked, leaning

against the back of the island, arms folded over his chest. His muscles bulged with the movement; my gaze navigated the hair from chest and along the small line that followed below. "I've punished girls for calling me less."

I poked my tongue inside my mouth, really liking this side of Eric. "Do the other girls like to be punished as well?"

A low growl escaped him as if in warning and it vibrated through me, creating an unfurling beat in my pussy. His gaze was intoxicating, consuming, and heated.

"You're half my age," he warned.

"I'm not. I'm sixteen years younger. And if you didn't see me as a woman than you wouldn't have been staring at my ass through my yoga pants all morning." I harrumphed. And with all my strength, and libido going feral, I turned away and focused on the cookies again. "And besides I'm celibate and we're just making cookies. Nothing to see here."

"I never said I was interested, snowflake," he remarked, draining his glass.

"No but your cock does," I said with a satisfied grin and shamelessly stared at the bulge pushing against his gray sweatpants. "But in case you're wondering, if I weren't sworn to celibacy, I might've considered it," I said, wiping the batter off my nose and popping it into my mouth, sucking on it in the same way he'd teased me. His glare was ruthless, his jaw tight. "I think it's ready to put the chocolate in, Eric," I said sweetly.

Chapter 14

Eric

The space had become too small—too comfortable, and yet riddled with tension. Cassidy's proximity under a few drinks in was a dangerous mix. I was a man of discipline, but I wasn't immune to a beautiful woman, especially in tight yoga pants and somehow, even the off-pitch singing to Spice Girls hadn't deterred me.

"And now we just twist," Cassidy instructed. Her long limbs were far nimbler than mine. She was sitting down in front of the fireplace and stretching her back into a twist. After a day filled with more card games, boozing, watching a movie, and eating the entire batch of cookies, I'd somehow ended up twisting like a pretzel in an attempt at yoga. And damn was it hard to look away when Cassidy asserted herself in some bizarre positions in those torturous tight pants.

I awkwardly twisted my spine, feeling as if something was going to pop any moment. She began to laugh.

"Why are you laughing," I growled out. This whole thing was stupid. Yoga might've been her thing but a man my size wasn't used to the "flow of the movements" as she'd put it. It was harder and more infuriating than any gym session I'd undertaken. And I'd much rather chop wood for hours than have to be subject to this torture.

"You just look so awkward," Cassidy chuckled. "Here, like this."

She stood up and moved behind me, pressing her hand to my lower back as she pulled back my shoulders. "Straighter."

I did as she said, a great grievance falling over me. Why had I agreed to do this? Shadow watched us tiredly with his head nestled between his paws.

"If you hadn't told me you worked in IT before I would've believed it now by this slouch of yours, shoulders back, Eric," Cassidy lectured.

"I have a great posture," I quickly defended. She began chuckling and I realized she was goading me. I blew out a sharp breath as I twisted to the other side.

It was too easy. I bit at her taunts too easily, embarrassing myself in the process. "And it's not like I'm hunched over the laptop all the time," I found myself grumbling.

Her featherlight touch danced across my bare arms. It was a dangerous mix considering I still hadn't put a shirt on and her every touch reminded me that I was a man and she was a woman—age difference be damned. My cock twitched.

"Now get on your knees and spread your thighs," she instructed.

"What?" I twisted sharply, the sway of the champagne catching up.

She chuckled. "So filthy minded." But judging by the glaze in her eyes, I hadn't been the only one thinking of other things. The thought of having her over my knee and spanking that tight little ass came to mind vividly. I gritted my teeth as she not so innocently dropped to her knees beside me, spreading them and pushing her arms forward. "Like this. It's called *child's pose*."

How the fuck had I let her convince me to do this? I did as she instructed, awkwardly and almost painfully as my arms stretched forward. But then after a moment of breathing I could feel the stretch in my back. And not that I'd admit it out loud, but this pose felt okay.

"So, when you're not chopping wood, what do you do to keep fit in the city?" Cassidy asked, laying her head to the side and peering in my direction. I did the same, looking at her.

"I have a gym in my home. Morning and night, no matter the occasion."

She whistled. "Looks like I'm not the only one with an addictive personality."

I didn't consider it an addictive personality. Simply, I had my routine and it worked for me.

"And what do you do back in Manhattan?" I asked.

She sighed. "I exercise regularly usually in the evening but now that I'm between jobs I might have to figure out a new routine, I might just keep doing this."

"What did you do for work?" I asked.

She blew out an exaggerated breath, falling deeper into the stretch. "I was a receptionist at a popular magazine, *Candice Magazine*. But I quit, you know change of scenery. Mini holiday and all now."

Lies and truth. I could tell there was more behind

her story. It sounded like she was running away from something, but as I tried to keep my personal life separate, I chose not to pry into hers any further.

We lay there in comfortable silence, staring at one another in our awkward, and yet profoundly effective pose.

"Thank you, Eric, for letting me stay here. You have nothing to gain from having me here and yet you've let me into your home. And I'm grateful for that."

There was something about her sincerity that twisted my stomach. At the start, I hadn't had much of a choice, but if I was being honest, I'd really enjoyed today. It was very... peculiar. But the reality was this was also short lived—a novelty at best.

"I'm sure it's not as fun or elaborate as your friend's in Canada."

A pained and twisted expression appeared, the quick slip transforming into a beautiful smile. "This might even been more fun. You know in a rustic way and all."

I didn't share her same amusement. The mere mention of Canada flickered an uncertain expression over her and I wasn't sure why. And I didn't understand why I might care.

I let out a breath and the words had fallen out of

my mouth before I'd even registered their meaning. "If you want, you can stay for the month, if plans have changed in Canada or something." My heart froze. Why the fuck had I offered her to stay for longer? Wasn't her staying here an inconvenience in the first place?

Shadow barked as if in agreeance, grabbing our attention from silently staring at one another.

She stretched back into a sitting position, quickly giving him pats thoughtfully as he rested his head on her knee.

"You don't have to offer me that, Eric. I know it's not ideal and I'm imposing on your space."

Guilt weighed heavily in my stomach. I really had been an asshole when she first arrived. I'd actively avoided sharing excess time with any woman, certain they were all the same. But there was something about Cassidy—she was completely the opposite to Katia. Just the thought of her name rose bile in my stomach. I shoved it back down alongside her memory. Cassidy and her were nothing alike. But weren't they all the same? Wouldn't they all use me for something?

"It wouldn't be for free," I quickly said. "You could work around the café and odd jobs in the town. But if you wanted a change of scenery the offer's there," I quickly gritted out, somewhat regretting the offer and hoping she'd decline because I wasn't even sure why I'd extended the invitation. And that unnerved me.

She seemed to consider me. I wasn't sure why I was saying this and she seemed perplexed by it as well. But I saw the small glimmer of hope in her expression. "And where would I stay? Here?"

"Yes." It wasn't a question. Of course she would stay here. Her gaze rolled down my chest and stomach and my cock twitched. She watched Shadow intently, a sombre mood creeping over her. "Cassidy, if you're in trouble I want you to tell me."

Her serious expression didn't change. I felt the urge to shake, hug, or scream at her. It was uncharacteristic to see her like this, with no smiles and all seriousness. I hated how that played on my mind. I wanted to hunt down whatever demons she was running from, and that realization threw a cold bucket of water over me.

"Thank you, Eric," she plastered on a fake smile, that dark and sombre consideration gone. "Do you mind if I think on it tonight. I do appreciate your hospitality. Surprisingly, you're a big teddy bear, huh?"

"I'm not—"

Her laughter fluttered through the air as she rose. "If only you could see your face. Big *lumberjack* teddy bear, I mean. Don't worry your secret is safe with me." She winked. "I'm going to have a shower."

And just like that, she was gone. Leaving me with thighs spread, sitting on my feet and Shadow on her tail, far more interested in where she was going than staying with me.

Chapter 15

Cassidy

I twisted my hair into a ponytail and added mascara. Eric casually leant against the bathroom doorframe, his masculine heat forcing me to grit my teeth. Okay, the guy gave off big dick energy and my loins were screaming at me to make something happen. My thighs automatically squeezed together as I looked back into the mirror perfecting the second eye, trying my hardest to ignore the pounding that thrummed in my lower stomach.

"Do you always take this long to get ready in the morning?" He casually yawned, covering his mouth and stretching lazily.

"You have to start the day off right. Make your bed and be prepared for any occasion in the day, which includes hair and makeup," I educated. And besides, he'd woken up slightly earlier this morning. "But I'm done now so the shower's all yours," I said, scooping up my makeup bag and assessing my shimmery cheekbone one more time.

"You know there's no one to impress in this town, right?" he said casually as I stopped in front of him.

"I'll have you know this is for myself. It's habit now. And I'm sure Shadow appreciates it just as much as I do," I said, pointing my nose in the air.

His lips twitched and he intentionally blocked my way out. My heart picked up a beat as I held my own in front of him, my apprehension fizzing at his proximity. Eric casually leant a hand against the doorframe.

"You didn't have any makeup on yesterday and you still looked fine."

I pouted. "Just fine?"

"More than fine," he growled, his green eyes hooded as he lazily stood over me, as if holding himself back as well. I might've not been the smartest woman in the room but I knew when a man was into me—and to know the feeling was mutual was satisfying.

I harrumphed with a smile as I barged past him, deliberately scraping my nails along his bare chest as if to push him out of the way. If he was purposefully standing in my way, I could play a little as well. "Yesterday we were snowed in." I looked up through thick lashes. "But today I'm a free woman again."

A muscle ticked in his jaw. Triumphant, I left him alone in the bathroom. I liked the way he tried his hardest to not show interest. But a man's body never lied. Neither did the thrumming between my thighs, the fantasy of raking my nails down his chest and torso coming to fruition.

I tried to shake the thought, throwing myself into making another vegetarian omelette. I was pouring coffee into Eric's mug by the time he walked out towel drying his hair. "We used the last of the eggs," I said, plating it up.

"We?" he queried.

Casually, I cut a small piece of the omelette from his plate. He watched me as I gave it to Shadow, who gently took it from my fingers. Eric's eyebrows rose.

"The dog eats before me now?"

In the last few days, I'd quickly learnt what was okay and what wasn't to feed dogs. And Shadow had the cutest little face that I couldn't possibly deny him one damn thing. I gave Shadow a big smushy kiss on the top of his head.

"Shadow's nicer to me and you took your time to

sit down," I casually lectured. "And yes... we." I twisted my hands together nervously. I'd thought long and hard about his offer last night. It'd taken me aback. Like always, I was just taking it day by day. But it set a relief inside of me when he'd offered for me to stay. I wasn't sure how much Eric had caught on about my escaping Manhattan, if anything at all. But ever since the mention of Frederick, Canada wasn't a place I wanted to be. Especially considering Alice had a big mouth. If she'd told either him or my parents I was there, I'd be caught out. I didn't think my scapegoat would be a burly mountain man, but I wasn't going to deny the universe when it offered me a little magic.

I looked him in the eye as he waited cautiously for my next words. "We... About that offer you made last night. I thought on it some." All night actually because I'd hardly slept. "If you're really okay with having me here, I'd like to stay a few weeks and I'll totally work hard and do whatever you need me to do. But yea, might be more fun than Canada." I casually shrugged. Was I out of my mind? I could make friends with anyone and stayed at random places with strangers but there was something different about committing weeks to this cabin with Eric. Butterflies fluttered in my stomach at the thought.

He finished his mouthful of coffee. My breath hitched waiting on his reply. But what if he reconsidered his offer? Then I was at my original issue, drive until what? My fuel ran out? It was still three weeks until I received my payout from *Candice Magazine*. I was royally fucked. In some bizarre, as fate would have it, twisted way, this small-town lumberjack became my knight in shining armor.

"Okay. The offer still stands," Eric said. "His forest-green eyes seemed to seep into me, as if reading my every thought. I let out my breath, almost embarrassed by how long I'd been holding it.

I squealed, jumping up and down in excitement. "Thank you. You won't regret it, boss."

"Don't call me that," he quickly hissed.

"How about Daddy?"

His coffee sprayed everywhere. Shadow jumped back, staring at his owner in disbelief. I threw back my head and laughed, butterflies filling me once again. I'd been so nervous that he'd revoke his offer. And yet I just realized how exciting these next few weeks might be teasing this grump.

Chapter 16

Eric

I'd dropped Cassidy off at the café before grabbing supplies from the local grocery store. Whispers had spread amongst the locals about the "new beautiful woman" who was residing with me. Gossip spread around here quickly, and it irritated me to no means. And that was before they'd even found out she'd be staying with me for a few weeks more to come.

The snow had melted significantly, leaving the locals with the cleanup. Coots had informed us that the tree blocking the main road would be cleared today as well. I just hoped no one was reckless in trying to go around it in the meantime. Especially those who weren't used to the mountains and driving in this kind of snow. We didn't often get this kind of heavy fall, but when we did, there was always an idiot somewhere who'd try to pull off some stunt.

Shadow pranced by my side. I still didn't know why he was drawn to Cassidy. He hadn't taken an interest in anyone else and that was just his outright personality. I couldn't help but find irony in him being so much like his owner. But oh, how he doted on the bouncy blonde from Manhattan. It appeared she was making an impression on both of us.

Carrying a box full of groceries, I barged the café door open with my shoulder. I found Cassidy and Lori hunched over the counter looking at something. Cassidy had a freshly squeezed juice beside her. I'd shown her the blender in the café and gave her access to throw in whatever fruits she pleased. She had however been disappointed we didn't have any coconut water. And when I asked for it at our local grocery, Max looked at me like I'd requested something alien. Apparently, I'd have to "specially" order that in.

"Wow, Eric was helping you make cookies, huh?" Lori asked, crossing her arms over her chest, looking suddenly impressed. I grumbled as I walked past them, realizing what they'd been looking at.

Cassidy flicked through my cell, satisfied with the first image that appeared. "See." She'd asked to use my cell for a recipe while I was briefly gone but I should've known better. I was just lucky Thomas wasn't here or he would've been relentless in his taunts. Not that it was like he wasn't going to hear about it anyway.

I rolled my eyes; I still wasn't sure why she'd demanded to take photos on my cell. Her service was disconnected but not the features and certainly not her camera. But the moment she'd realized she couldn't contact anyone with it she hadn't pulled it out since. That meant the million selfies she'd taken of Shadow and her somehow wound up on my camera roll instead.

Lori laughed, grabbing my cell from the counter and looking between me and the image. "I wouldn't have believed you unless you showed me a photo."

"I know, that's why I took it," Cassidy chimed. I side-eyed her and she raised her chest, as if proud of herself.

Lori casually took over two mugs of tea to Ann and Patrice, who listened in with interest. "Been having a good time I see," Ann crooned from her booth. Patrice sat across from her, a mischievous twinkle in both their gazes.

"It's been so much fun!" Cassidy excitedly announced.

That was the worst fucking part, it'd be the talk of the town. Me in my log cabin baking fucking cookies. And yet I couldn't bring myself to deter the fun Cassidy seemed to be having. So much fun, in fact—at my expense. I was just grateful she wasn't sharing with my sister the sweet nothings we were whispering to each other while baking those cookies or the yoga session. Now that she wouldn't believe.

It was hard to believe Cassidy only arrived a few days ago. My sister and she acted as if they were long lost friends.

"What are you going to do about your trip to Canada?" Lori asked as she threw the tea towel over her shoulder. One of her trademark habits.

"Well, since the roads are pretty snowy and sluggish and even with the tree removed, the drive still sounds kind of dangerous. Eric suggested I could stay here for a little while longer and that I might be able to help around and pay for my stay?"

"Did he now?" Lori queried her mouth agape. My blood went cold. Fuck. My siblings would never let me live this down.

"She's not a confident driver," I said matter-of-factly. "You know how these roads can get." I ignored my sister's smug smile and stare, pulling out a sim card from the box of groceries. I handed it to

Cassidy. "This is for your cell, until you've sorted out your plan and server."

She seemed almost shy to accept my gift. "Thank you." Those big blue eyes pinned me into spot. "Sorry, I can give your cell back, I got carried away."

I placed my hand on top of hers that held the cell, again purposefully ignoring my sister's gaze. "I don't mind you using my cell. I hardly use it anyway. I just thought you might want to message your friends to let them know your whereabouts."

Genuine appreciation flooded her expression, the innocent and transparent emotion tempering my nerves.

Lori interrupted. Our hands broke apart as I cleared my throat. "Well, if we're getting chummy, and that looks to be the case, why don't you join us for dinner at our mother's this weekend?"

"That's not necessary," I gritted out. She was baiting me and it'd be like throwing Cassidy to the wolves. Worst of all, they'd ask questions that didn't need to be voiced. My siblings would tease and taunt me until no end. It was a complication I didn't need and had me immediately reconsidering my extended offer for Cassidy to stay longer.

Lori waved me off, her attention set on Cassidy. "Our mother would love to meet you. It's not like we get many visitors and besides all the brothers are going to be there and I'm sure they'll be dying to meet you as well. Our mother makes the best linguine." Lori reached out her hand and squeezed Cassidy's. I could see what she was doing, and it didn't help that Cassidy looked up at me with those big blue eyes, almost pleading.

She was a self-confessed socialite, the opposite to me. Invites to events, no matter how small, fuelled her curiosity and need to meet new people.

"I don't mind going," Cassidy alluded. "Maybe we should make some cookies for it?"

"That's a great idea!" Lori encouraged.

Cassidy lit up, excited by her newfound baking skill and I internally grumbled. If I rocked up with a plateful of freshly baked cookies, I was going to pay for it for years to come.

Cassidy excused herself to go to the bathroom. When she was out of earshot, I grumbled at my sister, "What are you doing?"

"Playing friendly neighbor. Not as friendly as some it would appear though." Her gaze narrowed on me as if she was trying to find something deeper and menacing. "She's young."

"I don't need your advice or opinion."

"Ouch, someone's on the defense." She had a

slow Cheshire cat smile. "I never said it was a bad thing, I was just curious as to how you'd react, but you've already answered my question."

"Your question?" I dared ask.

"As to whether you two are banging or not?"

"We're not."

Lori toyed with her expression, mock-believing me. "Then I must be blind as a badger that there's some serious chemistry playing between you two. I'm just curious what the twins will say."

At my effective glance, she began to laugh, throwing back her head as she walked into the kitchen. Fuck. I was going to be more miserable than usual at this dinner.

Chapter 17

Eric

Cassidy had been dragged to help Ann and Patrice, modelling a new dress Ann was making. She'd been gone now for an hour, not that I'd been keeping a purposeful eye on the time. Every second felt like it ticked by due to our lack of customers passing through. It'd most likely take a few days until it picked up as usual. Just in case we had customers, however, we'd parked Cassidy's rental car out the back.

Lori had finished with serving our only customer who'd stopped in for a coffee and was now suddenly fixated on trying her hardest to scrub off a stain on the counter that'd been there for years. I tried not to chuckle when frustrated, she blew a piece of her red hair that dangled away from her eyes.

I'd been chopping wood all morning and took a momentary break in the kitchen, taking a sip of my cup of joe and throwing back a breakfast sandwich. My muscles ached, satisfied by the workout so far. A cold sweat had spoilt my shirt and I intended on changing into the spare one in the truck once I was done with the day. Had it been just me, I wouldn't have minded, but I didn't want to get into the truck with Cassidy smelling like this.

The doorbell chimed as the door opened. Shadow's hackles raised immediately, a growl vibrating through him. I furrowed my eyebrows dropping the sandwich and dusting my hands to leave the kitchen and inspect.

"Good morning," Lori chirped as she threw the sponge to the side, obviously excited by the distraction.

Two men stood in the door, scoping out the café with displeasure. It was the obvious dynamics of the two I didn't like. The gentleman who wore a ridiculously over-the-top, expensive garment almost sneered at our café as if it was a dive. His blonde curly hair was slicked back in gel and those green snake eyes missed nothing. Behind him loomed what could only be described as his bodyguard.

I'd met plenty of his type before. Little pompous

pricks who felt entitled, and instinct told me this one was going to be a bigger pain in the ass than usual.

Ignoring Lori's welcome, they refused to step further inside. I rounded the counter with Shadow by my side. When I stopped, he sat at my feet, staring up at the man who easily became disgruntled by our appearance.

"Wow," the little pompous prick joked throwing a thumb my way. "They make them big out here, huh?" He titled his head back to the bodyguard, expecting him to laugh. But he didn't. Instead, the older man sized me up as a threat. These two were trouble.

I crossed my arms over my chest. "Are you here for breakfast?"

The man scoffed. "Here? God no. We're looking for a woman."

I expressed nothing on my face. "Yes. Less than half of our population here are women but I doubt any would have any business with you."

He rolled his tongue around in his mouth, evidently annoyed by my tone. He pushed back his hair, as if in fear that a piece of the gel had slipped. "A specific woman. And you might want to be cautious as to how you speak to me."

Shadow's growl was low and menacing,

reminding him that it was he who should watch his tone. Effortlessly, the bodyguard pushed back his coat to reveal a gun peeking out from the belt strapped at his pants. I snapped my gaze to the littler man. Who the fuck was this little prick?

"Eric, where do you want me to put this?" Lori sung out as she teased held up the rifle we kept behind the counter. A twitch provoked my lips, trying not to smile at my smart-ass little sister.

"Obviously we come in peace," the man laughed, almost amused by the escalation of events. Something told me this brat was used to getting what he wanted and when he wanted it.

"Let me assure you, coming into someone else's town and business with a gun and demand is not how it's done. Didn't your parents teach you any manners?" I growled out.

At the mention of his parents, a feverish anger washed over him, but then he revealed a deadly smile. "I'm after a woman, blonde curly hair, blue eyes..." he began detailing a description as his bodyguard pulled out his cell, displaying an image of Cassidy. Except not a recent photo. In the photo, she was holding a sparkler in hand with a cake the size of her height with twenty-one written all over it. She was in a bikini, laughing at nothing in particular. I noticed in that image the flashy surroundings and the way the others were dressed around her. Wealth. Prestige. Elite.

"Have you seen her?" the man asked again.

"No." My expression was deadpan.

"Really? We might be under the impression she stopped here last?" The man-child seemed disbelieving.

I said nothing. The low irritable growl of Shadow's pricked the air.

"We haven't but is she dangerous or something?" Lori asked from behind the counter. I felt the skin over my muscle tighten. I couldn't explain why I immediately wanted to kick this man out, but there was something about him, a dangerous and entitled kind of air. And I was grateful Lori played naïve as well.

He laughed. "Dangerous? No. Spoilt? Definitely. We're just playing a little cat and mouse, that's all." He charmed a smile as the bodyguard slid the cell back into his pocket.

He pulled out a slick card with a name, number, and a company logo plastered on it. He offered it to me but I simply eyed it. With a small grumble, Lori walked behind me, leant around my wide shoulders and plucked it out of his hand.

"Well, if we see her, we'll let you know," Lori said, flipping over the card to read it.

"Right," he drawled, giving me an unimpressed look. "Well enjoy your day." He turned and left as if he couldn't get out of here any quicker.

Lori whistled behind him. Slowly, I feathered a hand through Shadow's fur, easing the same tension that rippled through me. There was something not right about that man.

"He's the CEO of Taylor Oils," Lori said folding over the card. "Isn't that one of the big ones? And why is he looking for Cassidy?"

"We're not ratting her out" is all I said as I grabbed my coat with the intention to find her and make sure he didn't first. I doubted he'd try any other places on the main street. This was the most central for most people passing through. But I didn't like the threat walking through town either. People like him were not welcome here.

"Well of course not but," Lori called out to me as I shuffled my coat on, "don't you think you're going out on a bit of a limb for a stranger?" I paused and looked over my shoulder. "I mean it was only a few days ago you were reluctant to even breathe the same air as her and hold her up in your cabin. Don't you think it's risky going up against something like this and for what?"

Not that I had to explain myself, but my sister was one of few who understood me. And her best interest would always lay in the safety of the town where our parents lived. As did mine. But nor was I going to hand Cassidy over like some bargaining chip. I was certain he had something to do with the reason she was running away in the first place. "Something wasn't right about that man."

Lori seemed to agree with a grimace. And she liked Cassidy, I could tell. But she was right; we didn't know what kind of trouble she was caught up in either. "Where are you going now?" Lori asked.

"To make sure she's safe and doesn't leave Ann's house without me."

Lori's arms folded over her chest, a mischievous sparkle twinkling in her eye. I ignored it, stepping out into the slow sprinkling snow and heading to Ann's house with Shadow by my side. The two men had already driven off but I wasn't leaving anything to chance.

Chapter 18

Cassidy

I felt like a human burrito that had been wrapped in different materials. Ann's clever hands were gliding in and out as she positioned the layers differently in the dress I now wore.

"I haven't been able to work on a model with a waist this small in years," Ann said giddily. Patrice sat in a rocking chair nearby, reading a book and sipping a tea.

"These dresses are beautiful," I gushed enthusiastically. Perhaps outdated but they were crafted beautifully. She'd brought out a rack of various dresses and I was as of forty minutes ago her real-life manikin.

"It's only a hobby now," Ann crooned in lust-filled wonder.

"She used to own a shop back in Philadelphia," Patrice said fondly as she continued to read, gently rocking. She was reading some historical romance. There was something endearing about their setup, it flowed as if this was their everyday routine. Enjoying their own hobby amongst chatter and tea every day.

"What happened to it?" I asked.

Ann swatted a hand, as if embarrassed. "Well, I met Coots of course. We stayed in Philadelphia for a few years, traveled around some with our children and then ended up settling here fifty-odd years ago when Coots got a local mechanics job. Haven't looked elsewhere since."

My wildly-romantic heart swooned at their long-term marriage. Ann gestured a hand toward Patrice. "And Patrice and I were friends since high school. When she lost her husband who served in the military thirty years ago she moved out here as well. Didn't want to get in her children's way as they encouraged her to move close to them. She wanted a fresh start."

My heart sunk, unable to even imagine her loss.

Patrice rolled her eyes. "Don't want to burden the young ones? They're running around in their own busy lives and although I appreciated the gesture there was no way I could keep up with them.

My two sons both had young families then too. I didn't want to become dependent on nobody." She lifted her nose indignantly.

"I'm sorry for your loss," I said sincerely. She looked over her book, a small and gentle smile marring her expression.

"You're a sweet one with a good heart and I appreciate the gesture. We lived many years together and he was taken too soon. But I'm grateful for the years we had spent together. It took me a long time to come to that conclusion though, mark my words."

I couldn't imagine losing the love of my life. The thought paralyzed me. And yet I didn't seem any closer to finding any kind of forever relationship to truly envision its magnitude. I'd watched all the Disney movies, read all the romance books, and advocated the dramas. I'd grown up on love stories despite my parents displaying none in their marriage. It was all I craved, and yet I couldn't have been any further from it—despite actively searching for it in New York.

"That's why it's so enjoyable for us to watch you and Eric flutter about each other. I haven't seen that man crack a smile in years," Ann goaded.

"We thought he was a lost cause," Patrice agreed as she took another sip of her tea.

I blushed. "Oh, there's nothing happening between us. He's very kind though offering me a place to stay."

The two shared a mischievous smirk. "We might be old, love, but we aren't blind."

Ann hissed as she pricked her finger. She waved her hand back and forth before staring at dollop of blood. Patrice, without a second glance, handed her a tissue as if the two were in unison.

"He's a fine young man to look at it. It's a shame how burnt he got from the last one. It's been what? A decade since her?" Ann asked Patrice.

Patrice sighed. "Maybe even longer. He *was* a lot younger."

"Everyone's younger to us," Ann squabbled.

"I'm sorry who?" I interrupted, suddenly interested by who this "last one" was.

After placing a plaster on her finger, Ann pushed my back. "Taller dear, don't slouch."

I did as I was told.

"It was the talk of the town for years," Patrice began.

"Damn right it was," Ann crooned in reply.

"Katia moved into the town and it was probably within six months that the two were living together," Patrice continued.

"Youngsters falling in love quickly." Ann sighed.

The two bounced from one another conversationally, retelling the story.

"Two years into their relationship, she took him for everything he was worth. Everything had been signed over into her name including the home and three businesses the family owned including the café."

My jaw dropped and Ann nodded with eyebrows raised.

"Mmmhmmm." She clicked her fingers. "Just like that, she vanished and no one heard or saw from her again."

My heart dropped.

"Took the family another year to buy her out and get everything back. As the oldest they'd given Eric everything. But just as quickly, that one woman was able to deceive and take all of it," Patrice said glumly shaking her head.

"A con woman," Ann added as she lowered to her knees, establishing a new length for the dress. "Shook him up real bad. After everything settled, he fled to Chicago and started his own business."

"I think he must've felt guilty or didn't want to hinder the family," Patrice pitied.

"And from what Audrey's said, he hasn't brought another woman home since."

"Maybe he's gay," Patrice whispered.

Ann waved her off.

"Umm who's Audrey?" A twist of emotions bundled in the pit of my stomach. Eric went through all of that? I immediately pitied him. I'd gone through my flings and waves of men who'd only used me for sex—even when they promised sweet words and futures. The ones that hurt me the most were the two who'd never told me about their wives or true intentions. But I'd never been *conned* out of all my belongings.

"Oh, sorry dear, Audrey is Eric's mother. Lovely woman, very sad what happened to her in the accident though. Makes it hard for her to leave the house much in this weather."

My heart dropped again. "The accident?"

Patrice gave Ann an uncertain look. "Perhaps we've said too much."

"We can't very well stop now," Ann reprimanded. I looked through the mirror at the rich red reflection of the princess-cut dress.

"She was in a car accident six years ago and has been in a wheelchair ever since."

My heart physically ached. Had Eric been

dealing with this all on his own?

"Shh," Ann hushed. Patrice's eyebrows furrowed and she stood up to peer through the window. Eric approached the front door, his hands casually tucked into his pockets.

"But you didn't hear any of that from us," Patrice said, swatting the comment away and continued rocking in her chair casually, sipping her tea.

"The door's open!" Ann crooned and gave me a wink. "Looks like your knight in shining armor's come to save you from us old croons."

Before I could object, his hulking form filled the room. His gaze raked down the dress and back to me. "What are you doing here?" I asked breathlessly. Guilt and anguish rolled over me. I hadn't dealt with any of the things that he had in his life, so I could only empathize. And that just made it so much worse. Guilt also niggled at me for knowing some of his deepest hurts, and yet I couldn't share a wisp of mine. Not that he probably cared to hear them.

"Yes, what are you doing here, Eric? You never visit," Ann said, already packing up her equipment.

"I've come to pick up Cassidy."

"Do you have work for me?" I asked.

Eric looked sheepish as he glanced at our onlook-ers, who were hinged on his every word with curiosity. A tension filled the room, their looming romantic expectations obvious.

"Something like that."

I looked at Ann and she waved me off. "Go, go. Now that you're staying in town for a few weeks, I can have you anytime I want. As long as Eric's willing to share." Ann raised an incredulous eyebrow in Eric's direction. Patrice, ever quiet sipped, on her tea, her gaze drifting up occasionally to watch the tension throughout the room run its course.

Chapter 19

Cassidy

After dropping piles of wood off to the locals, we made our way back home to the cabin. The snow had begun to slowly melt away the frostbitten blanket of white, revealing a few streaks of green beneath. Apparently, it'd been unusual to receive this much snow at this time of year. But part of me secretly enjoyed the days. In Manhattan it might've hindered my social life but here I could appreciate its beauty.

It was so different to most vacations or places I'd been. My schedule was always busy with social events and for the first time in a long time, I kind of had nothing to do. I still had so much to figure out but I didn't feel as stressed about my whereabouts or how I might step forward. I just had to believe it was going to work out, and by the time I had to move on, I'd have my pay check and could take it from there.

I stared at my cell. Eric had installed the new sim card, and so I'd messaged Clover and Issobelle to tell them I was safe in my travels and asked if anything exciting was happening in Manhattan since I'd left.

I realized then there was no one else I particularly wanted to reach out to. I was surrounded by so many people in Manhattan, and yet I genuinely thought the only two who cared about my whereabouts and safety were those two.

I also sent Alice a short and cryptic message. *May be longer. Got stuck on the way but having fun. It's such a vibe!* The reality was I didn't trust her not to inform my parents or Frederick about my whereabouts.

A light tension filled the truck. It wasn't unusual for Eric and me to sit in comfortable silence. In fact, it was one of Eric's favorite pastimes, but right now I'd actively avoided conversation, too scared he'd see straight through me and the discussion I'd had with Ann and Patrice. Eric had been right, the folk here loved to gossip and now that I had all of this information about his deepest darkest downfalls, I wasn't sure what to do with it—if anything at all. I couldn't mention it if he hadn't told me himself, right?

And besides, what could I do to help? Wouldn't he hate my pity? Spite my curiosity? And yet all I wanted to do was give the big tower of a man a hug. I'm sure someone had been there to support him through it all, but I wanted to convey my apologies and tell him that situation was never okay.

"You're awfully quiet today." His voice was like an electric shock slicing through the air and straight into the pit of my stomach.

"Am I?" I squeaked. He side-eyed me.

"I have a question for you, and I want you to answer me honestly or as much as you can."

That statement alone had my heart racing. *Crap.* Did he know about the conversation I'd had with those gossipers. But how? Then again, Eric seemed like the type of man to find out everything.

"A man dropped by today in the café looking for you."

I stopped wringing my fingers together. This wasn't about Eric? And a man looking for me? Shock and a cold chill ran through me. What if it was *him?* My breath hitched, mortified at what Eric might say next. But instead, he sat in silence. It was far more effective and revealing than I'd like to admit. It made me uncomfortable as he waited for an answer. His one simple statement suddenly felt like an interrogation.

"That's a statement not a question," I deflected. He gave me one of his grumpy effective side glances.

"Is there any particular reason why he might be looking for you that I need to know? Will it affect the town?"

Ah. The town. Of course. After losing everything before, wouldn't the town always be his priority? I was still an outsider, after all. I swallowed the hard lump in my throat, trying to act nonchalant, but I wasn't fooling anyone. It unnerved me because I knew his answer before he'd even given it.

"What was his name?" My voice was small, and I began running my finger down the door handle trying to act blasé as I stared out the window. *Please don't be him. Please don't be him. Please don't be him.*

"Frederick Taylor."

My blood ran cold and my hand furled around the handle. A wave of nausea passed through me. Had he seen me? If he had though, he would've confronted me, right? How many years had I been running away from him, now? He was going to be angry and that wasn't even the worst of it.

"Did you say you knew me?" I asked in the quietest of voices—foreign to even me. I couldn't break out a smile or pretend like it was okay. My body headed automatically into fight-or-flight response.

"No," Eric growled out, and I stared at him, aroused and terrified by his dominant tone. Heat filled my lower abdomen. In his own way, without realizing it or caring to admit, had he been protecting me? All the while I was gossiping about his con ex-girlfriend.

"He's someone I can't get caught up with again. I guess you could describe him as an ex of sorts." Bile crept into my throat just by referring him as that. I closed my eyes, praying that Eric wouldn't ask any more questions. I hadn't had to deal with my parents or even the mention of Frederick for three years now. That's how long I'd been in Manhattan, and yet I still wasn't ready to face any of them.

A warm hand covered mine and squeezed. My eyes burst open, and I stared at Eric. "If you're in trouble, I need to know."

Involuntary tears welled in my eyes. I'd waited for so long for someone to sincerely offer me that help, drowning under paranoia that Frederick would show up in Manhattan at any time. But after a year, I'd realized they didn't care and no one would come. Until now. And even so, it'd felt so long since I was associated with that world that I never thought to bring it up in conversation or entertain it to my new group of friends I'd made in Manhattan.

By the time we'd arrived at the cabin, tears had slipped down my cheeks at the thought and release of all the pent-up emotions and fears I'd held back for so long. Eric pulled on the handbrake, a fiery rage burning through his beautiful green eyes.

"I'm sorry it's dumb," I vigorously wiped away the tears, embarrassed. I needed to get out of this car. I needed to forget again. I needed a moment to breathe and bounce back to my usual bright self. "I just remembered something bad is all." I undid my belt and tried to open the door. Whiplash took hold as Eric tugged me back into the car. When I turned around, his mouth crashed onto mine and everything immediately dissipated.

My mind went blank but my body opened up to him, melting into him as my hands furled around his collar, pulling him in and asking for more. Everything about him was rough and demanding. His hand cupped my cheek as I tried to lean further over the awkward box between us in the car, my thighs urging me to straddle him instead.

He smelt of pinewood and masculine promise, my toes curling at the prospect. All the tension rippled from me, morphing and gripping me with a new kind of buzz. One that promised dirty words and thick masculine thighs spreading my own.

I bit down on his bottom lip with a groan and both of our eyes sprang open, breaking the spell. He pulled back, a small growl rumbling through his core. My body quaked in anticipation. I was breathless, my hair a mess. His thick, calloused thumb rubbed against my cheekbone as realization dawned on us. Did we just... kiss?

My mouth opened and then closed. For the first time ever, I was speechless.

"I don't like seeing you cry," he said. Simple and matter of fact.

"So you kiss women into silence?" I hiccupped, still in disbelief.

"No, I usually kiss them into submission," he growled.

My core flooded, my pussy pounding with the first real excitement it had since... well a long time. Sure, I'd been celibate for three months, but even before then I'd been going through the motions with men. *All types of men.* But there was a hungry need and urgency that filled me now. I felt *wanted* by Eric. And as I dipped my gaze to the hard bulge in his jeans, I realized that couldn't be any clearer.

He slipped away his hand and jerked open the door. I sat there stunned. What was happening?

I kicked my own door open. "What was that?" I asked, still in a dreary state.

"It was a mistake. It's not a good idea if you and I get involved, snowflake."

As quickly as it happened, I was rejected in the same breath. I felt stunned and frozen in the snow, moving mechanically to open the door for Shadow.

"And trust me when I say it's in your best interest," Eric reinforced matter-of-factly. All passion had drained from him, and he'd returned to his stoic state.

I snorted. "It's not you, it's me, right? What a classic line." And one I'd grown too accustomed to hearing. As uncomfortable as the rejection was, I found myself grateful for one thing. Despite Eric's confusing methods, that cold gripping terror had vanished, and he didn't look like he was about to press for any more answers about my past. For now.

"Trust me, I'm not the one for you," Eric said as he all but ran for the door, leaving me and Shadow behind by the still open and unlocked truck. We gave one another a dubious look. Shit, I knew I'd scared off men in the past, but this was a whole new level. And yet I couldn't help reach for my lip, reliving that moment of pure intoxication. I felt alive and hot. And despite his words, my heart and pussy pounded defiantly, demanding more, now that it had a taste of what was possible. I found it difficult to believe his words when his actions had told me something entirely different.

I wanted to slap my cheeks in an attempt to calm my libido down. I'd sworn to celibacy until I found the right man. For once, I wasn't using my body first. Wouldn't this be betraying that notion? I realized after two dates, most didn't bother to stick around in the past three months when I didn't put out.

Was this any different? Or could it be that it was a convenience for him to have a woman in his cabin and why not? But if that had been the case... he wouldn't have run away so easily. Right?

Chapter 20

Eric

Thud. The wood split into two. I was surrounded by mounds of chopped wood but no matter how much I chopped, it wasn't enough to burn away any of that unwanted and remaining energy. I'd kissed Cassidy impulsively. The moment I saw her eyes fill with tears, sheer terror in her expression and that bottom lip wobbling, I was a goner. I wanted to distract her in any way I could and my body moved of its own accord.

The kiss was fucking amazing and scorched straight into my memories. My dick became so uncomfortably hard that had it been anyone else, I probably would've dragged them out and fucked them against the truck's bonnet, driving us both into oblivion. But Cassidy was different. I couldn't do that. We were temporarily living together, and I still wasn't entirely sure why I'd extended the offer, but I wasn't going to screw it up because I wanted a release.

Thud. Another piece of wood split. Flashes of her soft lips and skin against my calloused hands. The way those big blue eyes stared back at me with total submission. I could've done anything to that woman no matter how dirty my fantasy.

Thud. Fuck. My dick was twitching at the thought. She hadn't come out since we'd arrived at the cabin either. When I was chopping wood, she'd usually bring me a beverage but perhaps wisely for now, we were both keeping our distance.

An hour later, the sun completely set, I'd decided it was time to call it a night. I was satisfied by the ache and fatigue in my muscles. I kicked my boots off at the door, not letting any of the dirt or snow in since last time Cassidy had reprimanded me for it.

I quietly stepped inside, eyeing Cassidy and feeling uncomfortable by the lump in my throat. Fuck she was beautiful. She was coiled up with a hot cup of tea and blanket in front of the fireplace. Shadow lay at her feet as she scrolled through her cell.

"I just sent an article to you about the benefits of yoga," she said, looking over her shoulder at me. I was surprised she knew I was inside. Again, her gaze deceived her as it dipped before she looked away again.

I quirked a smile. Despite my clear attraction toward her, I enjoyed taunting her slightly just as she did so often to me. I rounded the couch, admiring her messy top bun. She'd showered and removed her makeup, revealing smooth glowing skin. I tried my best not to reach out again, remembering the softness of her cheek.

"Read it to me," I growled, lifting her legs so I could sit.

"Hey! You smell!" She hissed as I plonked myself beside her and let her legs fall over me. I was playing with fire, I knew that. It was only a minute ago I had the resolve to keep my distance. And yet now I found myself taunting her, enjoying the light blush that spread across her cheek. I casually hung my arm over her legs, avoiding my own urge to slip my hand underneath the blanket and her sweatpants and stroke her.

"Read it to me," I repeated.

She harrumphed, lifting her chin. A small

chuckle escaped, rewarding me with a slow smile of her own, even as she pretended to be mad.

I sat there comfortably as she read the article about the benefits of yoga. Her voice was soothing. The piece itself, I wasn't so much convinced on, no matter how much she tried to coax me. I found my eyes slowly shutting with ease as I succumbed to her soothing voice, feeling oddly content.

Two hours later, I woke up, still sitting upright but now with a blanket spread over me. I rubbed at my face, realizing I'd fallen asleep. I pulled back my sweaty shirt with a low grumble. I still hadn't showered. The aroma of crackling firewood and something cheesy filled the room.

I twisted on the sofa, peering over at Cassidy whose hips swayed as she silently cooked. "Did you set up the fireplace?" I asked groggily. I'd been intending on doing it for her when I'd come in from chopping the wood.

"Oh, you're awake." Shadow left Cassidy's side and waltzed over expectantly for pats. "And yes, I might've watched you a few times." She cursed under her breath. "But I broke a fricking nail doing it and I'm not impressed."

I chuckled, throwing the blanket off. She held out her hand, an angry pout on her face. "Do you know how long it's been since I've broken a nail? I'm going to have to trim them all now *and* it hurt."

I had the urge to grab her hand and kiss it better but brushed that off as simply grogginess. "What are you making?" I asked peering over her shoulder. It was self-explanatory. "Grilled cheese toastie?"

She perked up, proud. "Lori explained to me what the secret was, you know flattening it on the pan and all. I wanted to make you one."

I looked over at the plate. She'd already made three. She quirked a smile. "Okay so maybe I got overly excited because I learnt something new to make so I hope you're hungry."

The truth was, I was starving. Again, I ignored the urge to dip down and press a kiss to her forehead in thanks. What was happening to me? All these urges were compromising my better judgement. "I'll have a quick shower and then be your guinea pig."

"Hey!" she called from behind me, spatula in hand. As of late, I'd hardly had to make anything in the café to eat because of Cassidy's sudden fascination with cooking. And I wasn't complaining.

Chapter 21

Cassidy

I'd avoided Eric's gaze ever since he stepped out of the shower with steam rolling off him like some mountain god. The bare chest and chiselled stomach most certainly had something to do it; those grey sweatpants evoking all kinds of fantasies. Since he'd kissed me, my bravado changed shamelessly. A heated thrum coursed through me constantly. Desire. Heat. Him.

Out of the four cheesy toasties, I splendored on the greasiness of half a piece. I was aware Eric watched me like a hawk around my eating habits. It certainly wasn't the portion sizes he was used to but I was almost smaller than half his size and so he'd stopped inquiring as to why I ate so little after pointing out that fact.

When I started unfurling the blanket on the sofa, the sweaty masculine heat rolled from it since Eric had been sleeping with it. There was a comfort in knowing I'd be sleeping beneath it tonight, shamefully intoxicated by its smell. And I didn't want to explore that any further. I was scared my deceitful little heart was becoming too attached like it always did. Okay, so I finally found a man who offered me a nice gesture and hadn't asked me for my body yet, but I still didn't trust myself.

Eric cleared his throat as he fluffed his own pillow, a thick tension rising between us across the room. "You don't have to keep sleeping on the sofa, Cassidy. You can share the bed with me, it's big enough."

My eyes widened as I looked between him and the bed, the stunning backdrop of the mountains behind it taking my breath away. Him and me... in the same bed? The vision of entangled limbs and sweet nothings whispered created a heated stir in my lower abdomen.

He chuckled. "You look like a deer in headlights. Relax I'm not going to do anything to you. That sofa can't be good to sleep on for so long and I doubt any amount of yoga is going to help fix a jarred back."

"Yoga helps with a lot," I said quietly and pointedly.

He chuckled. "If my mother finds out I've been letting you sleep on a sofa she'll tear me a new one."

So, was this him attempting to be a gentleman? Or, more importantly, fear from the wrath of his mother? Both of which was kind of funny and endearing all the same.

I was clutching the blanket and nibbling on my bottom lip. Well, it hadn't been the comfiest, nor was it uncomfy. But the temptation of his big bouncy bed was alluring. I swallowed hard, pushing down my wild fantasies. "If we sleep in the same bed, we're sleeping head to toe."

His lip twitched into an arrogant smile. "Head to toe?"

"Yes. That way we're not tempted by any... unsavory business."

He threw his head back laughing as he strode toward the wall, switching off the lights. By way of the flickering flames from the fireplace, I could still see his outline and the way he patted the end of the bed. "As you wish."

Thoughtfully, I dropped the blanket on the sofa and grabbed my pillow. I cautiously stepped around the bed and he growled. "I'm not going to bite you, Cassidy, even if that's all you can think about."

"I am not!" I was.

Another laugh. How was he not effected in the same way that I was? Or was that simply my foolish girly heart betraying me again?

"Wait I have a term," I said pointedly as he slid under the blankets, his sheer enormity filling the space. I hadn't done head to toe since sleepovers as a child. And even then it'd never been necessary, but I'd seen it on movies and it looked fun.

"What's your condition, Cassidy?" he growled. Those penetrating green eyes glimmered from the dark via the flickering flames. But I could see him... all of him, including the curled hair on his bare chest. I pushed down my temptation to feather my fingers through it.

I inhaled. No man was left behind. "Shadow gets to sleep on the bed too."

I pointed to the dog curled up on his own pillow on the floor. If there was a dog in the bed, I was certain that would be the best kind of buffer to anything happening. Not that I was assuming something was going to happen... but I didn't entirely trust this heated thrumming in my core. Or my chest.

"Shadow doesn't sleep on the bed," Eric said gruffly.

"Neither did I, up until two minutes ago."

As if understanding and hopeful, Shadow propped his head up staring at me.

"He can even share my side of the bed, so he doesn't take up too much of yours," I encouraged, like he was really lucking out here. Silence filled the room, and I could sense Eric's displeasure.

"Fine," Eric gritted out eventually. I squealed excitedly, tapping on the bed and encouraging Shadow to jump up. He seemed perplexed but it didn't take him long to join me as I shuffled underneath the blanket, then spooned Shadow like some giant teddy.

I wriggled comfortably around him, casually patting his fur.

Silence. Nothing but pure masculine heat radiated next to me. He shuffled slightly, his thigh pressing against my leg. My attention and focus drew toward to that spot and I closed my eyes. Why was I acting like a teenager? I'd slept in the same bed with many men before.

"Are you comfy?" he eventually asked, his voice a husky whisper.

"Mhmm," I lied. The bed itself was divine, like a

soft marshmallow. The proximity however... was too much to handle. I opened my eyes again, staring at an already snoozing Shadow. In my peripheral was the dark but beautiful view of the mountains beyond the window. Trying to take my mind off the palpable tension, I asked, "Why did you call him Shadow?" We'd already been laying here for ten minutes, and I felt more alert then when I'd originally set the intentions to sleep.

"You'll laugh," Eric said flatly.

A smile curved my lips. "Now that sounds promising." I continued patting Shadow's head, trailing a finger down his nose and between his eyes.

"You ever heard of Sonic the Hedgehog?"

I scrunched up my nose. "Vaguely. Wasn't it some arcade game?"

He sighed. "It's moments like this I realize how old I'm getting."

I laughed. "You're forty-two, that's not old. Stop being dramatic." I nudged him with my leg.

He sighed as if disbelieving. "I used to play it as a teen all the time and Shadow was the character I'd often select. I adopted Shadow when he was already six months old from a shelter, he didn't have any history, they'd found him malnourished on the streets, so he hadn't been given a new name at the time. It was Lori who dragged me to the shelter six years ago and it was her idea that I adopted, actually. When I refused... she did it on my behalf. I woke up in my Chicago apartment with a six-month-old German shepherd mix Christmas morning. In the end... it turned out she might've been right. And the only name I could think of at the time for an animal was Shadow. Not a very spectacular story is it?"

I patted Shadow thoughtfully and considered Lori. I wondered if she thought Eric was lonely and that's why she adopted a companion for him. Granted, I didn't know what Eric's life looked like in Chicago but I doubted he was a social butterfly. I would fall back in surprise if he was.

"Your sister really cares about you and I think the name suits him fine." Although it was hard to envision Eric as a teenager who played video games, it was endearing to think of.

"She's also meddlesome," he gritted out. I smiled. From the few friends I'd had over the years with siblings, I thought that was normal because they all said the same thing. It was nice to look in on from time to time.

My blood went cold as a long howl echoed through the night. Shadow shot up, growling with ears pulled back. Eric placed a hand on my leg as I shot up beside him.

"It's okay," Eric said gently, rubbing over the spot his hand burned onto my leg. My heart pounded.

"I thought wolves weren't meant to be in this area," I said breathlessly.

"They're not. It could be a wild dog. It's okay," he reassured. "Shadow." His singular word silenced the dog, who licked his lips and reluctantly laid back down. Following suit, I tucked back in beside him. Although Eric spoke sweet things calmly, I could feel the tension in his body. Was it possible wolves lived in the mountains? I mean if there were bears and coyotes, surely wolves weren't a stretch.

Not that anything could get into the cabin... but still. It was a reminder that we were far from any city.

"Good night, Cassidy," Eric said gently, his thumb still stroking over my leg. I curled a little further into Shadow, a part of me wishing that it was Eric instead. I was grateful for my genius of using the dog as a buffer because my heart was starting to betray me. But didn't it always?

"Good night, Eric, don't dream too many naughty thoughts of me," I threw in with tongue in cheek. His growl rippled through me, his hand squeezing tighter.

"You keep that talk up and it won't be wolves you'll be scared of."

I bit my lip, smiling, and tucked into the comfiest, most insulated sleep I'd had in months.

Chapter 22

Eric

After getting caught in chatter with Ann and Patrice thirty minutes after our café closed, Cassidy had finally been able to drag herself away and I was able to not so subtly kick the two croons out.

"You can't keep her all to yourself the whole time," Ann had said with a mischievous grin. I imagined she was filling time until Coots returned home this weekend. He always worked in the neighboring town during the week and so without Patrice, Ann often found herself bored. Every year I came back not much had changed. Well, except this year of course.

I wanted to make sure we returned to the cabin before dusk, especially considering I'd promised

Cassidy a personal lesson of wood chopping. I'd grumbled my complaint when she'd first asked me. And yet somehow she'd managed to twist my arm yet again.

We now stood around the thick tree trunk I used to cut the pieces of wood on top of. She looked out of place in her bright pink jacket, sizing up the smaller piece of wood I'd managed to find for her. Cassidy was staring at it with as much concentration as she did all the recipes Lori had given her recently. Shadow was laying on the porch, his head nestled on his paws as he napped.

"Okay so you swing over with all your might?" she asked enthusiastically.

I chuckled, imaging whatever that might've looked like to her. Cassidy had the height and build of a runway model and bulging muscles was not a part of her charm. She picked up the axe, and I took two steps forward. "Woah, there," I chuckled. Where she lacked in strength, she made up with enthusiasm.

I wrapped my arms around her, assaulted by her sweet honeysuckle scent. My nose nuzzled into her cascading blonde curls, and I envisioned what it'd be like to wrap them around my knuckles and tug. My cock twitched. I cleared my throat and spaced my legs wider, shuffling her hands down the handle of the axe.

"Like this?" she asked breathlessly. I was curled around her tiny frame, neatly tucking her in my arms. If I curled in slightly more I'd be able to rest my chin on top of her head, almost tempted enough to do so. "This makes it harder."

I found myself distracted by her smell, the blanket of cool air doing nothing to penetrate our collective heat. My cock twitched again, rubbing against her mid-back. Even holding her like this made my body react on its own. "What makes it harder?" I growled.

She licked her lips, looking up at me ever so slightly; her arms had gone limp around the handle; I was mostly holding the axe now. "You... holding me like this." Those big blue eyes looked up at me through thick eyelashes. Fuck. My cock was throbbing as I stared at those plump lips, considering how they might feel around my swelling cock. "You make it hard to focus."

Shamelessly, I wrapped my hand around her waist and pushed her back so she could feel the steel of my cock digging into her back. She sucked in a sharp breath, her eyes filling with immediate lust. "That makes two of us, snowflake," I growled.

She completely let go of the axe as she stood up on tippy toes, her back brushing against my cock as she wrapped a loose hand around the back of my neck and pulled me in. She strained to angle around, that heated gaze reeling me in silently. I crashed my mouth onto hers, losing all resolve.

A little moan escaped her as she twisted around fully and threw her hands around my neck, trying to pull me down further. With one arm still hanging loose with the axe, I bent over and rounded my other arm under her ass and lifted her, so she could hitch her legs around my waist.

Her hand tangled through my hair as her hips ground ever so slightly against me, her body pleading for what my cock throbbed for. I walked us into the cabin, consciously aware of the weapon in my hand. I hadn't yet made it to the door when I pressed her against the wall, my cock pushing hard against her jeans.

She moaned and I become entirely lost in her. She kissed along my jaw, her hands snaking under my long-sleeved shirt, those devilish little nails dragging down hungrily. Shadow moved out of the way as I carefully dropped the axe at the entrance and carried her through to the sofa.

"Eric," she moaned my name, her hot breath

filling me. Were we out of our fucking minds? Her legs folded around me as I sat on the sofa, my cock straining painfully beneath my jeans. Our hands were everywhere, her little hips rocking back and forth, the friction killing us both.

Her tongue was razor sharp against soft lips. Cassidy acted like a starving animal. We'd both been deprived and this tension had been rolling through us for weeks now. I wrapped my hand around her throat, pulling her back and staring into her lust-filled gaze. She couldn't move due to the way I handled her, but in the way she stared back with hooded eyes, I knew she fucking loved it. Those hips continued to try and work me through the jeans.

But I realized with sudden clarity that Cassidy was someone who would want more than just this. Sex I could do, but her obvious heart that showed beautifully and transparently wasn't something I could return in full. She deserved better than that.

"I don't have a condom," I growled. "And you're practicing celibacy."

"I was. I am," she corrected quickly, arising a chuckle out of me.

"Snowflake, we shouldn't act on impulse."

Her little nails dug down to the waist of my jeans. "Don't you want me?"

A low growl cleared my throat. "You know I do."

"Fine, I'll let you be chivalrous. We can buy condoms tomorrow. I'm not on any birth control anyway so I guess smarter is always best," she said reasonably, although her gaze was still feral. Her neck twisted slightly in my palm, the bobble of her throat beating under my hand. With my other hand, I grabbed her ass and squeezed. A little pained whimper escaped her.

"I don't know if you'll be able to handle how I fuck, sweetheart."

"Try me," she growled with an intense fever.

Gently, I released my hand from around her throat. Fuck. "If we stay like this for any longer, my cock's about to be ten inches deep inside of you."

She kissed me again, feverishly at first, until it smoothed into a slow warmth rolling through her as she began to kiss me gently. Her hand smoothed over my beard on my jawline and she nipped and dragged out my bottom lip, then pouted. "I didn't even cut any wood."

But if my cock was any indication, she was certainly splitting something.

"Are you sure about this, Cassidy? I can't offer you what you're after," I said carefully. She seemed like the type that believed in fairy-tale endings and love stories. And I didn't do that shit.

"You can't offer me a six foot six mountain god fucking my brains out?" she asked with a twisted smile.

I wrapped those blonde curls around my fist and yanked back. "You *will* be punished for that bratty attitude of yours."

"I want you to punish me, Eric," she said breathlessly. "I'm not asking for marriage here. I'm asking for something memorable. But do we really have to stop?"

I internally screamed "no." But I wasn't making any mistakes just because I was thinking with my cock. I'd done that once before and it burnt me so deeply it destroyed everything I thought love could be.

"Unless you'd like to take it up the ass?" I purred.

"Ew no. I'm not that type of girl," she said shrewdly. I threw my head back and laughed. "Not that there's anything wrong with those who do, but that hole is for well you know..."

"No tell me," I purred, loosening my hold on her hair and trailing my hand down her back, ass, and thighs. Everything about her was tempting and beautiful, her pussy only inches away from my throbbing cock.

She flipped me off. I threw my head back and laughed again, the rumble surprising even me.

"Now, sweetheart, I'm going to have to peel you off me and take matters into my own hands in the shower."

"Can I help?" she asked as I gently placed her on her feet.

"No, because I want to ram so fucking hard into you that I don't trust myself." I gently cradled her throat again. "You're a fucking temptation and my walking disaster."

Her throat bobbled. "And here I thought you were simply a part-time lumberjack. I didn't realize you were a poet as well."

I smiled ruthlessly as I bent over and kissed her again, longingly and passionately. Regretfully, I pulled away and toward the shower. What a fucking joke walking away from a bombshell who was temporary living with me and I was still about to fist my cock. Just like I had been every single night since she'd first arrived.

Chapter 23

Cassidy

Saturday evening Eric parked the truck in front of his mother's home. It was a ten-minute drive out of town, through windy paths, sitting on an acreage. It wasn't at all what I expected. Unlike some of the outdated township, their house had been well looked after and remodeled. It had a wraparound patio and was inundated with plants that hadn't survived the winter season, but I imagined in spring it was colourful, much like the town itself would be with rolling hills and mountains surrounding it.

I sat in the passenger seat with a box full of cookies Eric and I had baked that morning. We'd spent all day at the café which had been surprisingly busy. Apparently, that was normal on weekends because so many people drove through the town, but no one stayed more than a few hours.

I looked over at Eric; his knuckles were turning white over the steering wheel. Concerned, I placed a hand on his forearm, grabbing his attention. He looked like he was about walk into a warzone. Part of me wondered if there was worse history in this house or with his family than I realized. But as Lori had explained to me at the café, taking in his grumpy mood, he simply hated copping so much shit from his siblings and apparently my appearance was certainly ammunition.

"Don't take it personally," she'd said. "He's the big brother you know, we have to keep him on his toes and he's already such a grump that he easily bites back and gets huffy." She'd laughed. "It's fantastic. He's so easy to wind up."

"Eric," I said carefully, with mixed emotions as to whether I should laugh or be seriously concerned.

He blew out a frustrated breath. "Two hours that's it," he warned me as if I was the reason we were here. And perhaps my curiosity was what led us here. I suddenly felt bad; what if he disliked being in the same room as his family like I did? A cold sweat ran over me. *Oh shit, was it that bad?*

Shadow barked, grabbing our attention when

Lori parked beside us on her motorcycle. My eyes bulged. I'd seen her every day at work but never her means to and from the café. Eric had been "clocking off" early as Lori had put it. And I wondered if that was so we had time to buy ingredients and cook whatever new meal I'd discovered on my rapidly building Pinterest board of recipes.

I dropped my hand from Eric, forgetting sometimes how we'd become too comfortable around one another. The past few nights had been torture sleeping head to toe with him. As much as it had also been the best sleep I'd had in months. We'd spoken for hours some nights about trivial things or past vacations. Little by little he was opening up but last night had changed everything. Our dynamics were completely different. I wanted to touch him, but it felt like it should be a secret around others.

"Punctual as ever," Lori joked as she removed her helmet, shaking out her loosely pinned hair. "Looks like the boys are already here." She pointed at the trucks that were already parked at the front.

"Because they're mommy boys," Eric grumbled. She laughed and opened the door for Shadow. He bounded out, quickly running around the place and marking his territory.

Lori started walking in, looking over her shoulder

with a disapproving glare. "Y'all both going to catch a cold if you stand out here all day."

Eric pressed his hand to my lower back, encouraging me to step forward. Heat scorched in that very spot, vivid memories of last night rising to the forefront. The small hungry stares, the meddlesome promises and the brief touches, especially in the bed, had been fighting all of my chastity promises as of late. I wanted to jump the man's bones. And it might've been presumptuous to assume he wanted the same, but I'd never held out for anyone this long and it was starting to give me an anxious butterfly-like tension. And I sensed he'd felt the same after last night.

I squared my shoulders, but that was then and this was now. And I had an impression to make. Quietly, I whispered, "Are you using me as a shield right now?" He pushed me forward.

Despite his ill mood, he chuckled. "No, I'm using the cookies as the shield."

Beside the four steps onto the patio was a long ramp, a reminder that if what Ann and Patrice gossiped about was true, their mother was in a wheelchair. It wasn't that she was in a wheelchair that disturbed me but the pain and turmoil the incident must've caused. And the reason why Eric was so wary of the roads and especially non-locals driving them in poor weather. But instead of doom and gloom the moment Lori opened the door there was nothing but cheer and warmth that greeted us.

A redheaded man had Thomas in a headlock. I paused at the door, trying to take in the lively scene.

"I told you, the last piece was for me, little brother," the redhead hissed as he ruffled Thomas's hair. They grappled around one another, acutely aware of the furnishings around them and making sure not to knock anything around them. And despite the different hair color, there was no denying that this redheaded man was their brother.

"Already Jude?" Lori asked, hand on hip. "You guys don't waste any time." She shuffled around them, throwing her backpack on the floor beside a messy stack of shoes. The house had an open layout, with wide doors, wooden furnishings, and floorboards.

Eric cleared his throat and the two men looked up. The moment they did, they both broke out into wide charismatic grins, pushing away from one another, and Jude bound over with his hand out.

"You must be Cassidy," he said charismatically. Freckles littered his face with familiar green eyes. He was attractive, all of them were. Eric pointedly stared at his brother's hand, all heat behind me icing over.

I grabbed his hand and he pulled it in to press a kiss to my knuckles. I blushed unfamiliar with the gesture. A small growl, an actual warning, crept out of Eric. His brother threw his head back laughing. I couldn't help but smile politely because his laugh was genuinely contagious.

"I told you he's protective," Thomas beamed, waltzing up and giving me a bear hug. Surprised, I hugged him back awkwardly, trying my best to protect the cookies. I could sense him purposefully looking up at Eric.

"So, this her?" Another man stepped into the room, identical to Jude. This must've been Declan. It was hard to decipher between the two. The only differences being that Declan had grown out his hair slightly and had a more rugged beard. "She's more beautiful than Thomas led on."

"Maybe that's because I'm keeping her to myself," Thomas snickered, poking out his tongue.

"Oh, Eric, you're here too!" Declan enthused.

Tension rolled off Eric and despite my best efforts to side with him, a small snicker crept out. Eric sliced a look my way. I wanted to say, "I swear I'm not choosing their side over yours" but his reaction was comical. As Lori had stated, he *was* sensitive to his brothers' goading.

"Give the poor girl some space," an older woman's voice broke through the room. A beautiful dark-haired woman pushed herself into the room. The few wisps of grey in her hair might've been the only thing to indicate that she was somewhere in her sixties. "I'm sorry, my boys were raised on a farm. If you can't tell." She offered them an effective look and I charmed a smile. Now I knew where Eric got his looks from. But unlike his rigid demeanor, his mother was warmth and welcoming. Her children worked around her, parting the way so she could come at a stop in front of me.

"We don't often get guests here so it's quiet the pleasure to meet you. And it's nice to see a reason that forces my eldest son to make his way over. Despite him only being a short driveable distance away." She offered him a pointed glare. "I'm Audrey."

In an attempt to redirect her gaze from Eric, I perked up. "I'm Cassidy and thank you for having me over. We brought cookies."

"Ah yes." Audrey smiled, taking the box and putting it in her lap. "I heard you two had become quite the bakers." A mischievous glimmer twinkled in her eye.

The brothers snickered behind her. Eric said nothing but again, I could tell he didn't enjoy being the butt of their joke and I couldn't help but find it amusing.

"Come in, sorry they harassed you at the door."

"I'll give you a tour," Thomas said in a singsong way.

Eric's hand wrapped around my shoulder. "I'm very capable myself."

Declan whistled. "Wow you weren't kidding about his alpha-assholeness were you?"

"I told you," Thomas goaded, shoving him playfully.

Something told me this was going to be a long night.

I looked up at Eric, not entirely bothered by his possessiveness but more so confused. Despite his notion that we might be able to have a short-lived fling for the few weeks I was in town, he certainly wasn't trying to hide it anymore and maybe there was an underlying jealousy. I wasn't sure how that sat with me either. I didn't want it to make me feel good in the way that it did, because that could mean

I might be falling for him and that was something I didn't want to risk my heart with.

But as I looked up at Eric and his stoic expression, I realized this was all new for him too. And I couldn't help but enjoy seeing this new side to him—where he was taunted and teased. "One hour and fifty minutes," I mouthed.

And at that, his mouth twitched into a smile for the first time since we'd arrived.

Chapter 24

Eric

The little shits fluttered around Cassidy like moths to a flame. The twins purposefully positioned her to sit between them, despite my clear warning. I sat at the end of the table, beer in hand, watching them silently. Shadow was by my side, waiting patiently for the opportunity he'd be given a piece of anything. We sat around the wooden dining table my parents had owned for as long as I could remember. A table for ten, a little excess in size but as they said, "just in case we ever had guests," for moments such as these, I supposed.

I threw back another bitter sip. Cassidy also took a small sip from her beer one of the twins had given her. I wondered if it was the first time she'd ever had its bitter taste. She was a woman used to finer class and palates. She much better suited the backdrop of Manhattan—or even Chicago for that matter—but somehow, she seemed to fit into any space she filled but with a beer in hand... I wasn't so sure.

"And he actually did yoga with you?" Declan's eyebrows rose and the entire table stared back at me. *Fuck. It was exactly what I feared.*

"It actually has fantastic benefits and considering how active he is I was certain his muscles were tight," Cassidy chimed. Innocently, she was only feeding fuel to their fire. I'd never hear the end of this, but nor was I going to stop her. She appeared to be having fun. I took another swig.

"Wow, physical and tight, that does sound like Eric, doesn't it?" Jude gleamed.

"And notice how Shadow likes her too!" Thomas said spitting food across the table. My hand tightened around my beer. They were acting like a bunch of animals.

"Boys, enough! Stop giving Eric a hard time. And, Thomas, eat with your mouth closed," my mother chastised. Fuck, some things never changed around here.

Lori scooped a forkful of the potato bake, smirking through the entire dinner silently. Somehow that irked me even more because I knew exactly who was feeding them with all this ammunition. Lori and Thomas were no better; Declan and Jude were the last nails in my coffin and nerves.

"Eric's been very kind to let me stay in his home for a few weeks. And I'm grateful to you all for having me over for dinner as well. It's refreshing here, I'm so used to the city that I feel like this is the first time in a long time I've been able to breathe," Cassidy admitted with a smile. "So even if his *downward dog* pose needs to be polished, I'm definitely grateful for his hospitality." She winked at me, throwing in the last remark for extra measure.

My brothers laughed and Lori raised her drink. "To Eric. Because as much of a grump he is, he's come through for all of us in one way or another."

A heat spread across my cheeks. I didn't deserve their thanks. Not after my actions and last failed relationship affected them all. Sure, I'd been able to get us out eventually, but I'd been the one to put them in that comprisable position. And yet years later here we were, right where it all began.

"Here, here," my brothers cheered in unison. It was the bane of my existent how in unison they were. Even Thomas seemed to be on that train of telepathy, especially when they taunted my nerves.

My mother raised her glass of wine—the only

one drinking it. "Well since we're doing toasts, I'd like to thank all of my children for coming back here at least once a year to help manage the shop while your father and uncle go away on their hunting trip. I wouldn't be able to do any of this without you, and not to forget to mention I miss you all dearly. And to throw in for luck, because we're still in the festive season, I better get some grandbabies out of someone soon because I'm sick of waiting."

Inadvertently, mine and Cassidy's eyes met. I immediately looked away, my heart missing its beat. The glance wasn't missed by Lori, silently smirking and picking at her plate.

"What?" I grumbled.

"Oh nothing." She shrugged nonchalant.

"Eric's the oldest!" Jude chimed.

"If anyone's going to get anyone pregnant it's Thomas," Lori remarked.

"What? Why me?!" Thomas raised his hands in defense.

"Because you're such a little fuckboy," Declan announced.

"Rich coming from you!"

Amongst all the bickering, Cassidy's laughter fluttered through the air, tears wetting her eyes. The tension melted off me. If she was comfortable and enjoying herself, the night didn't seem so bad after all. Giving up on me, Shadow walked over to Cassidy and without a second glance she fed him a piece of cheesy potato. I was going to have to put this dog on a diet when we returned to Chicago. She had him wrapped around her little pinkie. Or was it the other way around, I wasn't so sure?

"So, what kind of meals have you been cooking together?" Mom asked pointedly, looking between Cassidy and me, ignoring the bickering of who was a bigger fuckboy at the table. Were we always this loud? I was surprised Cassidy fitted in so casually around my loud dysfunctional family.

"Umm, we've been baking sweets and Lori's been giving me recipes for vegetarian alternatives."

"Wait, are you vegetarian?" Jude asked.

"I told you that, you dimwit," Lori said, her fork suspended and pointed at him.

"So, what's big beast over here been eating?" Declan asked, pointing a thumb my way. Man, they were enjoying this way too much. I'd have to find a way to punish them for it later. Maybe I'd start with kicking them out of the apartment in Chicago I'd bought for them.

Cassidy seemed affronted by the nickname, but her lip curved into a stifled smile. "He's been eating the stuff I've been cooking," she said, somewhat confused. I took another swig because I knew what was coming and it was like watching a natural disaster unfold, there was nothing I could say or do to intervene and stop the inevitable.

Jude's jaw dropped. "No shit, you've got him eating vegetables? All he ever eats is meat and potato. I haven't seen him eat greens since we were kids and grew up to be bigger than Dad and he realized he could say no."

Again, my family stared at me like I'd grown a third head, and it was the smug smile and twinkle in my mother's eye that unnerved me the most.

"It's all carbs," I mumbled under my breath.

But Cassidy stared at me with surprise. Great, now I really would look like, as she would put it, "a teddy bear."

Declan fell back into his chair. "Shit, I thought I'd seen it all." They all glanced at my finished plate that had only contained meat and potatoes soiled in gravy. I wasn't a complete saint.

"And how long do you think you'll be staying?" my mother asked Cassidy.

Cassidy nervously tucked her hair behind her ear. "Um, I'm not sure yet, maybe a week or so?" She looked at me in question.

"Oh how lovely, why don't you take her target shooting tomorrow, Eric?"

"I'd be down for that," Lori was quick to assert.

"Yea let's do it!" the twins yelled in unison.

"No, you two boys can actually handle the café for once. Give Eric and Lori a day off."

A twitch threatened the corner of my mouth. Maybe I didn't have to serve out punishment after all. Because my mother had already done it.

They grumbled their complaint. Considering the twins were in town for a few nights, it might offer Lori and me a small break.

For once, I couldn't read Cassidy's expression. "You don't have to," I was quick to say.

"It's not that, I'd love to." She perked up. But there was hesitation.

"Sounds like a plan," my mother chimed again, that mischief was gleaming in her expression. She was up to something and in the way her and Lori looked at each other, it was like they were in on it together. I took another swig. When those two schemed, nothing good ever came of it. Well in my experience the result was always an inconvenience to my daily routine. "Now with that decided, who's ready for dessert?"

As expected, the twins found themselves elsewhere when it was time for cleanup. I stood in the kitchen, scrubbing at the dishes as I considered tonight and the silent promise that had perfumed the air all night between Cassidy and me. I'd claim her tonight, there was no doubt about it.

I imagined Cassidy beneath me, her thighs wrapped tightly around me. I considered her vow of celibacy and had I been a better man, I might've made the decision for her that this wasn't best. But I wasn't a better man and I wanted to fuck that sweet little pussy more than I needed my next breath.

My cock twitched and I sighed. Not in my mother's house, however.

"Eric," my mother's voice broke through my thoughts, and I almost dropped the plate I'd been absentmindedly cleaning.

"Mom, what's up?" I replied, pressing a kiss to her cheek as she came to a stop at the sink and began wiping over the drying plates.

"It's always interesting how your brothers find themselves busy elsewhere when it's time to clean up, huh?" she said with a knowing smile.

"I told you, you went too easy on them growing up," I teased. "And where's Thomas?" He usually helped out.

"He's with Lori and Cassidy."

A tension rippled through me. I loved my younger brother, but he was a fuckboy and on top of that, women seemed to love the whole "doctor" idea. He was in placement as of next year and closer in age to Cassidy. And I certainly wasn't comfortable with this mixed jealousy and protectiveness. She wasn't mine. I'd made that very clear to even her. She was in town for as long as I was and then that would be that. "Something memorable" she'd said. So why the fuck did I care so much?

"She's sweet, the little stray you've brought in," my mother said as she began stacking the dry plates on top of one another.

"You'd say that about anyone who compliments your cooking," I said.

"Not entirely true because everyone likes my cooking. It's only a select few I'd invite back."

I smirked. "You'd invite anyone into this home, even if you didn't like them," I said honestly. My mother was giving and loving in nature. She'd ensure everyone else was looked after before prioritizing herself. And I could never give back to her or my father what they'd extended out to me over the years. Even when I built the IT company from the ground up to pay them back tenfold for my fuckup with Katia, it never truly replaced what had been taken or those years of stress I'd put them through.

"You like her," my mother said, staring at my side profile. "I haven't seen you look at anyone since... *that woman*."

I blew out a breath. Katia was not something we'd spoken about for years, and I certainly wasn't going to relive the past with my mother over how badly and naively I'd fucked up.

"I see the way you two look at each other," she continued.

"She's just staying in town for a few weeks, Mom, just like me, that's it." I blew out a small, frustrated breath. I was a forty-two-year-old man still getting lectured by his mother. And I didn't have the heart to tell her that the supposed look she'd seen flash between us was made from us wanting to fuck one another's brains out, nothing more.

"Out of all my sons, I worry about you the most."

Frustrated, I placed the plate down. This is why I didn't come over as often, because every time I did, my mother would voice her concern. "You shouldn't. I have everything I need. I run a multi-billionaire company, own multiple properties and can provide my family with everything and anything they'd ever need. I've achieved my objective and I'm happy."

"Having money isn't happiness, Eric."

I kept my temperament in check. I didn't care for the money. What I'd wanted was being able to provide for them. I'd vowed I'd never be in a predicament again where I couldn't supply for my family. They'd never again go through years of stress and loss that I'd forced on them. That was my happiness and redemption.

"And it's time you start thinking about growing your own family. You're forty-two, Eric. You have to settle down at some time."

"Why won't you believe I'm happy alone?"

"Because I'm your mother and I know when you're genuinely happy and you, son, have just been going through the motions for so many years now. Just think about it a little. I'm proud of all of you, but I want you to consider being open to the idea of letting someone else in as family, not just us. Your father and I aren't going to be around forever."

I grimaced. I hated when she went down this route. No matter how many times I'd suggested they moved to Chicago so I could better look after them, they'd always denied me saying this was their home.

That's why we all came back the same time every year, so Dad could continue his hunting with my uncle until... until he couldn't anymore.

Thomas bound in with a bowl full of candy. "Are you guys talking about my awesomeness?"

"I can't believe you're still eating," Lori chimed as she walked in behind him. Cassidy was by her side, my disloyal dog on her tail.

"We don't need to mention your awesomeness you seem plenty capable of reminding us every day," my mother cooed. "But perfect timing, here." She threw the hand towel to my brother. "I'm about to find those brothers of yours."

"I don't mind drying," Cassidy insisted.

Lori piped up. "Yea and we have to check out Mom's engine real fast too, Thomas. Remember?"

"Since when?" he asked, confused. I felt my temple pulse at Lori's not so subtle mischievous workings.

"Oh yea," Thomas said slowly. "Cassidy can you help Eric. I've got some stuff to do."

The three left, leaving Cassidy, Shadow, and I in silence. She walked to my side, grabbing the first plate.

"They don't really have to check your mother's engine, do they?"

"No."

Her laugh fluttered through the kitchen and the tension from my conversation with my mother eased.

"Do you think they know?" she whispered quietly, leaning closer toward me.

"Know about what?" I asked, naturally leaning into her, tempted to tuck her under my shoulder, she was so tiny in comparison. I had to hunch over just to wash the dishes, and yet I felt like she somehow was a perfect fit. Or maybe I'd just had blue balls for so long that I was romanticizing shit.

"About you and me... you know... almost..."

I gave her a side-glance, trying at best to keep the smile away. She seemed so coy and delightfully naïve.

"We haven't done anything," I said incredulously.

She huffed out an irritated breath. "Don't I know it."

I laughed this time, her pouting lips and irritable expression rather adorable.

"Hey, your hands are wet!" she screamed as I scoped my arms around her waist and tucked my body around her. I wiped my hands all over her, eliciting a small shrill squeal out of her.

"Ew, yuck sod water!" she screamed. I trailed my

fingers along her neck as she playfully tried to duck and wriggle out of my reach. She tried to reach for the water, but I pulled her light weight back. She clung to the side of the bench, trying her hardest to be immovable. It didn't take me long to pry her fingers off. By now, my hands were dry as I played with the edge of her long skirt. She sucked in a sharp breath as my fingers trailed over her seam—it would've been so easy to tuck my hand beneath.

Goose bumps sprouted along her lower abdomen as my cock twitched at the thought of pinning her against the edge of the bench. Her breath became shallow as I pressed my growing cock to her lower back. "See the things you do to me, sweetheart." I nipped her ear. "You're not the only one frustrated. And what are we going to do when we get home?"

Her response was low and husky. So foreign to the usual bubbly little brat that treated annoying me as a full-time job. "You're going to fuck me."

I cupped her sweet pussy through the thin skirt, imagining what she might look like wearing only those leather boots. I played over the fabric, her sharp breath sending my cock rigid. "And you're going to be my little slut, aren't you?"

"Yes," she whispered.

"You're going to let me do all nasty things to you until your limbs can't move anymore, aren't you?"

"Except for anal," she breathlessly whispered.

I chuckled, gliding my hand up and holding her stomach. Holding her into me and taking in her smell. In only an hour I'd be smothered in her scent and taste. "You'll do as I say," I growled.

"Yes, sir," she said, again another loosed breath as she placed her hand over my forearm, tucking further into me. My mother's words echoed in my thoughts. Was this what she considered as normality in her eyes? Happiness? Companionship? The thought had become so foreign, and yet with Cassidy, it was easy to fall into this situation and feeling. And that terrified me more than anything.

Chapter 25

Cassidy

The truck jolted beneath us. True to his word, Eric excused us two hours after we'd arrived at his family home. His brothers had booed him for being such a buzzkill as we left. And despite his complaints, I had the impression Eric enjoyed his time with his family but there was something that niggled at me. If he came all this way once a year for an entire month to help his mother and the family business, then why didn't he visit them more often? Why did Eric choose to live in solitude during that time?

"I think my family really liked you. My mother's going to be asking you to go over every day now until you leave," he huffed as if the thought irked him.

I laughed. "They're a lot of fun."

228

"They're loud."

"And fun." I nudged him. "And I wouldn't mind keeping your mother company. She was very welcoming."

His chest puffed out in slight pride. Although loud, and maybe a little wild, his family were loving and welcoming. But that little nuisance kept niggling at me. Before I lost courage, I asked, "Why don't you see your mother often?" I stared at the road ahead of us. I'd learnt to admire the beauty and scenery, although at nighttime, it was rather eerie. Especially with the unknown howl last night. It was a reminder that up here in the mountain we were not alone.

He grimaced, looking through the rearview mirror at Shadow. Where he might've once told me it was none of my business or ask why I even cared, he looked conflicted with himself, and a small seed of hope sprang forth. Maybe he would tell me about his ex or perhaps there was another reason. And I don't know why I so desperately wanted to hear it from his mouth instead of gossip. It was strange in the way; I felt protective of him even though I had no claim over him. Who he was all those years ago had nothing to do with me, and yet I wanted to protect him from all the hurt he must've endured.

The moment I saw him start to pull away, I

impulsively grabbed his hand that rested on the center console between us. "You know you can tell me anything, right?" I added. "I know all I do is talk but you'd be surprised at how good of a listener I am."

He offered me a small smile. "I have no doubt you are, snowflake." A heavy sigh echoed through him and just when I thought he'd say nothing at all, his small voice filled the truck. "Guilt mostly."

My eyebrows crinkled together. He absentmindedly rubbed his thumb over my hand. This thing with Eric—this retreat into healing and companionship—was starting to unfurl a wishful hope in my heart, more intense than I'd had with other men. But again, I wasn't sure if I could trust that. Logistically, it was impossible. He and I lived completely different lives. And yet when I leaned forward and hinged on what he might say next, I realized my heart had thrown itself in too deep once again. It was attached and hopeful, probably to another man who wouldn't keep it safe.

"Guilt about what?" I prodded, trying to run away from my own hurtful realizations. I had the distinct feeling that Eric didn't express himself often and whatever he was willing to give me, I'd accept.

His hand tightened around mine, a reflex he

probably wasn't even aware of. "I got mixed up in a bad relationship when I was younger with a con woman. After dating her for two years she'd managed to write all our family businesses into her name and she fled. As the oldest son, they'd been passed down to me and I fucked it up.

I hadn't realized she'd been changing the papers. It took us a few years to get the businesses back but it cost my parents a lot in the process. And I've never forgiven myself for that. How could I? It jeopardized everything my family had worked so hard towards."

I placed my other hand on his big forearm, adjusting myself as the silence began to eat away at us. "Eric, you never meant for that to happen. That's a long time to hate yourself for something anyone could've done in a young relationship."

He shook his head to disagree. "It's because I was stupid."

"You're not stupid," I argued. It surprised me to even hear him say that. "How did she do it?" It might've been the wrong thing to ask but I was curious. Eric now ran a reputable company in Chicago from what his siblings had bragged about tonight. How could someone so smart be tricked?

He looked back through the rearview mirror

again, staring at Shadow as if for some kind of support.

"I'm dyslexic, Cassidy." My eyebrows crinkled in confusion. Is this why he'd thought he was stupid? "I let her handle all my paperwork. And I've never let anyone look over my paperwork and documentation ever since. Sure, it takes me a hell of lot longer but I'll never fall for that again."

Silence filled the truck. I wasn't sure entirely what to say. How could I prove to him that he was incredible? I didn't know what it was like to be dyslexic because I'd never experienced it but I certainly didn't want him thinking he was less than because of it. "Can you explain it to me?" He briefly glanced my way, skeptical and vulnerable. "Help me better understand," I elaborated quietly.

After another moment of silence, he quietly forfeited and said, "Sometimes the words just jumble together and it takes me a while to make sense of it. It's taken me a long time but I used to use it as an excuse until all of that happened. Such a stupid weakness to have. So now it just takes me longer. If I'm tired, its worse."

"I don't think it's stupid, Eric, and I don't want you to keep saying that." I patted his hand. I hated how he beat himself up. Hated that I couldn't do anything to support him and although I wanted to offer to read things for him, I realized that had been what got him in such a predicament those many years ago. "I imagined it wasn't just because of your dyslexia, Eric. Con people are good at what they do. Even if you weren't dependant on her reading your documents for you, she would've found a way. My dad's basically that type of businessman. I watched him manipulate a handful of business partners over the years. A con person is a con person, it has nothing to do with your intelligence and all to do with them. You're an intelligent man. Although perhaps a little broody."

I chuckled at the small pulse in his temple. "But I doubt your parents hold this against you. Especially your mother. I think if anything she'd want to see more of you. But you can't keep hating yourself for something you couldn't have navigated around differently. You're a successful businessman now, leave the past in the past and move on as best as you can."

He seemed to consider that for a moment, his thumb began to brush over mine again absentmindedly. "I think for someone who's great at listening you still have a lot to say."

"Hey!" I shouted, a dimpled smile forming.

"Thank you," he said sincerely. "It sounds different when coming from you. Everyone's said similar things to me but... I don't know, thank you." A slight flush spread across his cheeks. "Is your father really like that? He sounds like a right dick."

I chuckled. "People have called him worse." I realized as the silence filled again that it wasn't entirely fair that Eric shared something so personal and that I didn't offer anything in return. But I hadn't spoken about my parents to anyone in years. All those swirling mixed emotions had been neatly tucked away in a box not to be seen until I had to face them head on. And yet part of me knew that time was already upon me. I was simply avoiding it.

"No, he's not a good man but he's still my father. I watched him for years taking advantage of people. He even used my mother's parents in the same way. They were forced into an arranged marriage and I'm their only child from a loveless agreement." I might've been his heiress but I was nothing but a bargaining chip as well. "I left home three years ago and have lived in Manhattan and haven't spoken to them since. He used and took advantage of a lot of people, it's just how he does business, and yet for the most part I've lived off that money my entire life. I was raised on a lifestyle, judged the means to get it but still used the money because I was accustomed to it." I half-heartedly laughed at myself. Even when I'd applied to work myself, I could never survive off the wage it offered me, so I didn't give up anything at all, I simply ran away. "Isn't that a cop-out? It makes me as bad as him I suppose."

"No," Eric said firmly. "You're nothing like him."

"You don't even know him."

"I don't need to, to know that the man you're describing is nothing like you. And who cares if you use the family money, we all come from different advantages in life. You shouldn't beat yourself up because of the hand you were dealt."

"I could say the exact same thing to you."

He looked over at me, those forest-green eyes all consuming. I felt so small beside him, even in the truck. He just filled every space, in every room, drawing everyone to him and the only one that was pushing them all away was him. And I knew in time he would do the same to me. I don't even recall when I started looking for him in every room.

I stared down at our entwined hands. I wanted Eric, there was no denying it, but I didn't trust my heart amongst all of this. My body responded to his, fantasizing every hour what it might be like to have him in bed. To climb him like a tree. But I knew if I did, I'd only put my heart on the line. But hadn't I already?

"I like you, Eric," I admitted out loud. I'd never been good at hiding my feelings, so why try now? Men never gave me what I wanted in return, but I couldn't change who I was overnight. I watched my parents' loveless marriage with no communication and I'd vowed to be the opposite of that. And up until now, it'd always been my undoing. I'd learnt honesty and expressing feelings wasn't always reciprocated.

"I like you too, Cassidy," Eric replied. My heart fluttered and my stomach swirled with warmth. It was childish but pure. Intense but easy. And completely temporary. We only had two more weeks left to spend together and I was determined to at least make him mine for one night. To create a memory with this man who'd taken me in expecting nothing. Because in the end, I knew he had somewhere else to be and I had a past to confront.

Chapter 26

Eric

I threw back the clutch, jumped out, and rounded the truck in a few short steps, yanking the door open. Cassidy jumped into my arms, our mouths colliding in a heated clash. Her little desperate moans filled me as her legs wrapped around my waist, her little hips grinding feverishly.

Holding her with one arm, I blindly opened the back door to let Shadow out. Her nails raked down my neck and we hadn't even made it to the front door when she began busting open the buttons of my flannel shirt. For someone so tiny, she certainly had strength when she needed it. I fumbled around for the light switch beside the front door, slamming her against the wall as I searched for and switched it on.

"This stupid fucking skirt," I growled, pissed that

it wasn't as easy to slip my hands underneath the belt. I slammed the front door shut as soon as Shadow was inside. Taking the two steps up to the bed, I threw her onto it. She bounced slightly and I clicked at Shadow, who was preparing to jump on the bed beside her.

"Not tonight, buddy, sorry," I said and pointed at his bed. I wasn't going to be cockblocked tonight. Not again. Cassidy chuckled. Her hair was splayed around her, those rosy cheeks and labored breath making my cock twitch. *I wanted her.* I knew that from the moment I'd first seen her. But I'd never imagined she'd be laying in my bed. Not like this—panting, hot and heavy for me.

"Why are you looking at me like that?" she asked seductively.

"Because I'm thinking about what it will be like to taste you."

Her lips involuntarily parted. Perhaps I'd been too honest tonight. But my reality had become her. I woke up beside her and found peace falling asleep beside her every night. And my cock throbbed for her every waking hour, no matter how hard I'd fought it at the start.

Cassidy seemed conflicted. I stood over her, my arousal prominent and bulging as she gulped. "I'm giving you only one more out, are you sure you want to break your celibacy?"

She moistened her lips and propped herself on one elbow as she stared longingly at my cock. "I am. I want you too."

I slowly and deliberately wedged myself between her legs and leant against the bedframe.

"I've been running a pretty short leash these past few days, sweetheart. If you knew all the fucking things you did to me and the filthy thoughts I had of you, you would've never come back to this cabin again," I said as I traced her mouth with my thumb, studying it and imagining all the dirty things it could say and do.

She propped onto her knees, her hands on top of her thighs submissively. "Maybe that's why I've been coming back." Her big blue eyes glistened with mischief and arousal.

I reached out and squeezed her tit, testing her response. She hissed, her gaze never leaving mine. My cock twitched a full hard-on trying to press through my pants. How much of me could she accept? Would she be shaken by my filthy words and fuckery.

She tucked a loose blonde curl behind her ear as

she said, "You know I was going to try and seduce you tonight."

Everything she did was a kind of seduction, whether she did it purposefully or not. But it piqued my curiosity, how vixenish could this goldilocks be? Would she be able to handle me—all of me? "And how would you do it."

With that hooded gaze under thick eyelashes, she shamelessly cradled my cock through my pants and raked another hand down my chest, drawing thick pink scratch lines. The gentle sting aroused my cock into an iron-thick stiffness, entirely at her mercy, aching to be inside of her. Her touch turned featherlight as it drifted to my waistline, then button and zip. Her hands made quick work and she pulled my boxers and pants down. My cock sprang free and she gulped, licking her lips, eyeing my length and girth. I squeezed her tit again, reminding her this was just as much for me as it was for her.

"I wonder how wet I can make that tight little pussy of yours after three months of celibacy," I growled. She took a sharp inhale. Her eyes looked like she was hungry and desperate. Maybe even as desperate as me.

Cassidy leant over, her hair pooling over her shoulders as she indulged on my swollen cock. A tight tension twisted through me as her lips slid over my cock, her wet tongue pushing as far as she could go until she fisted the hilt of it and bounced those perfect little lips back and forth.

I twisted my fingers through her hair, my neck and eyes rolling back in pleasure from her sensual rhythm. *Fuck.* How long had it been since I was with a woman? Had I'd been on some unknown fucking celibacy as well? But this wasn't just any woman from Chicago. This was my little ray of fucking sunshine. I thrusted into her mouth, wanting and needing more. I wanted to fill her, dampen that sunshine with my cock and have her begging and screaming. I needed to show her what she'd really signed up for and if she'd regret all her taunts.

She worked me, fisting and sucking like I was her personal delicacy, pushing me to breaking point. I wouldn't last much longer if she kept using that perfect little mouth of hers. I'd blow all over her chest and she'd fucking love it. The visual of that almost sent me over the edge.

I jerked out of her mouth, grabbing her by the throat and pushing her onto her back. She gasped, shocked and aroused all in one. Extending over her, I undid the belt and pulled down her loose skirt around her ankles, and keeping those black leather boots on. All those taunting visuals came to mind. Those torturous mornings I'd had to deal with her bending over in those tight yoga pants, all served for this moment. "Did you really think you wouldn't be punished for wearing those tight little pants of yours every fucking day?"

"I didn't think you noticed," she breathed, her hot breath and scent swarming around me. I pinched her clit through the fabric of her panties. A sharp hiss escaped her as she bucked. I held her down by the throat and my thick forearm resting heavily down the center of her stomach as I dipped my head to her panties.

"You only move when I tell you to," I growled in warning. I didn't fuck sweetly, and I didn't care what kind of boys she was used to entertaining in the past, but I'd make sure to engrain myself so deeply into her mind that I'd ruin her for any other man.

Her nails dug into my hand clenched around her throat, marking me. I bit her clit through the underwear, another warning, and another little hiss escaping her. I pushed her pink panties to the side and my mouth watered. "You're going to let me have this sweet little pussy, aren't you?" I said, squeezing her throat.

"Yes," she breathed. A smile curved my lips as I

licked, my tongue stroking up through her slit, that first sweet taste of her filling me like a fucking starved man.

"You've tortured me with this pretty little pussy for weeks now," I growled. Her velvety softness and sweet taste elicited a satisfied purr through me.

"It's yours," she breathed. I bit her inner thigh, marking her. A primal sound escaped her. Damn right she was. I licked from her asshole and all the way up. She went rigid when I played with her ass but made no complaint. *Good girl.* To reward her, I dipped one thick finger into her tight pussy, the wet slickness of it eliciting another heated growl. I pumped into her feverishly, sucking on her clit as she kicked and stirred through whimpers of pleasure. It wasn't long before she was soaking my hand.

"I want you to fuck me," she whined. My cock twitched. I stood up, pulling her up by the throat and setting her back on her knees. The moment I did, she pulled me into a kiss. I realized then I'd have to fuck this snowflake differently, she needed and craved "connection." And I could taste and feel all of that need ripple through her. I closed my arms around her, reconsidering the way I'd take her.

I knew how to fuck women. But this, this was something entirely different and the way Cassidy melted into me, it was also new. Her little kisses were feverish and demanding and I found it both uncomfortable and inviting. I wanted her even more because she was so earnestly herself. She didn't just fuck. Cassidy gave all of herself over.

Her tight little budded nipples pressed against my bare hairy chest. She fisted my cock as we kissed, her softness a welcoming warmth to my rough and rigid form. I reached into my back pocket, revealing the golden packet of condoms I'd driven almost an hour for. "We have to treat these like fucking gold," I grumbled and she laughed, that flutter filling me with ease. For whatever reason, the tension left my body and for the first time in a long time, I found myself asking a woman: "What do you like, sweetheart?"

Without delay and assertively, she responded, "You. I want you to fuck me with all those promises you'd made."

Had I been a gentleman I might've lit the fireplace first, told her what she was in for, and whispered sweet things. But I wasn't and nor did I think she'd break. If she wanted to see all of me, earnestly, then that's what she'd get. I fisted her hair again, pulling her back and breaking our kiss as I handed her a condom. "Put it on my cock, sweetheart."

She ripped the corner of it away with her teeth, my savage little beggar desperate for attention. With quick efficiency, she glided it over my cock, cheekily squeezing tightly to the hilt to illicit a painful hiss from me. I tugged back her hair and she laughed.

I crushed my lips to hers, inhaling that devilish nature of hers. "Get on all fours," I growled into her mouth.

"Yes," she said, surrendering to me. She bent over, her ass on display as I grabbed the back of her panties and pulled them down to her knees.

My mouth watered as I fisted myself and stared at that beautiful pink shaven pussy of hers. I raked my hand down, pushing her panties all the way down to her black boots, spreading her legs wider. She looked over her shoulder, her gaze dropping to where I fisted myself.

"You want this cock, sweetheart?"

"Yes," she whimpered.

"Show me that *downward dog*." I slapped her ass, the noise echoing through the room. She jerked, a raw handprint left in its wake. Fuck, she was perfection. She did as I said, those long legs stretching up as I slid my hand around her waist and held her up, appreciating those black boots even at this angle. I rubbed my cock against her lips, soiling myself in the evidence of how wet she already was.

This fucking position had been the bane of my existence over the last few weeks. I drove into her, her body going rigid and lethargic all at once as I held her up with one arm. My other on her hips as I eased out of her inch by inch and dove into her again. Her tight pussy was a welcome sight and feel. My cock squeezed inside of her so painfully and perfectly.

"I want you to milk me, you filthy slut. I want to come so hard inside of you, you can feel me pulsing into this tight pussy of yours."

"Yes," she breathed as I drove into her again. Pound after pound, she slowly became a limp doll in my hand as I kept her body hanging over my clamped arm.

I flipped her over onto her back, spreading her thighs wide as I drove into her again, balls deep. The headboard began banging against the wall, back and forth, as I fucked her the way she deserved and begged for. She slid her fingers down to her clit and began to play with herself, those delicate little fingers circling with ferocity.

"Eric," she cried. "You're going to make me come."

I grabbed her neck and kissed her fiercely before growling into her ear. "You don't come until I tell you to. Is that understood?"

"Yes," she breathlessly rasped. She whined when I kissed her, her hot breath becoming mine as I fucked us both into oblivion. I closed her knees together and, with a roll of her hip, pushed so she was lying down on her side, trapping her hand between her legs as I took her from behind.

Her eyes and mouth went wide from the change of position. "What the fuck?" she cried breathlessly.

At this angle... and inside of her was my undoing.

"Come for me, baby," I said, grabbing her throat from behind and biting down on the side of her lip. My body tensed and when I ate her screams and moans, feeling the shudder of her pussy contract and milk everything my cock had to give, I blew, grunting into her mouth as I held her jaw firmly in place. I spilled into her, weeks of pent-up tension finally releasing.

Another wave hit her as she screamed out my name, her sweet pussy pushing around my cock like a tidal wave. Her hand cupped around my face as we lay there momentarily, clinging to each other.

I watched the ripple of tension leave her face, even when her eyes were shut, I saw every expression twist into a satisfied submission or smile. Her body slowly went limp and her thick eyelashes batted open revealing those big blue eyes.

"Wow," she said, catching her breath. I slowly pulled out of her and dropped to the bed, all masculine pride filling me.

I cradled her into my chest as she hooked her black boot around my calf.

"My underwear is still hanging around one of my boots," she said in disbelief.

"Next time I'll rip them off," I growled. She tucked herself under my chin, our breathing slowly creeping into unison. *Wow indeed. She'd been my perfect little toy, akin to my perverse talk and fucking.*

Her continued silence didn't sit well with me, however. I could spend hours like this, silent, but if I'd learnt anything about Cassidy, she always had something to say.

"Are you okay?" I asked, almost self-conscious. Had I been too rough for her? Maybe she didn't like the way I fucked. Her body certainly seemed to.

Tension rippled out of me when she finally spoke. Nervously she admitted, "If I'm being honest, I didn't think you'd want me in this way."

I angled my head so I could look down at her. "Any man would be crazy not to want you." And I realized then that I said the wrong thing because her expression flickered with hurt before she retreated into a weak smile.

"It seems most men like to have me and then discard me," she said vulnerably. My heart dropped out of my chest and bled all over the quilt between us. How could anyone discard her? They had a taste of this perfect woman and they threw her away? How could someone so beautiful and capable be so unsure of themselves?

I grabbed her hand and pressed a kiss to it. "Then they're all fucking idiots."

A soft, unbelieving expression rolled over Cassidy's features. But I felt guilty of the same, because what she was searching for, I wasn't entirely sure I could deliver. I hadn't been emotionally available to any woman for almost two decades now. And the thought and feeling of wanting to give Cassidy everything she asked for terrified me. Because what if she took it all away too. Or even worse, I couldn't be the man that she wanted me to be at all.

Chapter 27

Cassidy

We'd taken various bumpy dirt roads. Every time Eric and I made eye contact, a knowing smile crept over us both. Last night and this morning, hands down, had been the best sex of my life. Had someone told me I'd be called a slut while having sex and enjoyed it, I would've laughed in their face. Where I might've once thought its connotations were belittling, a heat rose to my cheeks and it turned me on. I liked hearing Eric purr it instead of my name. I liked knowing that I was his object, his sweet little toy to fuck as he pleased. I loved that I got him off.

I bit my bottom lip as we hit another bump. I was rather bemused. Here I thought he'd be a teddy bear in the sheets but he'd definitely lived up to his name and he was right, I was bruised and sore. But his aftercare made up for his bruising fucking and scolding words. I was already at his mercy and falling way too deeply. That sex last night had urged my ever-too-quickly falling heart. And there was nothing I could do about it.

"We're meeting Lori and Thomas there aren't we?" I asked.

"They should already be there," he replied. I looked down at our entwined hands and his thick calloused thumb rubbing over mine. I felt so petite, protected and at peace in his presence. And for extra measure, I had Shadow, who'd sulked half the morning because he'd been kicked out of bed. I'd realized now I might've created a habit that could bite me in the ass.

But then that would mean believing that this thing between Eric and I could be long lasting. That put a damper on my thoughts. The little bubble I'd been living in popped fast. I'd basically been freeloading and fucked the guy I was staying with. Wasn't I like a prostitute? Had I romanticized the situation because I had no grasp on reality anymore?

"We're here," Eric said as he parked the truck. Lori and Thomas stood in the frigid air, arms crossed over jackets. They leant against a truck, waiting.

"Hey, are you okay?" Eric asked, his eyebrows crinkled.

"Yea," I said and shook away my earlier thoughts. I'd always lived for the moment. So why was I trying to change that now. "Yea I was just thinking about how grateful I was that this was just target shooting and not animals or anything like that."

Eric grimaced. "That's not our thing. My father and uncle love it, but we tend to stick to it as more of a novelty. And besides, Lori's the only descent shot out of the lot of us."

I laughed. Somehow that wasn't surprising, and yet I imagined Eric was also being modest. "Shadow doesn't get spooked by the gunshots?" I asked as I opened the door.

"Nope," Lori answered on Eric's behalf as she walked toward us. "The only thing that dog's afraid of is his lack of snacks throughout the day."

I scowled at Eric. "You said you never gave him snacks?" He'd complained so much about Shadow getting fat from all the food I was slipping him.

Eric casually shrugged. "I said he doesn't *usually* get snacks. Not that many anyway."

"Uh-huh," Lori laughed as she pointed into Thomas's direction. "This one's trying to get reception for his make-believe girlfriend." I opened the back door for Shadow, who immediately sniffed out the area.

"She's not make-believe and she's not my girl-friend," Thomas replied without looking up. "I'm going back in two days, and I have an itch that needs to be scratched. You should all try it sometime soon, might remind you that you're not getting any younger and in Mom's eyes somebody better start birthing babies."

"Come here, you little shit," Lori hissed and chased him. He bolted, laughing.

Eric came to my side with a bag full of snacks and threw his arm around my shoulder casually.

I looked up at him. "Are you okay with them seeing us like this?"

"Like what?" he asked, dipping down and kissing me as feverishly as he had the night before and this morning. I moaned into his mouth, feeling limp by the anticipation of what would follow.

"Ew, yuck I knew it, but I didn't need to see it," Lori crooned.

I pulled away, red streaking my face. I'd gotten completely carried away.

"I'd rate it a six out of ten," Thomas remarked dryly to Eric.

"Do you want to be six foot under on this trip?" Eric asked, stone-faced.

"Mom wouldn't let you," he said, poking his tongue out. It was hard to believe this goofy guy, similar to my age, was almost in placement for becoming a surgeon and top of his classes. I wondered if there was a completely different version to him. Perhaps all of them were different when back at home.

"Alright, we've set up the targets so let's get shooting," Lori said pulling out guns from the back of the truck. "Ever held one of these before?"

I shook my head nervously. "No."

"It's alright, sweetheart, I'll show you what to do," Eric said, readjusting the strap over his shoulder. Despite the other two wearing jackets and me in my pink fluffy one, Eric only wore a patterned flannel shirt, a complete cliché to his lumberjack profile. How he didn't feel the cold would always escape me.

Two targets were already positioned against trees. And the rest of us took plenty of steps back, my heart pounding as I watched Thomas take his shot carefully. I jumped, shocked by how loud the gunshot was. Thomas cursed when he realized he'd only hit the outer rim of the target, lowering the handheld pistol.

Lori chuckled. "Weren't surgeons supposed to be good with their hands and aim?"

"Shut up, I save lives not practice with targets to take them."

"Must be hard for you with the ladies if you can't find the spot, huh?" she replied.

He looked back at her, mortified. Eric chuckled, lazily throwing his arm around my shoulder.

"Move over kid," Lori said, shoving him out of the way and taking aim. Thomas sulked as he walked over to the truck, grumbling under his breath. He began to search for a signal on his cell again, undoubtedly trying to connect to his "lady." Lori had a lollipop in her mouth, pausing with the stick poking out as she focused. A second later, she pulled the trigger. Bullseye. My jaw dropped.

"As terrifying as ever," Thomas grumbled and leant against the truck. "I bet the catering business is a complete cover-up and she works for the government."

"Then don't cross me," she said sternly before hitting another bullseye.

"Wait until I tell Mom," Thomas said, poking his tongue out. I laughed. Lori squeezed off another four shots before refilling the ammunition and offering the gun to me and Eric.

Suddenly I wasn't so sure, this wasn't and had never been my thing. "You'll be fine," Eric said, dragging me to the invisible line the other two had shot from. "I'll be here with you the entire way."

"Is this going to end up like the wood chopping where you don't teach me at all?" I sarcastically asked.

His calloused hands grazed along my arms, setting alight a heated fire all the way down as he placed the gun into my hands. "Do you want it to be a repeat of that time?" he growled into my ear. The heat spread through me and blemished my cheeks as I warily glanced behind us to where his siblings stood.

"You shouldn't say things like that around them," I reprimanded, embarrassed. His grip tightened on me as he maneuvered my fingers around the gun, my forefinger now resting against the trigger. My heart sped up, distracted by him and the lethal position he was putting me in.

"You're mine, sweetheart and I'll say and do whatever I please and you're going to like it. In fact," he purred, sending another shiver down my spine. "You're going to fucking beg for it like a good girl, aren't you?"

"Yes," I breathlessly and thoughtlessly replied.

But yes—one hundred times over. I was completely at his mercy and that thrilled and terrified me all the same.

"Should I teach her?" Lori called from her position against the truck.

"Perhaps you've gotten rusty sitting behind that cushy desk of yours on top of your big building," Thomas quickly followed.

Eric gave them both an effective glare over his shoulder. "Have you forgotten who's holding the gun?"

"No, we just remembered who was taking aim, and that's not on you, Cassidy," Lori teased.

Eric muttered his complaint before gently pressing against me again. "Now line it up and look along the top here. Prepare for the moment you pull that trigger because it'll kick back and flick up slightly."

My heart raced. "I'm not sure about this," I breathed honestly. The realization now that this was a weapon and I was holding it... the two just didn't seem to go hand in hand. It didn't seem like fun, it felt like a lot of responsibility.

"Don't worry, snowflake, I'm here with you," he said gently with his hands wrapped around mine.

"You just need to breathe and go whenever you're ready. I've got you."

I listened to him, allowing his strength to envelop me, believing every word and intention. *I can do this*, I thought. Nothing would go wrong, not while Eric was with me.

"On three," Eric said and began counting down. I exhaled. "Two. One."

Bang. The gun sprang back, surprising me with its force. What I wasn't surprised by was the lack of indent in the target board.

"I missed, didn't I?" I asked.

"No," Lori called out from behind. "You're very capable part-time lumberjack did."

Eric again grumbled his complaint and I laughed. His family were relentless in giving him shit. It reminded me a little of Issobelle. Her humor was so dry and quick witted and no one was an exception to her taunts. I thought about my friends back in Manhattan and grew slightly saddened. Was it bad that I'd been enjoying myself so much that I'd hardly thought about them or how or when I'd return? Guilt filled me again. They still had no idea where I was or the truth as to why I'd actually left. I'd just been so terrified that it'd somehow change our relationship entirely.

"Again," Eric said. "Don't worry practice makes perfect. And they're right, it was my fault."

I bit my bottom lip; I thought it had more to do with me than him because shortly after, I saw how terrifyingly well Eric's aim was with a gun. It was almost as good as Lori's. And I was content with letting him be a master with the gun and the axe and I'd stick to baking cookies—as cliché as that might've been.

Chapter 28

Cassidy

I'd realized not soon enough that Eric's excuse to go for a quick thirty minute "hike" and show me "around" had been code for "don't follow us." Shadow bounded in front of us, excited to explore a new area of the mountain. It was cold but it certainly hadn't been as cold as the weeks when I'd first arrived in Rosefield.

Not accustomed to hiking, I'd almost tripped over a fallen branch. Eric caught me, suspending me by our intertwined hands like a doll.

"Shit," I'd cursed. And he chuckled. My heart pounded and the thought of having scathing scars all over my face from being so clumsy came to mind.

"You know I think I curse more since hanging out with you."

"Yea?" he drawled, pleased.

"That wasn't a compliment," I corrected his attitude.

"Depends on who you ask," he purred.

I rolled my eyes. The rows of trees began to clear into an opening. My jaw dropped as I tried to gather my labored breath. We'd been walking on an incline for some time now. Yoga I was great at but hiking was not my friend. I clutched at my ribs in exhaustion, but my eyes widened at the view.

Rolling mountains and a deep blue lake stretched for miles. I realized with awe that you could see all of Rosefield from here. A small civilization a dollop in size against the lake. "Wow I didn't realize how big the lake was."

Pride seemed to fill his expression and I scanned the view with utter astonishment. It had literally taken my breath away. That or the walk up here.

"When I come back every year, I try to frequent this spot as much as possible. I find it peaceful," Eric contemplated aloud.

I admired his side profile as he scanned the vastness. At that, I wasn't surprised, he who chose to isolate himself in a cabin enjoyed to go on hikes to a solitude place such as this. And he wasn't even the slightest bit out of breath.

"You know you'll be carrying me back, right?" I said as I considered my already tired legs. No doubt Thomas and Lori had already packed up and left. We'd enjoyed a light lunch together before parting ways. The quiches and sandwiches Lori had made were divine.

Eric smiled. "I think I can manage that." He guided me over to a fallen tree, dusting it off for me and directing me to sit. I laughed, like he could make a fallen log any cleaner, but I appreciated the humorous gesture.

He sat beside me, throwing a casual arm over my shoulder. We stared out into the view, content.

"I can't remember the last time I did something like this," I admitted out loud.

"Go for a hike?" he asked.

"Well that, I mean obviously I've gone on one or two in my lifetime," I laughed. A trail hiker, I was not. "No just... sit in a spot with a beautiful view. I've traveled over the world so much and seen some incredible things, but it was always only to grab a photo and post on social media. Half the time I was still partying and drunk or hungover from the night before. And despite that, I've loved living in cities my entire life. This is... different and beautiful." Eric was different but beautiful too.

"I appreciate it more now," Eric confessed. "Not until I was about your age though." Reminding me again that we were years apart. I'd momentarily forgotten and a small part of me questioned whether the years in age would ever become a problem. Would he find me too immature? Was I not enough for him? I closed those thoughts down. No, I couldn't think like that. I wanted to barricade my heart knowing that this—whatever this fling was—could never eventuate into anything. And yet it felt so comfortable, I couldn't imagine anything else at this point.

Eric continued, eyeing me warily as if he'd caught onto my inner thoughts. "I hated this town so much. When I left for Chicago it was like a breath of fresh air and gave me a purpose. I set my roots but still came back every year to help my mother and father, especially because it was my uncle's and his tradition to go hunting this time of year. After everything that had happened with Katia, I owed them at least that much. At first, I almost begrudged coming back because it reminded of how badly I'd messed up here. The same pitying faces, the gossip that remained consistent and never forgotten." Ann and Patrice came to mind. "But besides all of that, the people mean well. It's quiet and it's a change of pace working in the café and not crammed in the office."

"What's your job like?" I asked curiously, swinging one leg at a time.

"Tiring. Stressful. But enough that I can manage. In the first two years I went from only myself, to four employees to two hundred."

My jaw dropped. "Wait, so when Lori and Thomas say you run a big IT company, they're not shitting around?"

He chuckled. "Shitting around, huh?"

"Shut up, I told you I swear more now because of you."

He again seemed pleased by that. My rigid and classy parents might beg to differ. The thought of them spread a painful guilt through me.

"Yes, I have an effective team. When I'm gone for the month my second in charge takes over. He only calls me in cases of an emergency but since he's been working with me for the last fifteen years he's able to de-escalate most issues."

"Wow, you trust him?" That came as a surprise. Considering how much he'd made a point to not trust anyone after Katia.

"I've set the correct things in place with lawyers so that no one can fuck me over again." I smiled. His own faltered. "What are you smiling at?"

"It's just hard to picture you as some big CEO in Chicago."

"Opposed to you being a receptionist at some fancy magazine." I stared at him. "Actually, I can see that very clearly."

"And ex-receptionist, remember?"

"Ah that's right, life change," he said thoughtfully. Another twinge of guilt ran through me. So not only was I young immature brat, I was also jobless with no direction. And part of me thought he'd already caught on to the fact that I didn't have a dime to my name. I'd just been grateful I'd paid the rental car upfront before my parents cut my credit card.

"When do you go back to Chicago?" I asked. I'd been here for two and a half weeks, and yet it'd felt like a lifetime.

"In less than two weeks." Silence fell over both of us. "Cassidy, I can't offer you what you're looking for."

My chest twisted. "I know," I said quietly. I'd known that every step of the way and still fell for him. Not that I'd be so desperate as to admit it to him. I'd imagined so many times what my conversation would've sounded like with Issobelle and

Clover. Issobelle would've reprimanded me for trying to settle in the first place and Clover would've told me to follow my heart. But glumly, I realized a relationship like hers and Damon's was one out of a fairy tale with happily ever after. And if I'd learnt anything at this point, that was not designated for me.

"Hey," Eric said, placing his finger under my chin and raising it. "Trust me, it's for the best. You don't want my baggage and you're young, Cassidy. You could have any man you want."

I chuckled, surprised by the tears that sprang to my eyes. I'd been so sick of hearing that same statement and although I'd tried to mentally prepare myself for it, I hated how easily Eric discarded me as well. Was it because I'd finally had sex with him? Had that been all he was after? And yet the only way I knew how to properly convey my feelings was through sex. Because when I'd been open with my feelings, it always made the other person uncomfortable and me an embarrassed bubbly mess.

"Fuck," Eric growled, picking me up and placing me in his lap as he nursed me. "Cassidy, trust me when I say this is for the better."

"I know," I said, realizing that my time here was coming to an end, but also that I'd soon have to face what I'd been running away from for so many years. "It's more annoying that you don't think I already know that."

"I don't want to hurt you, Cassidy," he said quietly. "I haven't had to deal with something like this." He pointed between us. "And I want to put a clear expectation on it."

I laughed. He sounded like a businessman through and through. And yet, even though he said it, I didn't believe him. That barrier and wall he kept erecting between us, as formidable as ever. But this time, I wouldn't fight him or challenge him on it. I wouldn't make the mistake like I had in the past to believe something else than what he was telling me.

"Two weeks, huh?" I said seductively as he wiped away my remaining tears with worry lines marring his forehead. How could something that felt so right be wrong? I battered away the mixed feelings. I truly was crazy falling for a man I barely knew, and yet I couldn't help it. But I could enjoy it with the little time we had left. "Then we better make the most of it, huh?" I said, brushing my lips against his, inviting him to dance. I nudged his mouth open, the brush of his beard tickling mine as I pressed my tongue against his.

A rough growl crept through him as he planted a

hand against my lower back, pushing me against him. I rocked my hips back and forth, quickly working his cock until I felt it press against me. He bound my wrists behind my back with one calloused hand.

His other hand clutched my throat and forfeiting to the submission was sublime. The ability to hand him over the control and use me as he pleased sent an electric thrill through me. I anticipated his filthy profanity, my toes curling in my boots at the thought already.

"You keep that shit up out here and you'll be punished over this log."

"Don't make promises you can't keep," I challenged breathlessly.

His gaze went hooded and a low guttural noise escaped him. "You're going to be my fucking undoing, Cassidy."

I could feel his rock-hard cock pressing against his jeans. "Please?" I begged with anticipation. I just wanted him, buried deep inside of me, making me forget all the shit I'd have to figure out soon. Right now, there was only Eric and me. "Fuck me, old man."

I hissed when he tugged back my hair, exposing my throat. "I think you've become rather cheeky recently," he growled against my neck before taking a bite. I hissed under explosive pain, my wrists still bound behind me, and yet my nipples ached and my core pounded. I was already wet for him, and I could tell as I ground my hips into him unapologetically and shamelessly he was as turned on as I was.

"You wet for me, sweetheart?" he asked, removing his hand from around my throat that'd felt more like a tight collar. He pulled a condom from his pocket. He'd taken his vow of never going without again seriously.

"I'm wet for you," I breathed.

"Stand up," he instructed. I did as he commanded. "And push those jeans down so I can see your bare ass."

I did as he said, neither of us breaking eye contact as I unbuttoned my jeans, pulling them and my panties to my knees. "Bend over," he growled. The cold chill of the day quickly soaked into my bones. "Press both your hands against the log."

I grabbed onto the wood, entirely exposed as I looked over my shoulder, my mouth watering at his engorged cock. I bucked under the sharp painful slap on my ass. I bit down on my lip, the aching thunderous pain jolting a thrill through me. "Did you like that, sweetheart?"

"Yes," I admitted, heat streaking across my

cheeks. I'd never known or enjoyed something so filthy. Another hard slap and I bucked again, this time, my scream carried through the trees.

Eric circled his thumb over my entrance, my knees rubbing together with anticipation. I wanted his cock, and Eric loved when I begged for it. *I loved when I begged for it,* reassured that in time his punishment was also my pleasure.

"Fuck me, Eric."

Another slap and this time, he pulled back my hair, jerking my neck. He rounded behind me, his thick thighs bracing me as his tongue came down on mine possessively. I groaned, the angle twisting my neck painfully, and yet I fucking loved it. Eric was all masculine and possessive. Anything could jump out of this woodland right now and I knew I was safe.

He rubbed his cock against my opening as he passionately kissed me, wanting and hot. He edged in, taking my breath as he continued kissing me. He slid into the hilt, swallowing my pain-filled murmurs. The guy was built like a fucking mountain god and my pussy had to stretch to new levels to fit all of him. And yet with that pain, tension rippled through me, easing into the most brain-numbing, potent banging I'd ever known to exist.

"You like my cock, snowflake?" he asked, shoving

back into me hard. I braced my arms against the wood as I cried out, his every thrust driving deeper into my being.

"I fucking love it," I confessed in a high sex-crazed state. "Eric, I want you to come inside of me so bad."

A guttural growl in response. His hand drifted down to my clit and circled the bud of nerves, a tightness starting to build in my core. My eyes burst open. Surely, I couldn't almost be there already?

He removed his hand from my hair and grabbed my hip, pounding into me, my moans and cries only challenging him to bruise me further. Momentarily, the hand on my hip was gone, followed by a hard, bruising slap on my ass. I cried out in pain, a jolt shooting straight through me and taking my building tension from a low thrum to an avalanche.

"Fuck, Eric!" I screamed. He jerked into me with a grunt and my pussy quivered around him, flooding around his pulsing cock and milking him. I hurt. I was satisfied and somehow, I only wanted more.

His forehead dropped to my shoulder, pressing a small kiss in appreciation. "Fuck me, Cassidy," he said with a somewhat shaky breath. "You're my fucking undoing."

As he pulled out, I turned around to face him,

jeans still at my knees as I curled my arms around his shoulders. He pushed back part of my hair, staring at me like it was the last time he might be able to memorize my face. Behind him, the mountains continued to roll as the deep blue of the lake silhouetted him.

I tipped onto my toes as I gently brushed my lips to his. He cupped my face, all libido and harshness of the man who'd just impaled me against a tree trunk gone as he kissed me gently and endearingly. Every time we'd fucked, he'd made up for it in the same way. Tender and sweet. Like having to go through the storm to get to the peace and quiet within. And yet I liked both of these sides of Eric.

"Thank you," I whispered. For showing me all of you. Even if he'd never admit or was even aware. He might've claimed I'd been the transparent one. But as he brushed his nose against mine, pressing a small kiss to the corner of my lips, I hadn't seen any truer form of Eric. He was complicated and grumpy. But he was also sweet. And temporary.

Chapter 29

Eric

Cassidy was my undoing. I'd meant it when I said it. There was no denying how easily she'd crumbled away my secrets and insecurities that I didn't even let those who I worked with closest know about me. But she was young... too young for me, but she held a maturity I doubted she'd given herself much credit for. And on top of that the woman drove me fucking crazy in the sack.

It'd been a long time since I'd mentioned Katia. But in its wake, it left something raw and vulnerable.

We were back in the cabin with the fireplace crackling. We'd fucked in the truck on the drive back, on the kitchen bench, and in the shower already. Now that we'd crossed that line, we just couldn't keep our hands off one another. I was certain it'd get to the point where we just wouldn't bother wearing clothes anymore.

I sat on the sofa as she lay across, her head propped up on my lap and her legs suspended over the armchair. Her curly blonde hair was damp and loose. This little ray of sunshine randomly appearing in town had begun to shift something inside of me. And I was conscious of what it might've been and was conflicted by its realization. It went beyond just being physically attracted to her. Cassidy was so unconventional to my daily routine, and yet I now found myself looking forward to what bizarre notion or activity she'd be sending me on next. In those few short weeks, I'd become accustomed to her and wanted to spend every waking hour with her.

She was reading out loud some romance novel a friend called Sotiny had given her an advanced copy of. Cassidy had told me of her friend's great love with a playboy called Alex and worked with her friend Clover and her partner, Damon. She preached about their relationships and the progress made in recent months like it was some grand fairy tale retelling. I had to keep up with how everyone was connected but what I purposefully engrained was Clover and Issobelle were her best friends, and yet I hadn't seen her text or call them once since being here.

"This book's good," Cassidy said only one chapter in. She flicked to the cover again where a man's chest was splayed across the cover. "You could do this you know?"

I furrowed my eyebrows. "Write a romance novel?"

She laughed. "No be a cover model with your body."

I scoffed. "In your wildest dreams."

She purred. "Oooh but you already show up there. Then again, I don't know if I like the idea of sharing you with millions of other women."

I chuckled. "Keep reading. You were up to the part where she'd spilled the coffee on the new handsome stranger in town."

She chuckled and flicked back to the page reading out loud. I played with her hair, content and soothed as I brushed it out, strand by strand, mesmerized by her voice and the crackling fireplace in the background. What she was reading was irrelevant, but her voice and drama filled expressions in telling the story had me chuckling and staring at her endearingly.

I felt like an utter jerk telling her on the mountains this couldn't be any more. I knew it hurt her and I knew she understood. But I did this for both our sakes, and yet I couldn't help noticing my comfort and ease with her. I couldn't even imagine what returning to Chicago would feel like without her. And that terrified me.

"Eric?" she asked, looking up at me with those big blue eyes inquisitively.

"What is it, snowflake?" Snowflake, I'd started the nickname on a whim. She'd been so fragile looking and out of place when she'd first arrived to town but her beauty was immeasurable like the snow.

"How do you think it'll end?"

"You've only read ten pages."

"But these things can be predictable. Come on, we'll have a bet."

I rolled my tongue around in my mouth thoughtfully. "I think it'll end on a happily ever after."

She chuckled and shook her head as she looked back at the book. "That's so vague."

"Does it matter how it ends?"

She seemed affronted. "Of course it matters how it ends. Have you no heart?"

I laughed, a belly full, as she smiled brightly. "As I was saying..." she said, continuing the story.

Chapter 30

Cassidy

When I'd woken up in Eric's arms, his dead weight pinned me into place. There was no way of escaping or making him an omelette before he woke. I'd been barely able to shuffle so I could stare up at his sleeping expression.

He was curled up around me, his knees trapping me in his warmth. Out of choice though, I wasn't so sure. I tried not to laugh when I noticed Shadow, sleeping at his feet and forcing the bulky man to shrink his size around me.

He'd kicked off most of his blankets, his body heat radiating off him in waves. I brushed a hand over his beard lightly and soothingly. After our many discussions, I'd realized he wasn't as harsh on anyone

277

else as he was on himself. Especially when it came to his family and his dyslexia. *I'm stupid.* Those words resonated with me since the moment he'd first told me in his truck. I'd been subject to so many "pretty blonde" jokes and "only good for one thing" statements. So, in a different way, I understood how he felt but that didn't take away the fact that I wanted to melt away any ill thoughts he had toward himself.

And last night had been nice... really nice, being able to read to him even if it was a sweet contemporary romance that he might've not ordinarily been inclined toward. I'd snagged a free advanced copy from Sotiny before I'd left Manhattan when she came back into town since Alex still lived there on and off.

And reading it to Eric felt intimate. He'd watched me the whole time, laughing and tugging at my hair when I'd throw in a cheeky comment.

His low snore came to a stop, and without even prying his eyes open, he tucked me in tighter and murmured, "It's creepy to stare at someone while they're sleeping."

A slow smile crossed my face. "You don't seem so scared." And also, how did he know I was staring?

Still sleepy, he said. "The only thing I'm scared of is you leaving."

My heart flipped in my chest and I hated how easily it was carried away. He was half asleep, and I wondered what part of Eric I was talking to. His heavy snore followed through once again. It had only been yesterday he'd outright told me this couldn't be any more than what it was already, and yet... when he said things like that and cared for me... like when he intimately washed over my body in the shower and told me pretty things without sex attached to it— okay we had sex before then but my heart fluttered and in its own way, it was cruel. We were both trying to fight this thing but it felt strangely inevitable. Or maybe I'd just watched and read too many romances.

When I asked him last night how he thought the story would end and he said happily ever after, I wondered if through all the hurdles, like the main characters in books, maybe somehow Eric might change his mind. I nuzzled in tighter, embarrassed by my girly thoughts. But he wouldn't, and I had prepared myself for that but with every given chance my heart would react before my head could think logically. That this felt right... That no matter what, we could somehow make it work. But then there were things I'd have to address and cut away.

Sadly, I realized that all this time I'd just been trying to find a place to belong. To be loved. And not for my money or my last name. But simply for being me. And the place I thought I might've found that had made it abundantly clear he wasn't the one.

It felt strange Eric not being home. Even more so, not going into town with him. He'd given me the option but I decided to stay back and make some cookies, which cooled inside. He threatened me not to read any more of the novel until he returned. In such a short time, this little cabin had become familiar to me. While he was gone, I decided to experiment with my newfound skill at wood chopping. He'd been gone for a few hours now, and I patiently waited until I could try the new recipe Lori had given me when he returned with the ingredients.

I blew out a heavy breath as I slammed down the axe on the piece of wood. Damn, it only splintered it. I yanked it out. Okay another time. Eric made it look ridiculously easy and sexy as well. And although I was clearly not a natural, I could see how he got carried away with time. In its own way, it was therapeutic. And it was rewarding to know the locals would use it for their fireplaces.

Shadow lazily snoozed on the porch, disinterested in my wood chopping attempts. I wiped away the sweat on my brows and glanced at the small little pile I'd managed to form. I turned to look out to the mountain view behind me. It was stunning. I'd never stayed in a place like this long enough to enjoy its beauty and peace. I closed my eyes for a moment, enjoying the frigid air. It was hard to think about returning to Manhattan. I wouldn't say I was a local or accustomed to living this lifestyle, but I felt like I'd changed. Had an appreciation for somethings that I might've previously overlooked in the busyness of Manhattan.

Something brown flashed in the trees, grabbing my attention. A deer walked away from me and further into the woods. My curiosity unfurled as I dropped the axe and stepped into the woods, trying to be quiet as I followed it. I hadn't seen many deer in real life. Especially in the wild.

Crunch. A branch broke beneath my boot and the deer paused, its ears pushing back. Shit. After only a moment of hesitation the deer bolted. I threw my hands up in the air. Well, what did I expect? To have some kind of Disney princess moment and pat it?

Crunch. I burrowed my eyebrows in confusion. I

hadn't moved my feet. A low, menacing growl raised all the hairs on my arms and I slowly turned, terror pumping through my veins. A grey wolf padded toward me, its fangs bared. I took in a sharp breath.

Snap. There was another one to its left. And another behind that. Three wolves surrounded me. My heart hammered in my chest as I briefly eyed every direction. *Use your legs, Cassidy. Use your fucking legs.*

A wolf barked and I screamed, bolting for the cabin. The wolves began snapping and snarling as they gave chase. Within seconds, one yelped. Shadow barged into it from the side.

"Shadow!" I screamed, stopping. The others had stopped chasing me and sized up Shadow. Without thought, I looked around, finding a branch. The two dogs toppled and rolled over each other. Adrenaline pumped in my veins as I picked up the large branch and charged, swinging it at the other two wolves. My heart pounded in my ears. I was going to die. I acted on impulse. But I'd be fucked if I was going to let them hurt Shadow. There was a yelp as Shadow flung the other wolf off.

No longer deterred by my stick, one of the wolves lunged for me instead. I screamed, throwing my hands in front of my face. I was pushed out of the way, a grunt the only audible sound through my heart pounding in my ears as Eric wrestled with a wolf latched onto his arm.

He gripped at his fangs, opening its mouth and flinging it off. Shadow chased as the three wolves scampered away with tails between their legs. Eric whistled, calling him back immediately. The dog returned obediently. Everything had happened so fast. Like a dream. My mind was whirling and catching up to what had just transpired. My eyes went wide at the sight of red dripping blood.

Eric dropped to his knees in front of me, his hand cupping my jaw. "Are you okay?" he said, panicked.

"Am I okay? Eric, you're bleeding!"

"Are you okay?!" He yelled. I was stunned by the fierceness in his tone. He looked like he was about to burst into tears. Although his eyes surveyed every part of me, he wasn't seeing me at all. A sheer panic had swept over him.

I grabbed his hand that cupped my face, pushing myself onto my knees as I grabbed his other hand and placed it to my heart. "Eric, look at me."

He did but was still in that haze. Did he even realize he was the one bleeding? "Eric, look at me!"

He blinked, my tone finally getting through to him. Tears filled his green eyes. "I'm okay." Tears threatened to spill down my own cheeks, adrenaline coursing through my veins.

He dropped his forehead to mine. "I thought you were hurt," his voice wobbled. "I should've been here and—" he choked.

His undoing broke me apart. I kissed him gently and sweetly, its power and force becoming desperate. "I'm okay," I breathed. The realization that he'd literally just saved me from three wild wolves forcing me into a shaking fit.

"Coots mentioned there might've been wolves recently in the area when I first arrived. And we'd even heard howling a few nights ago. I should've taken it more seriously," he choked out, furious with himself. Shadow whimpered and I made space for him between Eric and me. We quickly searched over him. Surprisingly, Shadow hadn't been harmed at all, the wolf taking far more of a beating. I sighed in relief.

Eric, however, bled all over my jacket. "We need to get you to a hospital."

"No, just call Thomas he'll be able to stitch me up and should have a tetanus shot somewhere."

"Eric," I said, cupping his face again, tears spilling over my cheeks.

"I know," he said, cupping my face desperately. "I thought I'd lost you."

Tears streamed down my face. "You shouldn't have jumped in, you're hurt."

He chuckled, almost hysterically. "As if I'd let anything happen to you." His expression softened and he dipped his forehead to mine again. "And thank you for defending Shadow."

I looked down at the courageous dog, stroking his head in appreciation. I'd just found my new hero.

With a wince, Eric pulled out his cell. "Let's go back inside in case they come back." I helped him stand, although he insisted he didn't need it. He tucked me in tightly, kissing the top of my head and squeezing me as he called Thomas. I squeezed into his ribs, my heart pounding, my bottom lip quivering. With the adrenaline wearing off, exhaustion began to quickly take hold.

I held Eric tightly, my heart in my throat as the thought of losing either Shadow or Eric more terrifying than I'd realized. I clung to Eric as tightly as he clung to me, staring at his bleeding arm, tears streaming down my cheeks that there was nothing I could do to help him. He'd risked his life to save me —not for my name or money. Simply to protect *me*.

Chapter 31

Eric

When I'd called Thomas he was at our family home and somehow managed to force my mother back into the house as she made a commotion in the background. I'd also called Lori to warn the locals and any tourists who were stopping by to hike locally.

Thomas had already given me the tetanus shot, stitched me up, and bandaged my arm. I hadn't realized at the time that one of the others had nipped me on the calf as well. He said I was lucky that I was such a hunk of meat in the first place and they didn't snag anything too important. It didn't give me much reassurance, as he cocked a smirk while saying it. What I was grateful for was the heavy drugs he'd given me.

Cassidy had fluttered around me ever since, and now she was re-evaluating the bandages even when they didn't need to be. I watched her groggily. I didn't feel like the lucky one. Shadow had been waiting for me in front of the door. When I'd jumped out and closed the truck door, that's when he suddenly bolted for the trees and I heard Cassidy's scream. I'd never run so fast in my life, my heart pounding in my chest. I acted on impulse and instinct, the rest was a blur.

I hadn't even thought twice about throwing myself in front of the wolf. My entire world had flipped upside down the moment I'd seen her defending herself and protecting *my* fucking dog. It should've been me. She should've never been in that dangerous situation and the thought of anything happening to her... My fist curled into the blanket and unsettled anxiety filled my chest.

"Cassidy," I said quietly as I shifted to sit more upright in the bed. The drugs Thomas had given me were strong.

"You should rest," she said quickly, sitting at my side and pressing her hand to my chest. I could see the worry in her gaze and it knotted something deep in my stomach. I grabbed her hand, rubbing my thumb over it; she looked like she was about to cry, but much like me... I noticed the tension ripple away ever so slightly with the contact. She'd avoided my eyes ever since Thomas had left. But the only thing I wanted right now was her, to know she was okay and safe. In my arms and protected where nothing would dare touch her.

"It's looking good," she said solemnly, staring at the bandage. "I'll get you more water." She grabbed my empty glass from the side table but I pulled her arm down instead, leaving her face only inches from mine. Finally, those bright blue eyes noticed me. I cupped her chin and she nuzzled into it.

"I told you I'm fine," she said quietly. Even though I saw her, felt her, that sheer terror still coursed through my veins.

"Stay with me. Read me another chapter," I said lazily. I didn't like this fretting side of Cassidy. It had us both on edge. I just wanted her by my side. Safe and warm. With me.

A soft expression twisted her face. "You should rest," she said.

"I will while you're reading to me. I want to see if they get there happily ever after." The truth was I didn't give two shits what happened to the couple in that book. But what I did care about was Cassidy acting her usual self. She'd since changed into her long sweatpants and that little crop top she'd often taunted me with while doing yoga. If the drugs weren't so effective acting as a tranquiliser, I might've taken her and explored every inch of her again.

But I could barely move. I grimaced. Fuck I *was* turning into an old man. She slowly unfurled my fingers and walked over to the fireplace, stoking it. I thought she was running away again but before I could argue, she collected the book from the side table near the sofa. She patted Shadow considerately, who lay at the end of the bed and had been there ever since. He seemed spooked as well. And much like I yearned for her touch, he seemed to relax slightly under her attention too. She tucked under my shoulder and curled into me, bringing the blanket up with her.

"We've only got four chapters left. What do you think's going to happen?" she asked.

"Well, they're obviously going to get back together, aren't they?" I said with a yawn.

"Maybe it's not so predictable," she murmured as she laid her head on my chest, cautious not to hurt my other arm. I tucked her in tighter.

"Then prove me otherwise," I murmured, stroking her hair as she began reading. When I looked down on the page it was a jumble of letters between the drugs and the dyslexia, and I couldn't concentrate on a damn thing. But my gaze drifted to Cassidy, the only thing I cared for in this very moment. And in the moment of truth—when I thought it'd be cruelly taken from me—I risked my fucking life to protect it. Maybe when I was sober and not on such heavy drugs, I'd consider its meaning further. Maybe tomorrow. But for now, I simply enjoyed the sound of her voice, trying to drown out the echoing scream of her voice in the woodlands that still haunted me.

Chapter 32

Cassidy

Eric had only made it through one and a half chapters before falling into a deep sleep. I stayed up most of the night, checking on him even when he swatted me away and said it was nothing. It hadn't looked like nothing. He'd literally been attacked and bitten by wolves. All because he'd been protecting me.

By the time morning broke, I'd hardly been able to sleep at all. The gruesome images kept replaying in my mind. Eric was curled up in bed, the sun barely risen when I slid out from underneath his arm and made way to make his breakfast and coffee. Shadow hadn't left the end of the bed all night either. It was remarkable he hadn't sustained so much as a scratch and for that, I was grateful. I gave him an appreciative pat, proud of my little hero. He'd not only saved my life but protected Eric as well and I could never show this furball my deepest thanks enough.

I'd only just switched the coffee maker on when I heard bouncing wheels come up the dirt road and a vehicle park outside the cabin. I looked over my shoulder where Eric was now sitting up in bed, an effective glare in my direction.

"Were you expecting someone?" I inquired. He shook his head. It was probably Coots or Thomas but even for them it was early.

I made my way to the door, startled by the low growl that crept from Shadow, my hand lingered in front of the handle, heeding his warning like a bad omen. He must've still been spooked from yesterday. Eric rose out of bed, his feint limp noticeable. "Stay in bed," I instructed. But I couldn't shake the foreboding sense as I opened the door.

When I did, all the breath left my body and the chill from outside ran deep into my bones. Frederick's unpleasant smile greeted me. "Well, it's about time I found you," he said, pushing past me and into the cabin.

"You can't be here," I panicked. *Not in here.* This was Eric's home. Not a single part of Frederick should be in here, contaminating everything he came in contact with.

"You?" Eric's voice cut through as Frederick's bodyguard shoved his way in as well.

"Consider me surprised when I find out you've been staying with the small-town café owner... even when I came through town two weeks ago and asked if he'd seen you." Frederick's cutting gaze went from Eric to me. "You played cat and mouse for longer than I'd given you credit for but I'm sick of the game."

"You need to get the fuck out of my cabin," Eric said, throwing an arm over my shoulder and pulling me back.

Frederick began to laugh, bemused and disgusted. "I should've known she'd have no issues with fucking the local old man for a place to stay as well."

I flinched under his harsh words. I was shoved back, and Eric swung. I screamed as Frederick's bodyguard lunged for Eric. Instinctively, I grabbed Shadow's collar, the poor dog yelping as he was yanked back. No, no, no, if he got involved, they'd have him put down. Everything happened so fast that it took me a moment to try and figure out what I could do.

In his weakened state, the bodyguard easily grappled Eric to the ground in seconds, pinning him headfirst and twisting his arm behind him with a knee in his back. Eric looked feral, probably still groggy from the medication, as he gritted his teeth. Red began to seep through his bandages.

"Get off of him!" I screamed but Frederick stood in my way, coming between us—as Frederick always did. Bemused, he played with his glove, the power he held over me pinning me in place.

"What a disgrace. If you weren't my betrothed, I'd publicize this humiliation and blackmail the Carrington family without a second thought."

I flinched under his regard.

"What did you just say?" Eric growled as he tried to shove back the man holding him down. Suddenly, he seemed to have less resistance, more interested in Frederick's reply. No, no, no. Tears streamed down my face as I held back Shadow, still keeping him safe, but ut it left Eric vulnerable and bleeding on the floor. His harsh green eyes met mine.

Frederick looked between us both and chuckled. "Oh shit, he really doesn't know?" He clicked his fingers all the more amused. "Listen here, old man, I'm not sure if your little, small-town brain can comprehend the status and situation those from money have, but the little runaway you've been cozying up with is actually an heiress." He pointed a delicate finger at me. "An heiress, that was promised to me when she turned twenty-six. We were meant to have the announcements and formalities dealt with already but someone decided to run away."

"I hate you!" I screamed. Those three trembling words felt like the only form of defense I had against him. This ugly man that my parents had promised me to. All to bring two families together in fame and wealth. It disgusted every part of my being. *He* disgusted me. The moment our fathers had made the agreement on our behalf, Frederick's polite mask wiped off and he'd only ever shown me this hideous thing beneath ever since.

"Ohhh but, wifey, you only have one job to serve." He made sure not to step any closer as Shadow snapped and snarled, trying to wrangle free. "You will go through with the plan so I get my inheritance. I didn't convince your parents to cut your funds and cell just for you to say no and walk away with some poor person. I'll burn this fucking town down before I let you humiliate me any further."

Tears welled in my eyes, not at his threats but the silence that overtook Eric. He wasn't looking at me anymore. "Eric," I said with a wobbly voice. "Please I can explain."

"You lied." His voice was distant. Miles away from me. Cold and reserved.

"Don't believe him, I don't want to go back. I won't go back. I—"

"Is it true?" Eric asked pointedly and finally, his green gaze landed on me. I saw the mixture of hurt, grief, and anger all infused in one and I choked. "Are you engaged to this man?"

My mouth was dry. All words lost as I tried to hold back the tears, realizing that no matter what I said, he'd only compare me to Katia now. A woman and a snake. Someone who tricked him. A person like who he hated the most.

"Not officially but as soon as we return to Manhattan it will be. And you will be forgotten, nothing but the small-town trash you were raised to be."

"Don't speak to him like that!" I snapped, cowering on the floor as I held back Shadow. In fear for what they might do to him and me. I'd seen Frederick's cruel side, a part of him that no one else saw. But I'd resigned myself to being a coward, because I found it easier to shout my hate at him than meet Eric's gaze again and suffer under that hurt.

Frederick laughed. "You really were always so naïve, sheltered and a brat. Just do as you're fucking told for once and make it easier for both of us. Do you truly plan on running away forever? What can *you* possibly do on your own other than just sleep around? That's all you've ever been good for."

"Jealous because it's never been you?" I snarled with all the acid I could muster.

His smile twisted, revealing his hideous nature. It reminded me far too much of the week after my twenty-first birthday. It was my first memory of seeing Frederick like this, his cruel and vile intentions seeping through. A powerful man who would do more harm than good. A memory I'd run away from for years now.

We'd both been at a party and despite our parents agreeing to a pre-organised marriage, I still didn't want to get to know him any further. Tears pricked at my eyes when I thought about him pinning me against the wall, hidden away from other members of the party.

"You're mine and you will give me what I want" *he sneered.*

"I won't sleep with you," I hissed. *"Get off me."*

Slap. *The cold air and his palm struck me. I*

clutched at my face, the alcohol in my system and the hit forcing the room to sway. Or was that me?

"You've never been pretty in the first place. I was showing you a mercy tonight. I hope I don't have to see you for another five years until our wedding day. Fucking disgusting." He walked away, my shallow breaths felt like they were bringing in the walls as I slid down it, holding my burning face.

Had I been only good for one thing? Was this what my loveless marriage would look like? Tears streamed down my face. How could my parents give me over to someone so cruel and all in the name of status and growth? And as much as I'd hated the sting on my cheek, I'd welcomed it. Relieved he'd hit me and walked away instead of the alternative. Terrified that he might not have stopped and taken something that was never his to take.

I'd wrapped my arms around myself and cried, disgusted that I was so pitiful but determined to find someone that genuinely loved me and cared. That I wouldn't be an item shipped around, that I had a meaning to someone. That I wasn't only judged for my looks or last name.

The few years after that were hell, Frederick was everywhere, sneering at me from the shadows but boasting his glee in front of friends publicly. Every party and every event. We had the same friends and circles. I'd just become known as the party girl when he'd become known as some golden goose to watch out for. My father's eyes sparkled with pride that he'd made the right investment.

And so, I ran away to Manhattan determined to find a man who would actually love me. To prove to my parents that they were wrong. That I wasn't just some bargaining chip and marriage was something to be cherished and filled with love, respect, and passion. And yet here I was... Him and me in the same room again. The only reason his hand probably wasn't raised to me was because of the snapping and snarling dog that came between us.

A tear slid down my cheek, my only focus now Eric. I was terrified as to what Frederick might do to me, but this wasn't Eric's mess. I'd only brought trouble to him.

"I didn't mean to lie," I squeaked. I'd only brought him pain, literally as he bled on the floor of his own cabin. This retreat he frequented. I'd tarnished it unknowingly because I'd been selfish and tried to run away from my own responsibilities. "Eric, please look at me." But I could feel he'd already slipped through my fingertips, leaving me as cold as the air sweeping through the front door in the early hours of the morning. "Eric, I don't love him. I love *you*."

Frederick laughed. "You'd really let anything put its dick inside of you, wouldn't you?"

Eric tried to wriggle free, but he was shoved painfully back down. The bodyguard was straining but I could only stare as the bandage thickened with red.

"She lied to you, dude. And you fell for it."

Silence. Eric's face was shoved into the floor. Tears streaked my cheeks. I wanted to hold him and say that I was sorry but I felt the distance stretch further between us. A layer of ice keeping me further away. My warm-hearted lumberjack had frosted over again, and I only had myself to blame. I was no better than the con woman who tricked him the first time.

"I swear to God, Cassidy if you don't get off the fucking floor and get in the car, I'll demolish this entire town."

Eric and I both flinched under that statement, and I knew with painful clarity that if Frederick threw a big enough tantrum, he had the money, power, and status to do it.

"Please don't hurt anyone," I begged. This was because I'd run away, not anything they'd done.

Frederick pointed at me. "Get off the floor. And

you, shithead." He pointed at Eric. "If you or your fucking mutt try anything I'll put a bullet in both of your heads."

I flinched at his words. And then Frederick's cruel smile stretched. "But don't worry, wifey, nothing will ever happen to you. The golden child of Mr. Carrington. We can't have anything happen to his precious daughter."

The bodyguard slowly stood. Eric shook him off and stood painfully, his limp more pronounced.

"Eric, I'm sorry," I cried. He looked away from me and my heart thudded to the floor.

"I really don't like having to raise my voice and go to these measures," Frederick said, adjusting his gloves. "But you've really created some trouble for me this time. So, get in the car and we'll pretend like none of this happened, okay?"

"Eric," I cried out again. But he was already lost to me. Slowly, he walked over, and my heart froze as he gently slipped his hand around Shadow's collar and took a step back. I choked on a sob.

"I won't let anything happen to this town," he said, finally eyeing me. "And you know I don't believe in fairy tales. If I had just been some fun for you to pass the time, then let's leave it at that."

"It wasn't—"

"Leave!"

I winced under his guttural growl.

"Ah a smart man after all," Frederick applauded. His bodyguard, despite his size and previous show of brute force, gently pulled me up from the floor. I hated this. I hated this family. I hated this hurt. I hated these chains.

Tears streamed down my face as I realized I was tired of running. I'd found what I'd been looking for. Someone to love, and in the process, I'd hurt them more painfully than I could've ever imagine I was capable of.

Shadow whined behind me as I made for the door, scratching at the wooden floorboard to follow. I felt numb as I was escorted to the car, in complete disbelief that not only had my father bargained me off, but Eric had so easily let me go too. But I couldn't blame him for it. I hated myself. I'd brought this upon him. If I'd told him earlier, would it have been any different? Or had I really been that stupid, thinking that I could keep running away and avoiding my responsibility?

After Frederick's bodyguard collected all three suitcases and slammed the trunk shut, I finally looked up and out the window. The cabin's front door was closed, a fitting metaphor for the memories shared and now, the disbelief of my heart being ripped out, discarded and bound to remain in the mountains. It'd been the last place I'd ever thought I'd wind up and feel at home. I curled my arms around myself, the cold chill of coming day seeping into the car. No, it wasn't this place that made me feel at home—it'd been Eric. And I'd fucked it all up.

I began to sob in the back of the car, the calamity of everything that was about to happen unfurling. My biggest nightmare had finally caught up to me, and yet I felt like I'd just left behind an even bigger disaster.

Chapter 33

Cassidy

I wrung my hands, anxiety fueling me as I sat on the expensive white sofa. I knew my mother had been silently staring at the dirt mark on my jacket since the moment I'd walked in. Frederick hadn't so much as allowed me to stop, let alone shower or change my attire since he'd dragged me out of Eric's cabin in my pajamas. My parents seemed disgruntled by my attire, but appreciative for him having brought me.

I hadn't seen my parents for over three years now. My mother's silky blonde hair was highlighted with a few lighter blondes mixing in the gray and my father, twenty years her senior only had flickers of gray through his molten brown hair. They hadn't changed or aged a bit.

We sat in the lobby of their penthouse in Manhattan. Frederick's bodyguard waited outside the door and Frederick poured himself and my father a glass of whiskey as they stood, peering over me as if I was some scolded child.

My only semblance of decency was that my mother actually hugged me and voiced she'd been concerned for my well-being when I arrived. But that affection was now long gone as my father adopted his usual business demeanor, appraising me as if I was some supervisor lacking in one of his projects.

"Do you know to what lengths it took us to find you? We were terrified as to what would happen when we cut off your credit card and cell."

"You didn't have to listen to him," I mumbled in Frederick's direction, since it had been his idea to begin with.

"Don't give me attitude," my father said, defeated. "These were our terms. You and I set an agreement before you left for New York. You had three years to enjoy your youth. More lenient than we were initially going to allow you. And this is how you repay us? Running off like a child?"

"I don't want to marry him," I gritted out, digging my nails into my leg.

"What we want, sweetheart, and what is our

duty are two different things," my mother said gently. My throat locked up on any smart remark because of her tender tone. I'd watched my parents in a loveless marriage. And as harsh as my mother might've been, she cared, and I knew my father did somewhere deep down as well. But it didn't mean they could still treat me like their little girl, bargaining me off.

"We live in the twenty-first century. I feel like I'm being bargained off like some goat," I argued.

"Watch your tone," my father reprimanded. "Your mother and I were married in the same way. And we've lived a happy beneficial life."

I almost choked on mock-humor. Was that between the silent affairs or "pushed under the rug" deals to protect the families' images? And that was what he deemed to be a "happy beneficial life"?

"You're our only daughter," my mother said carefully. "We want what's best for you."

"And this is what's best for you," my father said, pointing to Frederick. He'd said very little at this point, but his presence loomed over me like an axe. Neither of us mentioned the cabin or Eric. My heart ached at the thought. But Frederick's threat still lingered and was very real. If the only thing coming between him and what he wanted was me having fallen in love with another man, he'd destroy it within an eyeblink.

I couldn't drag Eric into this any further than I had already. And because of that, I couldn't expose Frederick for his nature because I didn't want Eric involved or dirtied in this mess. We were at a standstill. My heart pined at the thought of having so many things left unsaid. But the way he'd looked at me... disgusted and horrified... How could I ever dare face him again?

It was hard to tell my parents about Frederick, the mask he wore and the ugliness of his true nature. He'd spent years perfecting it, fine-tuning what he wanted the world to see. And I only looked like the silly girl, running away from a forced marriage.

"Please, Dad." My bottom lip wobbled. Today had been a long day. I wanted to sleep and pretend like it'd never happened.

"Cassidy, my darling," my father said, placing his glass of whiskey down. "Please don't make us look unreasonable." He tucked a piece of my hair back. "This was our agreement. You need to contribute to this household in your own way. What did you think would happen? That you'd continue living and partying in New York? There is expectation of you and with your skillset you can do very little to maintain the name or its funds." Not that we needed any more money. "Your place, to support your family is by Frederick's side."

My shoulders caved in. They'd never expected anything of me. I knew in my heart if I'd been born a son and not a daughter, my father might've expected something different of me. And my mother had never suggested anything else. And yet I'd allowed it to happen as well. I'd been ignorant and naïve running away. And for what?

"Cassidy," my mother spoke up. I didn't look at her. I wasn't going to convince anyone else otherwise in this room what was best for me. Defeated, I began to believe what they were saying was true. "You've always dreamed of a big love. But sometimes those things just don't happen in real life. Instead, you should seek an agreeable companionship. It's not easy maintaining this lifestyle. You can have anything you want—and this is how to keep it."

"I think maybe we shouldn't pressure her so much tonight," Frederick spoke chivalrously. I death-stared him, channeling all my hate and fury. My parents both looked at him admirably. "It's a lot, I don't want my future fiancée thinking I'm taking everything from her. We should give her a few days. I know she'll come around."

Had it not been for my upbringing and my parents standing in the room, I might've spat in his face. But all I wanted to do was curl myself into a ball and cry. I was back in New York, this city that I loved but didn't feel like home anymore. It just felt like an extension of the cage I'd been trying to flee.

Chapter Thirty-Four

E**ric**

Two weeks later

"Mr. Dawson, your sister's here to visit," Lucy, my receptionist, dialed in. I sighed. Whenever my sister visited unannounced, it was never a good thing. I'd returned to Chicago the moment shit went down with Cassidy. I needed a distraction and throwing myself back into work was the perfect excuse. And so since then, I'd purposefully ignored all of my family's calls—especially Lori's—for this exact reason.

Shadow yawned beside me in his "office bed" as Lori had once called it. Chicago was a bustling stream behind me as I sat at my desk, staring at and struggling with the documents that only I could look over and approve. I'd barely been able to make sense of much of the documents I'd read over since getting back. My mind completely elsewhere, thinking of the very person I wanted to never think about again.

But it was hard when you'd been given literal wounds as a reminder of a different time. Most of them had healed, leaving nothing but blemishes that would most likely scar.

Lori pushed in through the two wooden doors and I grimaced. Yep, she was definitely in a mood and I'd be fucked if I knew why. Then again, I had ignored her phone calls and any means of trying to reach me. And yet I wasn't surprised that she'd flown from LA just to bust my ass in typical Lori fashion.

"Don't you have a business to run?" I asked dryly, feigning interest in the documents I'd been studying for the last hour.

"Don't you have any balls?" she retorted. A tick ran through my jaw.

"I'd told Lucy not to let anyone in," I said casually, trying to keep my composure.

She snorted and threw down a paper. I glanced briefly at it. In the section of paper visible was a photo of Frederick and Cassidy, her hand glistening with a ring. I didn't even need to attempt to read the paper for its context. I pushed it away, feeling bile rise up my throat.

"You're okay with this?" She folded her arms over her chest.

"You flew all the way to Chicago to throw a newspaper at me?" I growled.

"You're a bigger idiot than I thought."

"Stop sticking your nose into shit you don't understand," I warned.

She mock-chuckled. "Don't understand? You do realize our mother's beside herself after Cassidy abruptly leaves and then you shortly after with no explanation other than "she's engaged." I don't have to be a rocket scientist to see she's miserable even with a fake smile plastered on her face in that photo."

"She looks plenty happy to me," I begrudged.

"No, she was happy when she was with you!" When I said nothing, she slammed her hand down on the table. "Damn it, Eric! Shake that shell of yours for once. You were fucking happy!"

"It was a few weeks. Do you know how many other women I've fucked in the past and yet you're not throwing their engagement papers in my face? Why does everyone think they can have an opinion about my life, I'm happy as I am!" I could feel my red hot temperament rising. Had it been one of my brothers, this discussion may have gone very differently. I almost wished it were one of them instead so I could flex some of this pent-up... discontentment.

"You guys were right for each other. And if you're not willing to fight for your happiness then I'll do it for you."

"She lied to me! She's no better than the con woman that took everything from our family!" Lori flinched under my words as I stood. "Or did you forget about that? Because I haven't. I let my guard down again. And this is what happened. I got carried away with a pretty little blonde and I got burnt. And I'm not letting that near the family again!"

A ripple of tension rolled through me, and yet saying it out loud made me feel lighter. I took a seat, pissed off with myself for standing over her like that. Sister or not.

"Eric, no one blames you for that. You need to let it go."

I stared at her, disbelieving. "I have built all of this." I swirled my finger around the room. "For you. For Mom and Dad. For Thomas and the twins. Isn't that enough? Why do you always expect more from me?" My words caught in my throat.

She eyed me, her own bottom lip wobbling. Fuck, this is why I hated dealing with Lori out of all my siblings, because despite all her bravado and

314

braveheart spirit, she empathized with others and could express herself freely. And I hated when she looked at me with such... pity.

"And what happens when we all start our own families? When Mom and Dad aren't around anymore and Shadow's on his last years. And you're all alone. In this big office with a puddle of cash at your feet." Her voice wavered and she took a breath. "You could have anything you want, brother. So why not be honest with yourself and actually fight for something that's out of your control. Why not take a chance *now*? You've built plenty security to fall back on. Just please honor yourself for once. I'd never seen you so damn happy until those few weeks. And I know you know deep down, that you were too."

The silence was palpable.

She raised her hands in the air. "You know what, Eric? One day you'll end up despising yourself and your stubbornness. It doesn't make you a smart man or a brave man to avoid your emotions. It just makes you a fool that I pity. I love you but you're still such a child sometimes."

I tightened my jaw, letting her words sink in. She nodded at nothing in particular, biting her bottom lip and almost laughing. "Fine." She threw her hands in the air again. "That's all I flew to Chicago to say to you, brother. Enjoy wallowing in your misery."

She slapped her hands on her thighs and left. The door slammed behind her. I stared at the door for a moment before slipping my gaze to the newspaper she'd left on my desk. My heart dropped and the apple in my throat bobbled at the sight of Cassidy. The memory of her crying on the floor as she clung to Shadow, provoking everything I'd been trying to shove down.

I'd been a bastard to let her leave with him, and yet I'd only cared about myself and my own pride. She'd lied but she'd done what she had to do to protect herself. But even then, I don't know if I was conveniently making an excuse for her. I dragged the paper closer and looked at her properly. Her beautiful smile was on display, but the sparkle and joy in her gaze had vanished. And that churned my chest more than anything. Despite my anger, there was so much hurt. And I hated how I considered what it would be like to forgive her. That had it been anyone else, I would've turned my back and never thought twice about them.

But would I really let her marry a man who treated her like that? I was almost disappointed in her for moving forward with the engagement. But if anyone understood the pressure and weight to carry a family, didn't I? Since that had been the very thing I'd grown my entire business on.

Shadow's paw stole my attention away from fixating and staring at the paper. He arched his head to the side staring at me. It'd been quiet since she'd left and we'd come back to Chicago, a city with so many people in it, and yet I felt more isolated than I had when living in the cabin every snowy month.

"I don't know, boy," I admitted. It wasn't any of my business and I grew angrier at Lori for pulling me out of my ignorant solace.

Chapter 35

Cassidy

I stared at the mirror, panic constricting around my throat at the sight of the wedding dress wrapping me tightly.

"I'd selected the three dresses I thought would best suit your figure," the lady called, standing outside the dressing room. And no doubt the most expensive because none of them were in my taste. This dress swallowed me whole, a princess cut with so many frills that the moment a gust of wind bristled around me I'd be picked up and be blown away.

"Cassidy, dear, come out and show us," my mother called out. This was all wrong. I could hardly move.

"Cassidy," Clover's voice gently encouraged.

"I'm coming in, okay?" She ducked her head behind the curtain. "Are you okay?"

From her reaction, I obviously wasn't doing a good job at hiding it. No. I wasn't okay. My parents were forcing me to marry the biggest jackass of all time, and yet I didn't have the will power to run away anymore, and now I was dressed up like a fucking Barbie doll. Man, it was getting hot in here.

"Cassidy, come out and show us," my mother called out again. I swallowed hard.

"It's okay," Clover said reassuringly and held out her hand. No, it wasn't, but I nodded and took her hand anyway, letting her guide me out.

My mother's glass of champagne suspended at her mouth as she looked over the dress, her lips going thin as she pursed them. This felt all kinds of wrong. And the airflow was clearly not working in here. I'd envisioned my wedding day since I was a small child and this wasn't it.

"Cassidy?" Clover gently pressed. I clutched her hand trying to escape the panic attack that was about to set in. When I'd told Clover and Issobelle about my true identity and circumstances, Clover had been understanding, whereas Issobelle had stormed out of the restaurant in a fit. Trust was one of her greatest values, and as she'd left, she'd said she felt like she hardly knew me at all.

"I feel like I'm going to throw up. Issobelle should be here," I said in short breaths. I felt the blood drain from my face and at the sight in the mirror, and Clover ran for a small bin. In a timely manner, I keeled over it, vomiting into the bin as she pushed back my hair. This dress made me feel physically ill. How was I supposed to go through with this if I couldn't even go through with the dress?

What was more flabbergasting was the woman who'd helped fit me into the dress didn't even think twice about trying to get the dress off me as I vomited, knowing we'd pay for the expenses anyway.

The wedding had been organized for in a month's time and I felt like a noose had been tied around my neck, gripping tighter day by day. Clover rubbed my back. "Issobelle will come around, you know she will." I tried my hardest not to sob into the bin. I felt like I'd lost everything, with no will or direction as to how I could change my course.

"I'd like a moment alone with my daughter, please," Mom said to Clover by way of asking her to leave. Clover sliced me a wary look. Pathetically, I nodded, unable to possibly bring up anything else.

Here I was, sitting in a who knew how expensive designer dress, vomiting into a bin. Had it been another time, I might've been elated, and yet this was becoming the worst day of my life.

My mother waited until I downed some water. When I felt stable enough and crossed the room, she patted the spot beside her. I grimaced, surprised that I hadn't damaged the dress in any way.

"You know your father does what he thinks is best for you, right?" my mother said patiently. Tears sprang to my eyes. I was sick of hearing this. It'd been so consistently rammed into my head that it made it almost inescapable to think otherwise now. "That's the role of a parent."

But panic spoke for me instead. Despite my lack of will to fight it anymore, sheer terror was now scratching at my insides. "Mom, I don't want to do this. Frederick isn't a good person."

She nodded and looked at her champagne glass with sudden interest. "You know, I was in love with someone else when my marriage to your father was arranged."

I sucked in a breath, trying to ease my sharp intakes. I hadn't been told this before, and it somehow derailed my panic attack. My mother, who often kept to herself, was opening up to me, and I clung to that desperately. "This is the first I've ever heard of it."

"Because some things are best buried away in the past. Are you in love with someone else?" she asked thoughtfully.

Tears welled in my eyes as I thought about Eric, left behind, bandaged and bleeding. How could anyone call that love? What I'd done to him? And yet I'd never felt something more fierce in my being. I thought I knew what love meant, but it wasn't until I met Eric that I could ever understand its magnitude.

My mother placed her glass to the side. "We've been given a very privileged life you and I. And I love your father in my own way. But I'd be lying if I said there weren't days when I'd wondered how it might've been different. And if it had whether I still would've had you as my daughter." I looked up at her, surprised. My mother and I had been closer when I was younger but as the years went by, we'd become distant and cold, mostly because of my father overshadowing everything we did. "Love's trifle, a lumberjack included."

My jaw dropped. "You knew where I was?" I asked quietly.

She scoffed. "My darling, never task a man to do a woman's job. A mother will always find her children. Even before they have to cut off their credit card and cell." There was slight amusement in her tone. Had she been so daring, she might've even given me a wink in that moment.

My bottom lip wobbled. "Why didn't you tell them where I was?" I'd later found out that it was Coots who accidently gave away my whereabouts. He was working in the neighboring town when Frederick had showed him the photo of me and innocently, he'd given my location. But if my mother had known all along, from the very start, why hadn't she said anything?

"Was there any need? You'd eventually come back. And I didn't see the point in stomping out your free spirit a day earlier than necessary."

Tears dropped down my cheek as I stared at her. Gently and gracefully, she wiped them away. "It's rare you and I can spend a moment alone like this." Especially in his older age, my father had grown attached to being by my mother's side. Tradition being only the women of the family were able to wedding dress shop. "I'd hoped to take this moment to offer you an early wedding gift."

I furrowed my eyebrows in confusion as she pulled out a little white box. Slowly, I took it. Receiving presents from my parents wasn't anything new but it was her tone and intent that prickled my skin, indicating this was something different. I opened the box, exposing a shiny gold credit card. "You know, my darling, one thing I've always been proud of is your ability to be free spirited and lift others and offer them courage when you don't even realize you're doing it."

Tears continued to spill. "Why are you giving me this?"

My mother uncharacteristically and nonchalantly shrugged. "It's attached to my allowance account. You'd be surprised how little I use it these days, one might consider there's an endless stream of funds in there if you need it, wherever you may go... depending on whoever you choose. I've paid the accountant a handsome bonus to overlook any withdrawals you might make so it doesn't alert your father." She tapped my hand lightly. "Use it whenever you need."

She went to stand but I grabbed her arm desperately. "Wait, are you telling me I don't have to go through with this wedding?" I choked desperately.

She cupped my cheek. "I'm telling you to follow

your heart, my darling. And don't begrudge your father. He's a stubborn man but he only wants the best for you. I'm sorry you ever felt so desperate as to run away from us. And this won't make amends for that. But perhaps it'll make your decision easier."

She pressed a kiss to my cheek and whispered, "And for what it's worth, I've never quite liked Frederick, he seems like a small fish in the pond, wouldn't you say?" I choked back a small disbelieving laugh.

The wooden doors sprang open, almost smashing one of the nearby vases off its stand. It shook back and forth and Clover dove for it as Issobelle waltzed into the room and pointed a finger at me. "I'm still pissed at you!"

My mother almost choked at her language, but then she shook her head, pretending she didn't hear it at all. "I'll let the woman know we'll buy this dress, since you made such a fine display in it. Do as you want. But choose wisely. And even if you make mistakes... I have a feeling you have those around you who can dig you out." She eyed Clover and Issobelle up and down as if our conversation had never happened.

"And I don't like that you're marrying this douche!" Issobelle exclaimed.

"Issobelle, shh that's Cassidy's mother," Clover reprimanded.

Issobelle stuttered for a moment. "Oh, shit sorry." She curtsied awkwardly as my mother left the room, shaking her head.

I laughed, a weight easing off me, that chain feeling slightly lighter. I stared down at the card, never more grateful for any piece of plastic in my life. Not because of the things that it could buy me but because of the freedom and understanding my mother offered. To know that I was loved and not some bargaining chip. That deep down, they cared— genuinely. Even if they were rigid in their thinking and beliefs, my mother gave me a choice without consequence of disappointing my family or being completely disowned. Had I hated them, it might've not been so bad. But I still clung to them, unable to leave them behind, which is why I found myself standing in this hideous wedding dress.

I lunged for Issobelle, hugging her tightly.

"I'm still mad!" She stomped a foot. Clover laughed, walking around to hug us both.

"Cassidy, if I'm being honest... I hate that dress," Clover admitted.

I laughed, tears streaming down my face. And despite the fact that my mother had gone up to purchase it, I said with a small smile, "I can't stand it either."

And slowly, I felt like the first piece was glued back together. A small glimmer of hope breaking through. My fairy tale might've not turn out how I'd imagined but at least I wasn't being forced into marrying a frog anymore.

Chapter 36

Cassidy

I 'd spent the afternoon with a very pissed off but able to tolerate me Issobelle, who did nothing but express how much of a mistake I'd been making since. I'd confessed to them everything that's happened, including Eric and how badly I'd fucked it all up.

"I just fall for everyone, don't I?" I laughed, almost hysterically so I didn't cry again. I was so sick of crying.

Issobelle had been slam-dunking her straw into her chocolate milkshake as we walked through Manhattan and to my parents' hotel building. My mother said she had errands to run, and she'd meet me there, giving me some well overdue girls' time.

"I've never seen you fall for anyone." I looked at her confused.

"But I have a reputation for being a serial dater," I laughed. At least I had up until four months ago.

"Serial dater and flings, Cassidy, but you've never declared your outright love for someone," Clover conveyed. And it'd been the worst time to tell him. I'd been so selfish, as if that'd been a scapegoat to make it all okay. *Because I loved him.* And only in a matter of weeks. He must've thought I was a silly little girl.

I tried to laugh it off. "But it was such a short time we knew each other. And he's so much older. Isn't that crazy?"

Clover and Issobelle looked at each other. Issobelle shrugged. "Don't look at me, I'm the furthest thing from the relationship type to offer you advice."

Clover sighed, defeated. "Well look at Damon and me. That all happened pretty quickly and in an unconventional way."

"Dating a billionaire male escort is definitely unconventional," Issobelle interrupted.

"Hey." Clover nudged her playfully. Even if she hadn't known his true identity at the time, circumstance led Clover and Damon together. "Despite our unusual meeting, it still felt inevitable. And I'm the happiest I've ever been."

"So, Clover meets a hot male escort, fake-dates him and then falls in love with him and has her dream job and a new shiny beau. I'm sure a little age gap isn't going to be that big of a deal in your love quest," Issobelle exemplified. Clover pinched her. "Hey!"

"You like to bring that one up when you can, don't you?" Clover asked, trying to keep a serious expression.

"I mean c'mon it's kind of a cool meet-cute," Issobelle laughed.

I considered her seriously. "I don't think it's the age gap that's the problem anymore. I lied to him... If you'd seen his expression when he'd found out..." I fell short, the emotion as raw now as it had been then. How could I ever ask for his forgiveness after I brought that kind of trouble to his home?

"Well trust is important but it's not like you lied to him on purpose. I mean the man saved you from a pack of wolves. If he can do that and not sit in a room with you and express his feelings then he's really misaligned," Issobelle casually shrugged.

Clover tsked at her.

"What?" Issobelle made light of it. "Putting him

to the side, you can't marry this Frederick douchebag. I don't care what your parents say. You can live with me for all I give a shit."

"You know you're always welcome to live with Damon and me," Clover added.

I scrunched up my nose. "No offence, Clover, but I wouldn't want to be third wheel to your household considering you and Damon just moved in together and can't keep your hands off each other.

"And besides, I can do this. I'm going to tell my father outright tonight I won't go through with it." A heavy weight sat on my chest. "And if he disowns me because of it... well I'll figure it out." Ironically, the pay check I'd been waiting on had been deposited into my account weeks ago. It was minimal but it was there and it was mine. And although my mother had given me a credit card to use, I wanted to try and stand on my own two feet and stay true to my decision.

I'd been so scared about my parents' disappointment and them disowning me that I'd been willing to sign my life away. And although I was blessed with my mother's permission—in not so many words—I realized vomiting in the bottom of that bin in that ridiculously hideous wedding dress that there was no way I could go through with this, even when I tried to force myself.

We'd finally arrived at the hotel my parents stayed in when they visited. I could see my mother waiting patiently in the reception.

"Do you need us to come with you?" Clover asked quietly. I inhaled a long calming breath.

"No, I need to do this on my own." Facing my father terrified me but other things terrified me more... Like a lot of wrongs and hurts I had to make up for. Like flying to Chicago and confronting Eric to apologize. That scared me more than anything else. Because it would be his final rejection, which I anticipated, that would break me completely. I owed him at least a proper explanation. And my fragile heart gave way to the hopeful thought that maybe he'd hear me out... that he'd look at me with something other than disgust. But first I had to get through this.

"Thank you. I love you both," I admitted and pulled them tightly into a hug.

"I'm still pissed," Issobelle called out, taking another sip of her milkshake. Clover swatted her arm, the two mock-bickering behind me as I walked through the doors, my mother studying her wristwatch, without looking at me as she stood. "You're five minutes late."

"I feel like five minutes late from ruining my father's day and possibly year isn't all that bad," I replied.

She nodded taking a harsh swallow. Because she'd be the one to deal with the fallout. And yet my mother had given me an out. One I could never admit to another person in case she was judged by my father for it.

My mother and I stood silently in the elevator and my heart thrummed in my chest. I loved my father, despite how messed up the situation might be in him palming me off like some bargaining chip, I still loved him. And the thought of him being displeased or even hating me sent a cold chill through me and my stomach swirled with nausea again. But I couldn't live a loveless marriage simply because I wanted him to be happy with a business deal gone right. He wouldn't be sitting in the marriage—I would.

When the elevator doors opened, commotion and chaos sounded through the halls. Walking straight out into the hallway of the penthouse, I saw Frederick round the corner with a sneer on his face.

He barged between me and my mother. I grabbed her by the arm before she lost her footing.

"Hey, asshole!" I hissed. When he turned, he looked ominous, a vile sneer and expression on his face.

"Couldn't keep your filthy mouth shut could you?" he growled.

My mother was indignant, and I stared at him, baffled. When the elevator doors closed, we turned to face one another. Neither of us knew what was happening. We followed the noise to where it sounded like my father was losing his absolute shit.

"Dad?" I called out as we rounded into the sizeable living room. A few papers had been thrown to the floor and with a bony finger, he pointed into the direction that Frederick had left.

"He was trying to trick us," he yelled furiously. Even in my father's rage, still not a single strand of hair was out of place.

"Marcus," my mother said calmly because she was used to his many spurts. "What happened?" She hurried to pick up the papers in case someone might see him having "such a moment." I hadn't envied my time away. The longer I'd been away from them the more relaxed I became and not caring so much what other people thought, if ever so slightly. But my parents, they hadn't and were never going to change a bit.

"Did you know they'd run out of oil," my father said, raising more papers in the air. "They planned on marrying in for the security of funds knowing I would've bought into the company."

My mother silently poured him a whisky from the bottle always conveniently placed on the side table. My mind was a whirl. Slowly, I took the bundled papers from him. It contained graphs and figures, some emails sent via management, and it was all in the negative. The last two years of earnings dropping significantly. How had they even covered this up from the media so far? Then again, Frederick's family cared about their appearance and reputation just as much as my own parents.

"You will not be marrying that man," he said, as if it were a punishment that I now couldn't marry him. "I forbid it." I tried to wipe the smile from my face, the mounted relief flowing off me. I lunged for my dad, taking him by surprise as I hugged him.

He didn't seem to know what to do as he carefully wrapped an awkward hand around me. "Thank you," I said sincerely. My mother slowly walked over, putting a gentle hand on both our backs in what I imagined was meant to be a family hug.

When had it become so stifled and awkward between us?

"How did you find this?" I asked. My father ran a hand over his tie, tidying his appearance.

He cleared his throat, still a little flustered, from the ordeal or the family hug, I wasn't so sure. Dad pointed to the library. "Your friend that works in IT, he'd managed to accumulate some things." My heart pounded. *My friend?* "He said you'd asked him to look into it. Thank you, Cassidy, and... I'm sorry."

I only knew one person who worked in IT. No, didn't work in IT, ran a staff of over two hundred people in IT type of guy. I swallowed hard. "Is he still here?" I asked in a distant voice.

My father combed through his pepper-sprinkled hair and cleared his throat as if the apology itself had singed him. But he'd done it and said it, much to my disbelief. But my breath hitched for other reasons now. Had it been Eric?

"He's in the library now, said he could wait for your return," my father said, throwing back the glass of whiskey.

"Let's sit in the other room," my mother said knowingly as she guided my father into the second lounge with the bottle of whisky in hand. I had the distinct impression my father would be waking up with a sore head in the morning.

When they'd left, I turned around facing the library, the wooden doors slightly ajar. I'd been surprised by my father so openly displaying his rage with someone else in the penthouse who could hear. I supposed it just showed how mad he was at the idea of being tricked by what had been a longtime friend. But I supposed some friendships came at a price. Especially in the inner circles that my parents danced amongst.

My outstretched hand paused at the door, my heart hammering in my ears. Tears welled in my eyes before I'd even pushed the door open, hopeful as to who might be on the other side. I continued on. Soundlessly, it exposed a thick, muscular, suit-covered back. He'd been looking over the classical library my father enjoyed collecting.

Slowly, Eric turned, that rugged beard and features looking like they were carved out of stone and squeezed perfectly into the suit. His forest-green eyes were trained on me as he slid the book back onto the shelf.

I wasn't entirely sure what to say, so I foolishly said the first thing that popped into my head. I waved a hand over him. "Wow Chicago Eric in a suit, huh?"

He looked over himself self-consciously. "It looks good," I blurted. "Not that you needed my approval or anything." *Why was I still talking?*

His mouth twitched at the corner, fluttering all kinds of emotions into me. No, I was reading into this all wrong. I tried to calm my jittery nerves.

"You found those things about Frederick's family?"

He nodded. Then more palpable silence. My heart pounded in my chest. Why wasn't he saying anything? Why was he here? I just wanted to run up and throw myself around him, but the last time I'd seen him he was bleeding on the ground with disgust and betrayal twisting his features. I was scared if I took one step closer, his disgust would reappear.

"How's your arm and leg?" I asked. He seemed surprised by my question. Whatever his train of thought had been it'd stopped.

"They're fine," he said roughly and cleared his throat. "And the information wasn't that difficult to find, I had a team on it, so it only took us a few days to find cold hard proof."

I nodded, still standing closely to the doorframe as if it was giving me strength to stand. "How did you know where to find us?"

I was saying all the wrong things. *Are you here for me? Do you still hate me? I'm sorry.*

He rounded the big wooden desk, coming to a stop before it and leaning against its edge. If my father saw him do it, he'd probably lose his shit. "When I began researching your family's name it wasn't hard to find your whereabouts, Cassidy. Or should I say your father's. And it's even easier to get in touch with him when you have the right contacts."

I gulped, almost too scared to ask my next question. "But you came to deliver them personally?"

He let out a slow breath, those intense green eyes boring into me. A mixture of hope and pain rolled through me.

He seemed to not know what to do with his hands as he nodded. "After that asshole took you from the cabin, I left straight for Chicago the next day. I thought I'd go back to normal, but I was more pissed off with the world than usual and I couldn't get you out of my fucking head." I winced at every curse word he used, feeling their impact of anger and hurt. "About a week ago, Lori flew to Chicago and kicked me up the ass." Sounded like Lori alright. He licked his lips as if parched. His expression turned innocent. "I realized I might've been unfair to you."

"No, I was the one in wrong," I quickly said. He

offered a lopsided smile that took my breath away and stopped me short.

"You turned my world upside down, snowflake." My heart melted at his nickname. "And every morning when I wake up, I still find myself looking for you fluttering about the kitchen or doing some weird pose for yoga, even in my Chicago home. I haven't been able to sleep right since that night and even though you're not with me, you're still somehow driving me absolutely insane."

My bottom lip wobbled.

"And I miss you reading that goddamn book. It doesn't matter what book it is your reading, I just miss your voice and commentary. And I miss us. I know it's unreasonable. I know we weren't meant to meet and I'm just an old fucking man but I'm also a tired one. And for the first time in a long time, I'm finding myself here, taking a risk with you, hopeful that you'll accept my apology."

My voice wavered. "That was an apology?"

He exhaled a sharp breath with a taut smile. "Yes, sweetheart. I didn't know you were under those types of pressures. I should've protected you but instead I locked up and selfishly thought about myself."

I shook my head, taking a step forward. "No, you

were thinking about your family, and I hadn't told you the truth. I brought a bad man into your town, and I'll never be able to apologize enough for that."

Breathlessly, I'd taken the last few steps between us somehow and now stood in front of him. My heart hammering in my chest.

"So did they ever live a happily ever after in that book?" he asked innocently, his gaze devouring me.

I felt my throat bobble, his gaze drawn to its dip and then my lips. "I never read the last few chapters without you."

Slowly, I reached out to him. He mimicked my action until his calloused fingers brushed against mine. My body lit with flames and the tears that had been building finally broke free. He pulled me in, hugging and squeezing me tightly as I cried into his shoulder. I was surrounded by his warmth and protection. Home. I felt like I was at home again. It hadn't been any particular place and certainly not the cabin. It had been Eric. And I'd make sure to send Lori the biggest present of her life for sending him back to me.

"You know," I said with a croaky voice. "I was going to come find you in Chicago after tonight. I was going to tell my father I couldn't go through with it."

He brushed back part of my hair, studying my face as if he might never see it again. "Shadow would've liked that. I haven't been the only miserable bastard without you."

I let out a hideous laugh through blanketed tears. "Well, I am still technically on vacay."

He smiled, staring at my lips. "Would you like to come back to Chicago with me on a temporary vacation?" he asked.

Warmth filled my entire body and I felt like I lit up like a Christmas tree. I nodded profusely. "Yes," I breathed. "I don't want to be anywhere else, Eric. Even if you are a grump half the time."

His lips twitched into a smile until finally, he bent down and kissed me. All that hurt, longing, and passion coiled into one. His tongue was dominant, and I opened up to him more so he could lick every delicacy that I'd happily give him. I could feel his cock twitching beneath the fabric of his pants, my own body heating with anticipation.

He growled, those hooded green eyes studying my lips as he pulled back. "I have a hotel room if—"

"Yes," I breathed, grabbing his hand and running for the door. He laughed, tugging me back.

"Wait, what if your father sees."

"I don't care who sees us together, Eric. I never have. Especially my father of all people. And besides it also turns out that my boyfriend's big enough to be scary."

"Boyfriend?" he asked, arching eyebrows.

Heat blasted across my cheeks. "I—"

His lips crushed to mine again possessively. "I never want you guessing where you stand again, Cassidy. You're the only woman for me. So yes, I'm your fucking boyfriend."

The way he growled it had my toes curling, as if the moment he'd said it I was trapped in some twisted dark ruin. A dangerous promise and one that I'd been praying for every single day since the moment I'd left him and Shadow behind in that cabin.

"Now take me to this hotel room of yours, boyfriend."

With ease, he threw me over his shoulder forcing a small squeal to escape my lips as he gritted out, "It's just one floor down." But I didn't even know if we could make it past the elevator.

I kicked and screamed playfully, my loose curls swinging toward the floor as he carried me like a caveman. My father and mother were nowhere to be seen. Most likely because my mother knew exactly who'd been in that room and she kept my father distracted.

Warmth flooded me as a lightness finally took hold. I finally felt free. My parents had shown their love in their own way. But now I'd found my own that filled me entirely and I wasn't ever willing to let it go.

Epilogue – Eric

Six months later

Clover and Damon's engagement party danced with life. So many guests fluttered about celebrating the pair. I absentmindedly rubbed Cassidy's belly. She'd only just started showing but I found myself protectively gravitating toward patting the baby and I'd be fucked if I gave a shit if others considered me doting or "too much" because of it.

What I considered "too much" was my mother, who now called every day delighted and offering advice on parenting. By now she'd stopped calling me directly and called Cassidy instead, who seemed more than happily obliging.

"So how are you finding it in Chicago?" Issobelle asked Cassidy. Issobelle was one of the few friends of

Cassidy's I did like. She was no-nonsense and gave no shits about what anyone else thought.

"It's beautiful. Not the same as New York but nothing else is. But this one makes it all worth it." She patted my arm. "Although he seemed awfully grumpy with me this morning before we flew out, maybe I'll reconsider."

I let out a breath; she'd been teasing me over it all morning. "Well, if I hadn't spent the entire morning freezing my ass off and letting Twinkles pee on the grass I might've had a nice sleep in."

Cassidy laughed. Twinkles, the newest member to our household, was a smart-mouth Chihuahua who I was still in the process of training to pee on the grass instead of our bathroom mat. Cassidy had pleaded to get a friend for Shadow and he'd stared at the rat-looking dog in the same way that I had. And despite promising that she'd look after and train it, I'd ended up freezing my ass off every morning. But granted, Cassidy had been dealing with some intense morning sickness.

It was only a month after adopting Twinkles that we'd discovered we were due for our own. Had it been a year ago, I would've been bone deep terrified at the thought of having a baby, but with Cassidy it felt right. I hadn't even been looking for her, and yet she'd been what I needed all along.

And despite their upbringing and expectations, her parents had finally come around to the idea of accepting me as any kind of son-in-law figure, although it was more the bank account and company I ran that "permitted" their blessings. But I didn't give a fuck; I wasn't in a relationship with her parents. I pressed a kiss to her temple thoughtfully.

"Your sister looks like she's getting pretty chummy over there," Issobelle pointed out. I scowled at Lori, who was laughing at some asshole's jokes all night. And I was not a fan.

"Apparently he's one of Hayden Zilch's players," Cassidy said thoughtfully. "Speaking of Hayden, I haven't seen him for a while."

"Or Megan," Issobelle said, raising a suspicious eyebrow. I'd since found out Megan was Clover's sister with two children who were already running around high on candy; and Hayden was some bigwig sports manager who also collaborated with Damon's company.

Cassidy chuckled. "Look at those two, they're so ridiculous." She pointed over at Alex, Damon's best man, and Sotiny, his wife. "How long do you think until they start their own family?"

Issobelle laughed, folding her arms. "She'll make him wait as long as possible, I reckon."

Thomas was surrounded by three beautiful models, completely in his element. I rolled my eyes. Although it was kind of them to extend an invitation to any friend of Cassidy's, including some of my siblings, it was still unnerving watching them flirt and mingle.

"Your kid brother's going to love it in Seattle, the women are beautiful there too," Issobelle remarked as she munched down on a bowl of nuts she'd stolen from the table.

"Yea his placement's soon. He's still trying to find a place to stay. I considered buying an apartment for him, but I'd made the mistake of buying my other brothers a place and now they're too comfortable and 'between' jobs."

Cassidy laughed; I didn't find it as funny.

Issobelle seemed to consider this for a while. "You know I have a friend called Nina, who has a spare room in her apartment. She recently had a friend who passed away and has holed herself up since. I think though it might be good for her to have someone move in, just so she's not so alone. I could ask her if you'd like?"

I rubbed my beard thoughtfully. "I don't think

it's the best idea if she's grieving. My brother can be very... charming with the opposite sex."

Cassidy laughed. "What a polite way of saying he's a fuckboy."

Issobelle chuckled. "Trust me I don't know anyone more uninterested than Nina and I've been thinking on it for a while, but I really do think she needs someone to move in. I'll send her a message and let you know."

"Okay that sounds good," I said politely. I still wasn't convinced it was the greatest idea but if anything eventuated from it, it could be discussed another day.

Cassidy sneezed. "Are you okay? Do you want me to grab your jacket."

"I'm fine," she laughed. "I'm pregnant not helpless."

"You seemed awfully helpless this morning when someone had to take Twinkles out to the toilet."

She laughed and my entire chest spread with warmth, my own smile forming. I kissed her on the forehead. "Well, I don't care, I'm getting your jacket anyway. I'll be back."

She sighed. "Fine but I'm going to go over to Michelle and Phillip and meet their new little one."

She pointed over to the couple. Michelle was Damon's sister and co-CEO of *Be True*. It was a mind whirl trying to remember who everyone was.

I excused myself and walked into the giant cloakroom. After pushing through one of the racks, I found Cassidy's jacket when a noise caught my attention. Curiously, I rounded the corner just in time to see a very ruffled Hayden Zilch and Megan Granture push one another away.

Right. I turned for the door and called out, "I didn't see a thing."

That was their business. Well, that explained why they'd been gone from the party for so long, but it wasn't my place to say. And from what I'd heard, Clover had sworn Hayden off her sister since they were university friends. She was strictly off-limits. I'm sure if anything eventuated I'd hear it through Cassidy.

I stepped back into the dazzling room filled with music, light chatter, and laughter. I found Cassidy, standing beside a small water fountain, the overhanging chandelier glistening the water's reflection against her face.

I watched from afar as Cassidy held a small baby, cooing and rocking it back and forth naturally. She'd always been beautiful; from the moment I'd first saw her, she'd taken my breath away. In a very uncomfortable way, because although I might've not been ready for Cassidy in my life back then, she'd burrowed into my heart, her smiles and light laughter melting away all barriers and resistance.

And every morning I woke up with her in my arms, I was shocked and terrified she'd decided to stay with me. And not that I'd ever admit it out loud, but once again, I found myself grateful for Lori's interference.

I watched my sister laugh and place a hand on the unknown player's arm and swallowed hard. I wanted her to find happiness. Just not with *that* guy who looked like a total hotshot.

"Eric," Cassidy called out, grabbing my attention. "Come and hold Rosalie."

My jaw tightened as I held back a tear, the dawning realization that soon that'd be us with our own child. Our family. Our love.

To connect find Kia on www.kiacarrington-russell.com

Thank you so much for reading my book. If you enjoyed this book, I'd love to hear your honest thoughts in way of a review. It not only helps support my writing but also gives me important feedback on how you felt and connected with the world and characters. I love connecting with my readers and would appreciate if you could take two minutes to leave a review or rating. Thank you so much and I hope you are having a wonderful day!

About the Author

Raised in the Darling Downs Region in Queensland, Australia, Kia Carrington-Russell, began writing as an angsty teenager, finding a passion for exploring creative realities and world building at fifteen. After graduating high school she decided to pursue a career in freelance journalism, and quickly amended that dream with something that made her heart beat faster and her mind race—fiction. With fresh eyes she went over her first manuscript, "Possession of my Soul" and began her publishing journey in 2014.

With a recognizable style of kick ass heroines, fast-paced action, and romance that dances from light to dark, she's been pronounced "the new up and coming author to look out for" and her writing style as "hauntingly beautiful."

Carrington-Russell's books have been recognized on multiple best-seller lists, most noticeably, her "Token Huntress" and "My Escort" series for which she's won numerous awards and notable reviews, including "Reader's Favorite" 5 star reviews for

"Token Huntress" and "The Shadow Minds Journal."

She has a firm belief in giving back to the writing community—sharing knowledge, promotions, and opportunities that might help other authors reach their readers, including running her own YouTube channel, Bound by Books, where she interviews fellow authors and other industry professionals.

With years in various industries, climbing the corporate ladders, Kia has now settled into a full-time writing career as a successful author and is always looking for the next adventure. She's travelled the world for both business and pleasure, including living in Edinburgh, Scotland for the past year.

Now back in her home country of Australia, she takes her Cavoodle, Sia along morning walks on beautiful coastline beaches, building worlds in the sea breezes and contemplating where she'll go next.